# THEY CAME FOR HIM

# THEY CAME FOR HIM

ZACHARY GOLDMAN MYSTERIES
BOOK THIRTEEN

P.D. WORKMAN

**PD WORKMAN**

ISBN: 9781774682630 (KDP Paperback)
ISBN: 9781774682647 (KDP Hardcover)
ISBN: 9781774682654 (Large Print)
ISBN: 9781774682661 (IS Paperback)
ISBN: 9781774682678 (Kindle)
ISBN: 9781774682685 (ePub)
ISBN: 9781774682661 (Lulu Paperback)

*To those imprisoned by lies*
*and the truth*

———————

# 1

---

Zachary's phone rang as he breakfasted with Kenzie. He knew better than to answer it at dinnertime unless it was an emergency, but he didn't usually have to worry about it ringing during breakfast, so he wasn't sure how to handle it. He glanced at Kenzie, who raised her brows questioningly. Zachary decided he'd better at least check to see who it was. It could be Heather, his older sister, calling to let him know that there was a client he needed to deal with urgently. Or it could be Lorne Peterson, his old foster father and long-time friend, who wanted to reach him while Kenzie was still home to invite them over for dinner or let them know something that was going on. It would be rare for a client or anyone else to call him first thing in the morning.

The caller ID was Jocelyn Goldman, his oldest sister.

Zachary's stomach plummeted. He couldn't think of any reason Joss would call him so early. The fact was that she never called him at all. He occasionally called her to see how she was doing, ask after Luke, or let her know that he would be in the area and was hoping to stop in for a visit. But Joss kept herself separated from everyone else, not getting close emotionally.

He swiped to answer and held the phone to his ear.

"Joss?"

"There's been some trouble," Joss said, bypassing any greeting or small talk.

Zachary swallowed. Had Joss gotten herself into trouble? Or had Luke? Was it something to do with Madison, Luke's former girlfriend, who Zachary had rescued from human traffickers? Or with Rhys, Zachary's young Black friend who was romantically interested in Luke? Zachary had been doing his best to keep them apart, but Rhys was a teenager and wasn't about to be told what to do.

As far as he knew, Joss hadn't had any contact with her old life and had been staying away from drugs. Still, he had thought the same of Tyrrell, his younger brother, before he had given in to his addiction a few months earlier. Was *she* the one who was in trouble?

Or was it something completely different? Since Joss kept to herself so much, there could be a hundred things going on that Zachary had no idea of.

He licked dry lips. "What's wrong?"

Across the table from him, Kenzie had put down her toast and was leaning forward, dark eyes worried, echoing his concern.

"Luke has been arrested."

Zachary swore under his breath. What had the boy done now? He knew that Joss had been worried about him lately, concerned that he could be tempted back into his old life. It was difficult to leave behind a life of addiction and almost impossible to leave a crime syndicate like the one that Luke had been involved in. Despite the abuses he had suffered at the hands of his bosses in the human trafficking ring, it was easier to be told what to do than to have to make his own decisions. It was easier to be supplied with all of the drugs and money he needed as long as he lured in new teens and brought in more business. The approval of his superiors was almost as strong a drug as the substances he had been addicted to. With long experience in the life herself, Joss had tried to explain to Zachary what a battle it would be to keep Luke not only clean and sober, but away from sex trafficking and the cycle of abuse that he had become accustomed to.

That was beside the fact that Luke had been making the organization a lot of money and they would do whatever they could to get him back if they knew where he was living now.

"What for? Drugs? Or…?"

"I wish that was all it was," Joss said with a sharp laugh. "If it was only that simple."

How could it be worse than that?

"It's murder," Joss told him baldly. "He's been charged with murder."

## 2

Murder?" Zachary repeated, his stomach tying itself into even tighter knots.

Kenzie's eyes widened. For an assistant in the medical examiner's office, murder was part of her everyday life. It was what had brought them together initially, as Zachary had been investigating the death of Declan Bond. But the deaths that she was involved with were not usually anything to do with anyone they knew.

There was a deep sigh from Joss. "Yeah, murder. You know that's what I said." Her tone was irritated. She had probably been up all night. And undoubtedly, she didn't really want to have to deal with it all. Zachary was encouraged by the fact that she had called him, but wasn't sure what she needed from him. Just a listening ear? Did she want him to call someone? Suggest a lawyer?

"Do you know what happened?"

"Apparently, he killed a pimp. Someone he knew while he was in the business. Not like they'll give me any details. I'm not even legally his guardian. But they had to call someone, and better me than child services, since *they* know nothing about him." Joss let out another sigh. "I don't know what I'm supposed to do about this."

"What did Luke say about it? Did he explain what happened?"

"He's not saying anything. Which is probably best because they'll just use anything he says to convict him."

"And he didn't tell you anything either?"

"I haven't talked to him. They haven't finished processing him yet, so he can't see anyone."

"He's allowed a phone call. He didn't want to talk to you? Did he call a lawyer? Public defender?"

"No. He didn't make a call. The cop who talked to me said that he hasn't had anything to say. Hasn't defended himself. Didn't want a lawyer. You know what's happened. Obviously, this pimp had contact with Luke in the past or was trying to pick him up."

"He'll probably get a lawyer in time. It's only the first day. Once he's had a chance to think about things, to talk to you and figure out what he's going to do…"

"Can you look into it?"

"What do you want me to do? Talk to the police? They won't tell me any more than they told you. They probably won't talk to me at all."

"No. I want you to find out what happened. Just ask around. Get the scoop from any witnesses."

Zachary tapped his finger against the table, thinking about it. "Sure… I'll do what I can to help. But the police won't want me talking to witnesses right now. They need to do their investigation first. And once Luke has been processed, he'll probably let you know what happened. He's just being careful right now. He knows how this works."

"They're going to railroad him!" Jocelyn snapped. "A kid like Luke isn't going to get any sympathy. They'll say he's in the business. He killed his pimp. He got into an argument over payment. Luke has got a record; they know exactly what kind of a life he was leading up until you brought him to live with me."

It wouldn't look good for Luke. Zachary knew that sex workers went to prison for much less. But he couldn't quite wrap his mind around what had happened.

"*Was* Luke back in the business? I know you were worried about him. What do you think happened?"

"I don't know. I'm not his mom or his babysitter. I don't always know where he is. I do my best to keep him out of trouble, but he's old enough to make his own decisions. I can't physically keep him from doing anything he sets his mind to. And he knows his way around. He doesn't need me to take him anywhere."

"I know that. I'm not saying that you should have kept him home or that you did anything wrong. You've been doing a great job with Luke. I can't think of anyone who could have done a better job with him. But you were worried that he might be tempted to get back into the life. The pull of the drugs and the money and positive strokes from the people he used to work for. Or a new boss."

"He's been out some nights. Not all the time, and not usually overnight. Just for a few hours. There's not much by way of entertainment around here. Popcorn and Netflix isn't exactly exciting for a kid who has been used to partying and the nightlife."

"So, he's drinking? Drugging?"

"I don't know. He says not, but…" Even though they were on the phone, Zachary could see her expressive shrug in his mind's eye. "Of course that's what he's going to say. Any addict who falls off the wagon is going to deny it to start with."

As Zachary had discovered with Tyrrell. Tyrrell had assured Zachary and Kenzie that he hadn't started drinking again. Until he'd disappeared on a drunken binge and Zachary had to track him down. He couldn't exactly deny it anymore at that point.

"But you must have seen the signs. If he was using again."

"He seemed fine to me. But if he stayed away for long enough to hide the signs… and those nights that he did stay out overnight…"

"Well… I'll find out what I can, but I don't know how much that will be. Do you think he'll talk to me? Once he's been processed?"

"No. Probably not. Kids are taught not to talk if they get scooped up. If you just keep your mouth shut, the cartel will get you out. Maybe you serve some time, but as long as you don't talk about anyone else… you can go back again when you are released."

Zachary made a noise of acknowledgment. His brain was busy, trying to figure out how he could do anything to help Luke. If the police wouldn't tell him anything, Luke wouldn't tell him anything, and Luke didn't even have a lawyer to defend him, how was Zachary supposed to get any information that might be helpful for Joss or Luke?

"I'll try to get in to talk to him later today or tomorrow," Joss said, lowering her voice a little, letting up on the anger that Zachary knew hadn't been aimed at him. "I'll find out what I can. I'll try to get him to get a lawyer and tell him to talk to you." She cleared her throat, but her voice still sounded tight as she went on. "You just had to bring him here, didn't you? You just had to go and let me get attached to someone. I care about what happens to him. You may think I'm a tough chick who won't let herself get hurt by anything…" That was certainly the image she tried to project. "But I do care about what happens to Luke."

"Of course you do," Zachary reassured her. "I'll do whatever I can to help."

## 3

After Zachary hung up the phone, he looked at Kenzie, shaking his head slowly.

"What exactly happened?" Kenzie asked. She pushed a few of her dark curls back over her ear, picked up her toast, and took a couple of bites, waiting for Zachary to fill her in.

"I don't know anything yet. Just that Luke was arrested for murder. Someone in human trafficking. Jocelyn doesn't know for sure whether he knew him from when he was in the business, or if this is someone that he's met since then. Maybe someone trying to pick him up. He's not telling anyone what happened."

"That's probably good for now."

"That's what Joss said."

"So… why did she call you? What does she want you to do?"

Zachary shrugged uncomfortably. "Look into it. I don't know what I'll be able to do or how helpful I'll be. But she's never asked me to help before, so I'll do whatever I can."

"Of course. I just wondered whether there was anything you *could* do."

"Probably not right now, but I can talk to him once he's been arraigned and everything. As long as he'll see me. Joss said she'll tell him to."

"If he lets *her* visit him."

Zachary rolled his eyes and nodded acknowledgment. "Man… Luke. I thought he was doing so well. I know Joss said that she was worried about him, that he might go back to the life, but… he seemed so strong when I talked to him. I didn't think he would."

"It's hard to wrap your mind around it. Like going back to an abusive spouse. I mean… he knows he's walking back into a violent, dangerous lifestyle, one that endangers him and where he'll be required to do things that he doesn't want to. And why? For drugs?"

"Among other things, yeah. There's an endless supply in the trafficking business."

"I thought he was doing well too. I'm sorry. You must be really disappointed."

Kenzie knew how hard Zachary had worked to get Madison and Luke away from the cartel and find them safe places to start over again, even going as far as planting false trails about both kids having been killed in the shootout during their escape attempt. He had hoped that they would be out of that life forever. But now Luke was right back in the middle of trouble again.

Kenzie reached across the table to put a comforting hand on Zachary's arm for a moment, then withdrew it. "So, what does this mean for the rest of today's plans?" she asked practically.

Zachary considered. "Nothing, really, other than being a distraction. I can't do anything right away, so we may as well just go ahead with our plans."

"Good. I think Tyrrell would be really disappointed if I showed up to pick him up without you."

Tyrrell had completed his program at the drug rehabilitation center, and it would be cruel for his brother not to be there to meet him and celebrate his accomplishment. Or to put it off for another day. Zachary needed to be there for Tyrrell, like he had promised.

He always needed to follow through on his promises to his brothers and sisters. They'd had to put up with enough crap from the parents who had abandoned them and the other challenges they had faced once put into the foster care system. They all needed him to be steady and reliable. A good big brother to Tyrrell, Vince, and Mindy, and little brother to Joss and Heather. Now that they were all back in his life again, at one level or another, he needed to show them that he wasn't the same Zachary as had burned the house down when he was ten, causing the dissolution of the family.

He would spend the rest of his life trying to make up for that.

"I have to be there for Tyrrell," he agreed. "I told him I would be."

"Are you going to eat?" Kenzie nodded to the granola bar and single-serving yogurt container on the table in front of Zachary. He needed to eat if he were going to get back up to a healthy weight and he couldn't take his newest meds on an empty stomach.

So he had to, despite the heavy, foreboding feeling that now twisted his guts into a solid, uncomfortable knot. Zachary breathed out slowly, trying to relax all of his muscles.

"Yeah. Of course."

He had started to open the granola bar wrapper before his phone had rung. He picked it up again and tore it open. He liked the chocolate chip granola bars, and now that he was on meds that didn't make him nauseated first thing in the morning, he could actually enjoy it.

---

Once they had finished eating breakfast, they got ready to pick Tyrrell up. They hadn't set up a specific time, but Zachary wanted to get to the rehab facility as early in the day as they could so that Tyrrell wouldn't be waiting around and they could spend as much time together as possible getting Tyrrell settled into his new life and celebrating his graduation with him.

Zachary drove. There was always a debate over which of them would drive, as they both enjoyed highway driving. Kenzie's sweet little red convertible was her baby, her pride and joy, and she loved any excuse to go out and show it off. Zachary's white compact, on the other hand, was meant to be as anonymous and unnoticeable as possible, looking like every other fleet car and rental out there. A solid, dependable ride that no one would even remember seeing later. Despite what Magnum, P.I. might have gotten away with in Hawaii, a private investigator couldn't conduct surveillance in a flashy red convertible. Vermont was not Hawaii.

Having enough space for Tyrrell and his bags necessitated taking Zachary's car. And taking his car meant that he got to drive, unless there was some reason to let Kenzie drive instead. When they had gone to the Lodge, he had been too wiped out to drive the whole distance, and she had taken over. But normally, taking Zachary's car meant he was doing the driving.

"I'm going to handle a few emails," Kenzie commented, taking out her laptop. "If that's okay with you. Did you want to visit?"

"I don't mind." Driving was like meditation to Zachary. It was one of the only times he could sit and do nothing and be happy about it. If Kenzie were paying attention to her email, he could probably go a little faster than he normally could drive with her in the car. Zachary's mouth twitched, and he had to make an effort not to grin at the idea.

"I saw that."

Zachary chuckled. "Saw what?"

"You'd better not get there in half an hour."

"Yes, ma'am."

The weather had been warmer the last couple of weeks. They didn't need to wait for the windows to defrost, so Zachary pulled out after ensuring that Kenzie had on her seat belt and was ready to go.

"Do you want music?"

"Whatever you want," Kenzie told him, her voice already far away, distracted by whatever she was reading on the screen.

Zachary turned on the radio and flipped through the saved channels until he found something good. By the time they reached the highway, he was already in the zone, blocking out all of his concerns about Luke and Joss and just how he could help Luke.

# 4

They didn't reach the rehab facility in half an hour. But it didn't take a full hour, either. Zachary caught Kenzie checking the time as they pulled up. She gave him a wry look.

"Time flies," she commented. "I expected to be able to get more done on the way here."

"It's supposed to be your day off anyway," Zachary pointed out. "You shouldn't be doing work email."

"Well, no. Not all of it was work."

Maybe she had checked her personal mail as well. Still, Zachary doubted that her bright red pursed lips and the small frown line between her eyebrows had been over something puzzling in her personal inbox.

"Maybe you'll be able to get a bit more done on the way home."

"Doubt it. The two of you will probably be jabbering like jays on the way home."

"Jabbering like jays?" Zachary raised his brows.

"At least I didn't say cackling like hens."

"We have a lot of catching up to do."

"And you'll have lots of time to do it. And you don't have to do it all today. I'm not saying it's a bad thing. You guys should talk and have a good time together. I'm just saying I know it will be distracting, that I can't focus on emails while you're having an interesting discussion."

Zachary smiled all the way from the car to the reception area. The lobby area that had been so bare and desolate when they had dropped Tyrrell off now seemed airy and was filled with bright sunlight, as if even the weather were celebrating Tyrrell's completion of the program.

"We're here for Tyrrell Goldman," Zachary told the receptionist.

She gave him a sunny smile. "Oh, believe me, I know! Tyrrell is over the moon about being finished and being able to go home with his family today." She tapped a button on her phone as she picked up the receiver. "And I would know who you are even without being told."

He and Tyrrell looked enough alike that people saw the resemblance between them and didn't need independent verification that they were siblings. Zachary briefly considered their shared genetic traits and the father they both resembled before pushing any thoughts of Berk to the side to stay focused on Tyrrell's achievements.

"He's here," the receptionist said into the receiver.

It was mere seconds before the security door to the right opened and a woman in burgundy nurse's scrubs motioned for them to join her. "Zachary Goldman?"

"That's me." Zachary gave Kenzie's arm a squeeze as they turned and headed toward the door. "And this is Dr. Kenzie Kirsch."

"Doctor." The woman gave Kenzie a respectful nod. "Glad to have you here."

"Don't worry," Kenzie said, to allay any anxiety the nurse might have about having an outside doctor in the facility. "All of my patients are dead."

The nurse looked at her, startled. "What?"

"I work at the medical examiner's office. The morgue."

"Oh!" The nurse laughed. "I see!"

"I don't have any kind of oversight here. I took a tour when we dropped Tyrrell off because I was interested in learning as much about your programs as possible, and I was very impressed. But there's no need to cater to me or even call me doctor. I'm just Kenzie here."

"Well, we're still glad to have you," the nurse said, but did look more relaxed about it.

She led them through a couple of short corridors to a common area where Tyrrell was sitting, waiting and talking to a few other residents. Like Zachary, he had dark hair and eyes, though his hair was not in a buzz cut like Zachary's, but a longer, shaggier style. He looked up at Zachary's arrival. His face split into a grin and he jumped to his feet.

"Zach! Bro! It's good to see you!"

He gave Zachary a vigorous hug and slapped him on the back. He turned to the other residents.

"My brother," he introduced, motioning to Zachary. "My big brother, Zachary. And this is Kenzie." He gave Kenzie a sideways shoulder hug. "Zachary and Kenzie..." he made a sweeping gesture toward the others to introduce them. "My buds. Worked our way through the program together."

Zachary nodded. "Good to meet all of you."

They made various comments and greetings. Zachary looked at Tyrrell, evaluating him, looking for any sign that he wasn't quite ready to leave the safety of the program yet. Of course, they had all talked it over before, but Zachary was worried. Tyrrell had seemed stable before too. Zachary hadn't had any idea that anything was wrong until it was too late. "How are you doing?" he asked. "You're ready to get out of here?"

"I'm ready," Tyrrell agreed firmly, giving a nod. "I'm doing really well. Don't know when the last time I felt this good was."

Zachary nodded, but he was still anxious, looking for cracks in Tyrrell's veneer. They didn't want to take Tyrrell away from the support of the program too soon. He needed to be ready.

"Are you ready to meet with Dr. Gable?" the nurse asked Zachary.

Zachary and Kenzie nodded. They both knew Dr. Gable and had met him on previous occasions. Zachary knew that today, Dr. Gable would be the one certifying that Tyrrell had completed the program and was ready to leave.

Zachary wished that meant that Tyrrell was cured and wouldn't have to worry about falling back again. But it didn't. He was a dry drunk. A recovering alcoholic, but never cured.

"This way."

# 5

They all went together to another room, one of the family visiting rooms like they had used before when they had taken Alisha and Mason, Tyrrell's children, to visit him. Comfortable surroundings, meant to look more like a living room than a doctor's office or exam room.

"Tyrrell Goldman," Dr. Gable greeted heartily and reached out his hand to shake Tyrrell's. "Can you believe it is time for us to say goodbye to each other already?" He was an older man, gray hair, wire-rimmed glasses, a lab coat that didn't quite cover his paunch.

"It seems like a long time, and like just yesterday," Tyrrell said. He looked around the room and at everyone assembled there. "I didn't think I would ever feel this good again."

"The time goes quickly." Dr. Gable sat down and motioned for them all to take seats. He laid a few papers out on the coffee table in front of him. "When Tyrrell came here, he was in pretty bad shape. Physically and emotionally." He looked at Tyrrell. "Over a month of very heavy drinking, and moderately heavy in the weeks before that. And, of course, his long history with alcoholism. It does a lot of damage to your system. Alters the way you think. Depresses your nervous system."

Tyrrell was nodding his agreement. He didn't seem to be embarrassed by the doctor talking about the specifics of the problems he'd had when he had arrived at the facility, as Zachary thought he might. But then, Zachary and Kenzie had seen. He had stayed with them for the few days between when Zachary had found him and when they had gotten him into the program. It had been a rough go.

"We have the results of some of the testing that you did and the medical examinations that were performed when you got here," Gable told Tyrrell, pointing to the stapled papers. "And pictures."

Tyrrell winced when Gable laid a few snapshots on the table. Zachary looked them over. They had been visiting Tyrrell regularly since he'd completed the first phase of the program. The physical changes had been gradual enough not to be startling. Still, when he looked at Tyrrell's admitting photos and remembered the way he had looked when Zachary had initially found him in that bar, it was a bit of a shock.

Tyrrell had grown gaunt during his drinking binge. Not as thin as Zachary when he went through his depressive cycle, but still noticeably thinner and less substantial than he was now. His eyes and skin had been dull, and Zachary remembered how he had done little else but lie around or sleep during the time he had been at the house. He had not been well. He had not acted like Zachary's brother.

Now, that mischievous smile was back. Zachary could see the twinkle in Tyrrell's eyes again, just like in the eyes of the six-year-old he had been separated from after the fire. Zachary leaned over and gave Tyrrell another hug.

"It's all thanks to Zachary and Kenzie," Tyrrell said. "Kenzie is the one who found this program and got me into it."

"The work has all been yours," Dr. Gable amended. "And it has been a lot of hard work."

Tyrrell nodded, not denying it. Zachary had seen their timetables, and knew that they kept the residents busy from before sunrise with programs, lessons, therapies, chores, and practical applications. If Tyrrell had made friends with the other residents who were there waiting with him, it was only because they had been able to talk while they worked and during meals and group therapy. There had been little time on the schedule for rest or recreation.

Dr. Gable flipped through one of the reports and read from one page, a narrative of the state Tyrrell had been in when he had arrived, the biggest concerns and challenges that the staff saw ahead of him. He put it to the side and picked up another, reading it aloud to Tyrrell. It was a graduation report listing Tyrrell's accomplishments and progress, the things that the other residents and staff admired about him, the areas he had shown strength in and the things that he needed to focus on going forward. Tyrrell's eyes shone proudly. He nodded as Gable reminded him of his responsibilities toward his children, the need to seek out gainful employment as soon as he could, and the need for ongoing therapy, mentoring, and group support. The facility provided employment counseling and other outreach services even after Tyrrell left. Dr. Gable gave him a brochure that listed various numbers to call and reminders of things to follow up on as he left the program.

"You said that you have a place to live," Dr. Gable said. "Fully independent?"

Tyrrell nodded. He looked toward Zachary. "It's Zachary's old apartment, where he lived before he moved in with Kenzie. He was still paying the rent and asked me if I'd move in there and look after the place for the first little while. It's rent-free until I get established, then working my way up to covering his payments to the landlord."

Zachary and Kenzie nodded. Zachary had been ready to terminate the lease on the apartment, and it seemed fortuitous that he'd still had it available to offer to Tyrrell. Kenzie had paid for Tyrrell's admittance into the rehab facility, and Zachary was making his financial contribution by covering Tyrrell's rent until he was making what he needed in order to support himself and pay his obligations for child maintenance to Lindsey. That way, Zachary didn't feel like Kenzie was carrying them. She was happy to put her trust fund to good use for Tyrrell's benefit, but Zachary wanted to do his part too.

Dr. Gable handed a medallion to Tyrrell. "That's a reminder of the time you have spent here and what you have learned in the program and marks the successful conclusion of your time with us. Keep it with you. Keep going to meetings. Don't get sloppy in your sobriety habits. Don't forget everything you've learned here."

"Thanks." Tyrrell rubbed the medallion with his thumb and then hugged the doctor. "Don't know what I would have done without you, Dr. Gable."

"You did the work. Keep it up. Keep working the program."

Tyrrell nodded seriously.

Zachary's mind wandered to Luke and how little support he'd had. What he'd been through in the years since his grandmother had died, and even before that when he'd been passed from one relative to another who didn't want to care for him, had been at least as traumatic as Tyrrell's early years. And his drug addiction was more serious than Tyrrell's alcoholism. But he had only gone through a short, publicly funded recovery program and had only Joss supporting him and trying to keep him on the straight road.

Had they really thought that was all he would need? Zachary knew Luke sometimes went to AA or NA meetings, or had in the beginning, at least. Other than that, his support network was woefully inadequate.

Without the proper support, it had only been a matter of time before Luke would slip and fall back into his old ways.

## 6

Z achary?"

Zachary looked at Tyrrell, who was gazing at him questioningly. Tyrrell shook his head slightly.

"Everything okay?"

"Sorry. My mind was somewhere else."

"Not a good place," Tyrrell said worriedly.

"No, it's okay. I'm sorry. I shouldn't be zoning out in the middle of your whole graduation ceremony."

Zachary knew that Tyrrell would assume it was something to do with their childhood or with Tyrrell's hard fall off the wagon. That would get him thinking about the abuse, their father, and Tyrrell's own difficulties in being a good dad to his kids. A domino line of negative thinking that could eventually lead to another setback.

He tried to smile reassuringly. "Nothing to do with you. Just about a phone call I had this morning before we came to get you. Not something you need to be worried about. Just my ADHD brain. You looking forward to seeing the kids?"

Tyrrell's smile blossomed once more. "Am I ever! It was good to see them when they came to visit. But it will be even better when we can be in a normal setting. Where they can actually play and enjoy themselves."

Dr. Gable held out his hand to Tyrrell, and they shook, two-handed, both grinning. "You enjoy it," Gable told him. "And remember that it doesn't have to be perfect. Kids have up and down times. Storms blow over quickly. They make mistakes, and you will too, but you can both forgive each other and move on to something more positive. Just keep moving forward."

Tyrrell nodded. "I will."

"When you fall down and are disappointed in yourself, pick yourself up, dust yourself off, and give yourself a pep talk. You can learn from your mistakes. It doesn't have to be a disaster."

"I know. I'll remember."

"Good. You can call me. Make use of our outreach services. We're still here to help you to stay on track."

---

Zachary and Tyrrell jabbered like jays all the way to Riverbrook, where Lindsey and the kids lived. Where Tyrrell had also lived until his last setback. Kenzie sat back, eyes closed or looking out the window while listening to their chatter. Zachary had to admit that she had been right; it would have been impossible for her to try to work in that environment.

Even though they had visited Tyrrell regularly once he had finished the initial phase of his rehabilitation, it seemed like there was so much more to share with him. Tyrrell regularly contributed, telling them about this or that class or therapy session at the rehabilitation facility, about the other patients there, about the personalities of the various nurses, therapists, doctors, and other staff.

They were not talked out by the time they got to Riverbrook, but Tyrrell fell silent, watching out the window. Replaying his failures in the past, Zachary was sure.

"Think about the good times," he urged. "You had lots of good times here with the kids."

"I did." Tyrrell nodded immediately. "And with Lindsey, too. When we were first married…" They passed houses, a green area, and a strip of stores. "Things were so good. We had so much fun together, and everything was ahead of us. We had such plans."

And those plans had been shattered by Tyrrell's alcoholism. Lindsey hadn't known anything about his addiction or past when they had gotten married. All of that had come out later. Secrets and addiction were not a good foundation on which to build a marriage.

"You had good times together," Zachary repeated. "And you're going to have lots more time with the kids. Just think of all of the things Mason is going to try before he's an adult."

Tyrrell laughed. "That's assuming he makes it to adulthood. I tell you, sometimes I wonder how he's survived this long."

Just as impulsive as Zachary remembered being himself, Mason had a knack for getting himself in trouble. It was a dangerous world for kids, and wasn't easy for the parents of creative, out-of-the-box thinkers.

Zachary found the playground that Lindsey had described and pulled up to the curb, finding a space among all of the mom vans. Tyrrell's door was open before anyone else's. Zachary took his time unbuckling his seat belt and opening his door. He and Kenzie both delayed as Tyrrell walked over to the climbing equipment so that Tyrrell would be the first one that the children saw.

Mason was hanging upside down from his knees and started to scream. "Daddy! Daddy!"

There was confusion evident on the faces of the other children in the playground as they stopped their conversations and games and turned around to look at him. Mason dropped too fast from the monkey bars, landing in a heap in the sand but, before Zachary had a chance to worry that he might have broken an arm or hit his head, Mason was on his feet and running towards Tyrrell. Alisha, who had been playing a game of tag with some of the older kids, was fast on his heels. Despite her longer legs, she did not sprint past him to get to Tyrrell first.

Mason rocketed into Tyrrell with an impact that Zachary could hear from the sidewalk. But Tyrrell laughed and picked him up and swung him around rather than getting after him. Tyrrell walked to where Alisha had stopped and hugged her around Mason. "Hi, sweetheart."

"I didn't know you were coming here. I didn't know you were out!"

"I just got out this morning. I came straight here before going anywhere else." He kissed her on the forehead.

"You're out, you're out!" Mason crowed. "I missed you so much, Daddy! And now you're home!"

Tyrrell didn't point out that he wouldn't be moving back in with them. Mason already knew that. Zachary and Kenzie got closer and gave the kids hugs and pats on the back as they clung to Tyrrell. Mason was already bubbling over with all of the news about school, what he had been learning, the new projects he was working on, and any trouble he had gotten into. Tyrrell just held him close, nodding as he took it all in.

## 7

Lindsey was standing a distance away. Tyrrell saw her and started walking with the children toward her. She didn't greet him with a hug or kiss, but nodded to him. "You're looking good," she commented, her voice flat.

"Thanks. I'm feeling really good. Physically and mentally. I'm going to beat this thing."

"Good. I hope you do."

They both understood that even if Tyrrell managed to beat his addiction and find a way to be happy and productive, they wouldn't be getting back together again. Too much water had already passed under that bridge. Zachary reached for Kenzie and pulled her into a gentle hug, reminding himself that he had someone now. After his divorce from Bridget, it had taken him a long time to accept the fact that they weren't ever going to get back together. Even when she beat the cancer and got healthy, there was no chance she was ever taking him back. He would never build a life with her. In their case, there had been no children to worry about. They would never have babies together like he had fantasized.

While he accepted that Bridget was now with Gordon Drake and Zachary was with Kenzie, he still couldn't help thinking sometimes about what it would have been like if they had stayed together. If things had worked out the way that he had hoped. And he still battled the obsessive thoughts or compulsions to drive by her house or see what she was doing.

Zachary shook off these thoughts and nodded a greeting to Lindsey. "Hi. Nice to see you again."

Their face-to-face interactions hadn't actually been very pleasant when he had been looking for Tyrrell. Still, Lindsey had apologized for that and thanked him for looking out for Tyrrell, something she didn't have the energy or desire to do. And she had appreciated Zachary and Kenzie taking the kids to visit Tyrrell a few times.

But Lindsey didn't behave the way that Bridget did toward Zachary, so that was a plus. He suspected she didn't even act that way toward Tyrrell, though she probably was more careful what she said and how she behaved toward him in front of other people than she was while they were alone. Living with Tyrrell's addiction, dealing with a man who had just walked off when their premature baby had been struggling for survival in the NICU, would not have been an easy job for even the most patient of spouses.

Tyrrell walked with the kids over to the climbing equipment so they could show him what games they were playing or introduce him to their friends. Zachary wondered how much their friends knew about the situation. Zachary and Kenzie sat down on one of the nearby benches to watch from a distance and Lindsey sat on the next one over. Not right next to them, but close enough that they didn't have to yell to be heard.

"The kids didn't know he was coming?" Zachary asked, though he already knew why.

"Would you have told them? I've seen them go through enough disappointment. They could have a nice time playing at the playground or have a great day with a surprise visit by their dad. Better than telling them that he was coming and then him not showing up. I already know what kind of a day they have when he doesn't show up like he promised."

Zachary nodded. "It was a nice surprise for them."

Lindsey mimed plugging her ears. "Mason's screaming, though..."

Zachary grinned. But he had noticed that she hadn't gotten after Mason for shattering everyone's eardrums. Better he was screaming in excitement than bawling his eyes out.

They all tried to relax. It was still chilly out, and sitting on the molded benches quickly made Zachary's tailbone sore. It had mostly healed, but was still tender if he sat down too hard. Or sat for long on cold, hard, unforgiving surfaces. He stood up and stretched, then leaned on the back of the bench while watching the playground.

"Too much sitting?" Lindsey asked. "Driving all the way out there and back?"

"Yeah." Zachary nodded. "How was your morning?"

"Nerve-racking. I'm always a wreck anticipating whether he will show up or not. Now that he's here..." she snuggled down into her coat. "I can relax. How was your morning?"

She probably meant how did it go at the rehab center, but Zachary's mind went to Joss instead.

"Didn't start out that great," he confessed. "I got a call from Jocelyn."

"That's enough to ruin anyone's day," Lindsey deadpanned.

Zachary chuckled. Joss wasn't exactly known for her sunny personality. She pushed people away from her and was frequently cutting and sarcastic.

"She wanted my help, actually. So, it wasn't too bad."

"Oh, that's good. What does Joss need help with? I got the feeling she is... fiercely independent."

"Yeah, she is." Zachary and Kenzie both nodded. It was a good description. Joss didn't want to have to rely on anyone else. It must have taken a lot for her to call Zachary and ask him for help. "It was... Luke is in some trouble, and she's hoping I can use my detective skills to help him out somehow."

"Luke. What's he done? Never mind, I probably don't want to know. Can you tell me exactly... who Luke is? Tyrrell tried to explain it to me once, but it was a bad time, or maybe he was drunk and not explaining it clearly. He's not her son, right? He's someone that she knew... way back when? They were both involved with the same organization or something?"

Zachary shook his head. "Not exactly. They didn't know each other back then. They didn't work the same area... though Jocelyn knows some of the players that are over the region... kind of like the godfather over Vermont or the northeastern states."

"Godfather?" Lindsey smiled and shook her head.

"I mean, nothing like that, but there is a hierarchy, and he was over the area that Jocelyn worked and the area that Luke worked. So she's familiar with some of those guys, up at the top."

Lindsey rummaged in her purse for a moment, but apparently did not find whatever it was she was looking for. She put it beside her on the bench. "And exactly what were they involved in? Tyrrell said something like trafficking, but I don't know if that means slaves of some kind or drugs, or what."

"They probably have their fingers in all of that kind of thing. But with Joss and Luke..." Zachary readjusted his position, uncomfortable. He was glad he was on his feet rather than sitting down. He didn't feel quite so squirmy. How much would Joss want him to reveal about her life? She had been very open about it with him, but he wasn't sure how she would feel about a relative stranger knowing any details. "They were in the sex trade." He grimaced about the way it sounded. "They were trafficked. Both of them were in the business for years. And Luke was involved in recruiting as well. Bringing other young kids into the organization."

Lindsey's eyes were wide. "Here in Vermont? That kind of thing doesn't happen here."

"It happens here. It happens everywhere. You might think that people have to go to other countries to see the sex trade... but the United States is actually one of the worst."

"Here? Like, right in Vermont? There wouldn't be enough business here to support it."

"Here in Vermont. All over." Zachary didn't know nearly as much about the industry as Joss and Luke, but he'd had an education over the past year. Since learning that Madison was being trafficked.

"That's really sad. So how did Joss and Luke end up together? They're not... involved, are they?"

"No. Nothing like that," Zachary waved his hands as if he could stop her brain from going down that path. "No. Joss is helping Luke. Trying to help him… to stay clean and straight. To have a better life than he could have in the organization."

"How did they meet?"

Zachary shrugged. "That was me. Luke was involved in one of my cases and I went to Joss for advice a couple of times."

"She says you don't listen to her," Lindsey said, looking away from Zachary. She said it in a neutral way, not mocking or teasing, but she didn't really say it as a question, either. Something for Zachary to comment on. Or not.

"Well… yeah, she says that. I try to understand what she's telling me about how the industry works. And I respect her opinion and know that what she is telling me is the truth. But… her advice when it came to Madison and Luke was to stay out of it. To just leave them alone and not try to help." Zachary shrugged. "I couldn't do that. I couldn't just walk away from it, knowing the torture those kids were going through, the kind of life they had to lead. Even if I didn't understand it fully, I knew that much."

"I don't think I could have walked away either," Lindsey agreed. "But I probably would have gotten the police involved. Not tried to do it myself."

"I did get the police involved," Zachary told her emphatically. "As soon as I knew where Madison was, I got them involved. They asked her if she wanted to stay there or go back to her parents, and she wanted to stay there, so she stayed. And there was at least one cop there who was involved with the cartel or looking the other way. So once the shooting started—"

"The shooting?" Lindsey interrupted. Her voice had risen, and everyone nearby looked over at her to see what was going on. Mason and Alisha, attuned to her voice, turned and looked to her for reassurance. Lindsey waved at them to go back to playing with Tyrrell. "Shooting?" she repeated in a lower voice. "I thought you weren't *that kind* of private investigator. That's just on TV." She looked him over, eyes sharp. "You're not carrying a weapon, are you?" She looked toward Mason, as if afraid for him.

"I've never owned a gun," Zachary assured her, "and I never will. I wasn't the one shooting. And believe me, if someone is shooting, I am going the other way as fast as I can. Madison and Noah—Luke— decided they wanted out. I was helping them to get away from there. But this is the kind of boss that doesn't take too kindly to you leaving. They did their best to stop us."

Lindsey didn't say anything for a minute, just looking at Zachary and thinking about this. Her eyes moved over to Kenzie as if asking her to verify what Zachary had said. Maybe she thought he was just being a blowhard, pretending that he lived a more exciting life than he did. But being shot at had not been in Zachary's plans, and he didn't intend to put himself back into that position again.

"Zachary is very careful," Kenzie told Lindsey. "He wouldn't knowingly put anyone in danger. But sometimes… things happen. Situations develop quickly." She was probably thinking about the cases that she had been involved in too. Investigating that she had done while working at the medical examiner's office. Questions that she had asked that had triggered the wrong people to take action.

Lindsey looked back toward the children again, shaking her head. "It would have been nice to know that you were involved in this kind of thing before."

"I'm *not* involved," Zachary repeated. "I stay as far away from violent people as I can."

# 8

It was a bittersweet goodbye. A couple of hours wasn't a long time for the children to be able to play and visit with Tyrrell. But they were delighted that he was back out of rehab and that he seemed to be his old self again. The daddy who didn't drink was much nicer to them than the daddy who did.

Mason cried, despite trying to be a little man and hold the tears back. He snuffled and rubbed his eyes and said brave things, but it was obvious that his heart was breaking and he was worried about when he would see Tyrrell again and if he would still be sober the next time. Quiet Alisha just grew quieter. She said a polite goodbye and just stood by, waiting for Tyrrell to finish saying everything he needed to say to Mason. Eventually, Zachary, Kenzie, and Tyrrell walked back to the car together.

Zachary didn't say anything. He knew how badly Tyrrell must be feeling about having to say goodbye and wanted to comfort him. But he didn't want to fill the air with empty, meaningless words, reassurances that Tyrrell would see them again soon and that they would be fine and that he would be strong and be able to get a job and do all of the other things he was supposed to do so that he could see them regularly. What was the point in that? No one knew the future and, given Tyrrell's history, he probably *would* have another setback. Hopefully not for a few months, maybe even a year or two, but he had not had two consecutive years sober since college.

They all got into the car. Zachary turned on the radio to cover the silence. Tyrrell had been smiling and cheerful the whole time he had been with the children, even when saying goodbye but, glancing in the rear-view mirror, Zachary could see that his expression was now morose, deep frown lines between his knitted brows. Kenzie glanced back at him after several minutes of silence.

"It was a good visit," she told him encouragingly. "The kids were so excited to see you."

Tyrrell nodded.

"You'll be able to see them again soon. We can set something up at our house. Or maybe the wildlife park or something else they would like."

"I can set up visits with my own kids, Kenzie," Tyrrell pointed out. "I appreciate you bringing them when I was in the program, but I can work things out now that I have access to a phone again."

"Oh. Right." Kenzie bit her lip and looked out her side window. "Sorry, I didn't mean to imply that you couldn't handle it yourself. I guess I just got used to having them around."

"I'm just being cranky. It's just that..." Tyrrell didn't finish the sentence. Looking back at him, Zachary could see that he was struggling to sort out his thoughts and put them into words. As someone used to keeping secrets and running away from problems, it probably wasn't easy for him to try to express those feelings.

If his brain worked at all like Zachary's, a crash almost inevitably followed a good time, especially if it was something where he'd had to remain "on" for other people. Even though he enjoyed himself, as Tyrrell had with the children, he couldn't seem to hold on to that happiness. Instead, as soon as it was over, or sometimes before events had officially ended, his brain started to analyze everything that had happened, worrying over whether he had answered every question the right way, remembering where he had stumbled in an answer, not said something when he should, or embarrassed himself some other way.

And it wasn't just the way that Bridget had criticized him after social events, even if he would have liked to put all the blame on her. His self-critical obsessive thoughts had started before ever meeting Bridget. He could remember it from a very early age. Maybe it had been exacerbated by Bridget's angry remonstrances and the many irritated foster mothers who had tried to bring Zachary up to be a polite and respectable young man, but the tendency to fall apart and disparage himself after a party or holiday had originated long before that.

"You're crashing," he suggested to Tyrrell.

Tyrrell looked in his direction, tilting his head slightly to consider it.

"Your brain is going through all of the things you did wrong or should have done better. Today and at other times. All of your failings."

Tyrrell's head bobbed up and down. "How do you know that?"

"I do it too."

Tyrrell cupped his palms over his eyes, leaning his head back against the headrest. "How do I make it stop? I know it was good that I got to see them today, but I almost wish I hadn't. I was calm while I was in the program. I had trouble after sessions sometimes, but we were so busy that it was just going from one thing to another and there wasn't really time to spend going over it all. At the end of the day, I would be so exhausted I would just fall into bed."

At that point, Zachary's hamster-wheel brain would happily have picked up with the hate-fest no matter how tired he was, going into overdrive trying to analyze everything. The more overtired he was, the harder it would be to shut off the voices and go to sleep. Tyrrell was lucky to be able to get straight to sleep after an overprogrammed day.

"Give yourself some time," Zachary said with a shrug. "Keep telling yourself that it was nice to see them so that you don't dread it next time. I don't really know more than that. You can talk about it with your therapist. Maybe they can give you some better advice."

"I know one thing that would calm it down."

They all sat in silence. Of course they all knew what Tyrrell was talking about. He was used to taking alcohol to numb the anxiety and self-recriminations. But he knew that he couldn't go back to it. Doing so would lead to more pain and heartache and would ruin everything he had accomplished in the rehab program.

Zachary pressed the buttons on the radio, looking for a faster song with a heavier beat to help fill the silence and distract them all from negative thoughts.

---

## 9

By the time they reached the apartment, the worst of the storm of emotions seemed to have passed. Tyrrell offered a few comments on his plans for the next few days and shared memories of some of the towns they passed through. Zachary pulled into the reserved space in the parking lot in front of the apartment building, feeling the satisfied "click" in his brain that he belonged there. He had been happy while he'd been in the apartment. Mostly. He was happier at Kenzie's, of course; that was his home now. But he'd felt good about living at the apartment. It had taken him a long time to get back on his feet after everything that had happened, but he had been able to move on and be independent again.

He let out a satisfied sigh. Kenzie heard it and looked at him, brows raised.

"Happy to be home?"

Zachary shrugged. "Good memories. I'd rather be with you."

"Of course you would," Tyrrell agreed. They all laughed. Zachary handed the apartment keys to Tyrrell and let him lead the way to figure out which key to use in the front doors of the building and in the door to his new apartment.

Tyrrell pushed the door open and there was a bit of a whoosh as the still air of the apartment stirred and mixed with the air from the hallway. There were a couple of flyers on the floor, and Tyrrell stooped to pick them up, then held them out toward Zachary. Zachary held up his hands.

"I don't want them. They're yours."

Tyrrell laughed and looked down at them. "Yeah. I guess they are," he said ruefully. He swiped back his hair with his free hand. "My first junk mail at the apartment." He still hesitated about what to do with it. He ended up putting it on the table to look at later. Zachary would probably just have tossed it out. But Tyrrell didn't know the neighborhood and might want to see what stores and restaurants the flyers were for.

Tyrrell took a deep breath and looked around, letting his breath out again slowly. "This is great, Zachary. You don't know how much I appreciate having somewhere to land. I'll make it up to you one day. Pay you back somehow."

"You already paid me back. By coming back into my life and introducing me to my siblings again. Before you came back, I didn't have anyone." He looked at Kenzie. "No biological family, I mean. I have Mr. Peterson—Lorne—and Pat. And I have Kenzie. But I didn't have any blood connections."

Tyrrell shrugged as if none of that meant anything. "So, how long were you here? Is this where you were when you and Kenzie met?"

"No. Two years ago, I was at the previous apartment. The one that…" Zachary trailed off.

Tyrrell looked at him expectantly. "The one that what?" he asked with a laugh. "The one that Kenzie didn't like? Did she make you get somewhere nicer?"

Kenzie squeezed Zachary's arm. "The one that burned," she told Tyrrell in a quiet voice.

Tyrrell's smile disappeared. "What?" He looked from Kenzie to Zachary, brows drawn down in confusion. "It was our old house that burned down. Back when we were little. When Zachary was ten."

"I know. And then there was another fire." She kept a close eye on Zachary, waiting to see how he reacted to the conversation. "Right after we met. Everything was destroyed. His wallet and ID too. It was a big mess."

"A pain in the neck," Zachary agreed. He wiped his perspiring forehead. He tried to focus on the details that Kenzie had mentioned instead of picturing the inferno, instead of letting himself go back there. "Do you know how hard it is to get your ID replaced when you don't have any ID? It took forever."

"How come you never told me that?" Tyrrell demanded. "Why wouldn't you tell me that you were in another fire?"

Zachary felt the heat of the first fire. Unimaginably hot, scorching his skin, the smoke filling his lungs. He had screamed for Tyrrell and the others to wake up, to escape the house while they still could, as he tried to squeeze himself into the narrow space under the couch for protection. Both times, he had been carried out by a firefighter. Carried out into the crisp, fresh winter air, so cold that it cut into his lungs already seared by the smoke.

"It's okay," Kenzie's voice told him. "Look around. Anchor yourself. What are five things you see?"

Zachary tried to see through the smoke and flames and confusion of the fires, both of them merging together in his memory and blotting everything else out.

"What do you hear?" Kenzie tried again. "Can you hear my voice?"

Zachary managed a nod. He could hear the sirens of that night, the crackle of the flames, his own strangled screams as he cried his throat raw.

"I can hear neighbors talking," Kenzie said. "Next door, I guess? It doesn't sound like they're arguing. They're just loud. And the ding of the elevator?"

Zachary heard the elevator and then the sound of footsteps in the hallway. He remembered the firefighters' heavy, clomping steps. Not like the light tread he heard down the hall.

"Yes," he whispered hoarsely. "Smell... fried food. Chicken? And... onions. Sweat." His own sweat, probably, rank with fear, clammy under his armpits and rolling down his back. Not smoke. The smell of the smoke was fading.

Kenzie rubbed his shoulders. "It's okay," she repeated. "Look around."

He blinked heavy-lidded eyes as if he were just coming out of a dream. The apartment looked just the same as it had moments earlier, but he felt like he had taken a journey back and forth through time. It was disorienting. Kenzie went over to the sink, ran cold water, and then filled a glass from the cupboard. She placed it on the table in front of him. "Okay?"

Zachary nodded. He was sitting at the table, though he couldn't remember how he had gotten there. Tyrrell hovered nearby, looking ready to jump into action but unsure what to do. Kenzie sat down in one of the other chairs, though she pulled it back and turned it at an angle so that she wasn't staring directly at him and he had a bit of space. Zachary picked up the glass and took a few gulps of the cold water, soothing the pain in his throat.

"*That* is probably why he didn't talk to you about it," Kenzie told Tyrrell.

"Uh… yeah, I guess so." Tyrrell flushed pink. He looked at Zachary uncertainly. "I thought that you didn't have flashbacks to the fire anymore."

He took another swallow of cold water. "I can be around a fire without being triggered now," he said hoarsely. "Not quite the same thing."

Tyrrell nodded slowly. "I didn't mean to do that," he said uncomfortably. "That looked like a bad one."

Zachary was thinking about it, wondering why it had been so intense, when he'd been able to head off most of his flashbacks recently, using techniques that Dr. B had given him to turn his mind to something else, or being able to anchor quickly before he became totally immersed in the experience. He sipped the water more slowly, not wanting to drain the glass.

"Double-whammy, I think. Because you were there the first time…" He turned his gaze from Tyrrell to Kenzie.

"And I was there when you fell asleep before the apartment fire," Kenzie finished. "Did you think that I was still there when you woke up to the fire?"

"I didn't know. I heard your voice—I dreamed that I heard you talking—before I woke up in the smoke. You *weren't* there…" He rubbed his forehead. "No. But I guess I got some wires crossed."

Kenzie nodded.

"It was like both were happening at the same time."

Tyrrell swore under his breath. "I'm sorry, bro. I shouldn't have asked you about it."

"It's okay. I *should* talk about it. Dr. B says that's the only way to get used to it, to get over being triggered. Just to look at it and talk about it normally, like this."

Still, his skin crawled and he was uncomfortable, worried that he might flash back a second time. Dr. Boyle said that he wouldn't once he was anchored, but he wasn't sure he believed it. His brain didn't always work the way it should.

"So you lost everything again," Tyrrell shook his head in wonder. "I don't know how you did it. You moved here afterward? How did you rent a place without any ID? How could you even get money out of the bank?"

"It wasn't easy. I couldn't get a place until my ID was reissued, and the bank was a whole other story. I had to see the bank manager and have someone swear an affidavit about my identity. They at least had a photocopy of my driver's license on the file so they could see my face matched. And I waited until I got my settlement check because I wasn't really sure what I could afford, and had all of the costs of getting set up again…"

"Did you stay with Kenzie?"

They both shook their heads.

"No, I barely knew her yet. We'd been on a couple of dates, that's all. But one of the cops that I know, he put me up on his couch for a few days." Zachary shrugged. "Though… 'a few days' kind of became a few months."

"Well, yeah. With having to get all of that done first. You're lucky you didn't end up on the street or in a shelter. Or living out of your car." Tyrrell gave a short laugh. He had been living out of his car when Zachary had tracked him down. Though really, he lived in the bar and only slept in the car when he got kicked out of the bar.

"I was lucky," Zachary agreed. "Kenzie helped out. I don't know if I would have gone to Mario on my own."

# 10

J oss called in the evening to tell Zachary that he should be able to visit Luke in the morning. Zachary felt pulled in two directions. He wanted to help Luke, of course. He wanted to see the boy and make sure that he was okay. But he also dreaded going to the jail and seeing him, knowing there was very little he could actually do. Joss and Luke were looking to him to solve this problem, to somehow get Luke out of the trouble he was in. But Zachary wasn't a lawyer, and it sounded like they had an open-and-shut case against the teen. He dreaded Luke's disappointment and the guilt of not being able to do the one thing Joss had asked him to.

It was a rough night, even taking sleep and anti-anxiety meds. Thinking about the visit with Luke, trying to anticipate what would happen and what to say to Luke to reassure him. Certain he wasn't going to be able to do anything to help, but desperate to do something. It didn't make for a restful night, even with chemical assistance.

Sunday was Kenzie's day to sleep in or at least to have a lazy morning, so she was just up, still in her dressing gown and blinking at her first cup of coffee, as Zachary was preparing to leave.

"Will the jail let you visit on a Sunday?" Kenzie asked. "And this early?"

"It won't be early anymore when I get there. And I checked their website. Looks like they still allow visits on Sunday."

"Seems like a wise thing to check before investing the time in driving down there."

"Yeah," Zachary agreed, checking his pockets for his keys.

"I mean… it doesn't sound like you talked to anyone and are only guessing that they'll let you in to see him. Don't you think you should call first?"

"What?" Zachary found his keys in a left-hand pocket, which was odd because he was right-handed. He shook his head, looking down at them. Maybe he had put them in his pocket while the coat was still hung up.

"You should call the jail. Make sure that you're going to be allowed in to see him before you drive down."

"Joss already made sure I'd be able to get in. I'm on a list somewhere as an approved visitor."

Kenzie rolled her eyes. "I still think you should do more than look at their website."

"It's easy to tell someone 'no' over the phone. It's a lot harder when they're right in front of you and had to drive a couple of hours to get there."

"But they could still tell you no."

"They could tell me yes over the phone and still tell me no when I got there too." Zachary shrugged. He was pretty good at talking his way into places, and he generally managed to get on with law enforcement officers, despite the reputation of his profession. He wouldn't tell them that he was there as a private investigator. He would just say that he was a friend.

"Okay…" Kenzie drew the word out and had that "Don't come crying to me when it doesn't work out" tone in her voice that he'd frequently gotten from foster moms. But things didn't work out the way he wanted when he tried to follow their instructions either. He might as well do things his own way.

"I'll try not to be too long," Zachary told her, giving her a quick peck on the cheek. "But even if I'm only an hour or two, then with the driving time…"

"Hopefully, you'll be home by supper."

Zachary nodded his agreement.

"Will you stop and see Joss as well?"

He thought about it. He had been so focused on getting through the visit with Luke that he hadn't thought about stopping in to talk to Joss.

"Maybe. I don't know yet. We'll see how the day goes. And she might not want to see me."

So far, she hadn't told him to get lost when he had just shown up on her doorstep without arranging something ahead of time, but she *had* told him to call the next time. She didn't seem to like meeting with him at her house.

"You never know," Kenzie said. "Though since you're doing her a favor, I would think she would show a little more appreciation and not just turn you away."

"Maybe. But we are talking about Joss here."

Kenzie laughed.

Zachary kissed her again and got on his way.

---

Zachary sat looking at the Kent police station when he got there. The trip had gone all too fast. He still didn't have any idea what to say to Luke or how to go about investigating what had happened in a way that would be beneficial to Luke's case. He would just have to find out everything he could and hope that would lead him to a solution.

Sitting in the car wasn't going to get him anywhere. If he lost the motivation to get out of the car and go into the police station, it was going to be that much harder. Zachary pushed himself to open the door and swing his feet out the door and hoped that the rest of his body would follow even though his brain was reluctant. The trick worked, and he locked and shut the door and headed into the police station without much more thought.

It was quiet. Apparently, not a lot happened there on a Sunday morning. There were no complainants gathered around the front desk, no shouting back and forth or ringing of phones. Just one cop sitting at a computer within view of the service window. Officer of the Day. Maybe someone who had screwed up and been punished by having to spend his weekend doing nothing but sitting and waiting. Zachary smiled as warmly as possible.

"Sorry, no services today," the cop told him. "Come back tomorrow."

"I'm here to see an inmate in the jail. He was just brought in recently. Luke—no," Zachary looked down at his notepad for the name Joss had given him. "Joseph Daniel Bryant."

The cop stood up and looked Zachary over. "You made arrangements?"

"My sister set it up."

The cop considered for another moment, like he might be able to come up with some excuse to send Zachary away. Then he reached for a rack of folders and thumbed through them. He pulled out one photocopied form and slid it across the counter to Zachary. "Fill that out."

Zachary had not anticipated having to fill out a bunch of paperwork to see Luke. He probably should have. The justice system ran on paper and red tape. Zachary was used to being able to skate by most of the paperwork requirements in Roxboro because most of the cops he dealt with knew him and didn't feel like doing extra work for a routine inquiry.

Zachary put the paper on the counter square in front of him and looked at the cop, who, after a moment, handed him a cheap stick pen to fill out the form. He stood there waiting as Zachary started to read through the headings on the form.

"I'm a slow writer," Zachary said. "You might as well read a book or something."

The young cop gave him a grin and sat back down in front of the computer. It was easier for Zachary to focus on each question and carefully scratch in his answers without someone hovering. He wasn't always so slow writing things down but, if he wanted someone else to be able to read it, he had to go slowly and form each letter with care. Sometimes even he couldn't read the chicken scratch that filled his notepads.

Eventually, he got down to the bottom of the page and went back to review each space to see if he had missed anything. When he looked up, the cop was looking in his direction.

"Done yet?"

"Yeah, I think so."

The young officer stood up again and took it from Zachary. Reading through the form, he asked a couple of questions and added notes to the spaces, sometimes striking out Zachary's answer completely. He glanced over it one more time, then took it back to the computer and started typing. He didn't seem to be transcribing all of Zachary's answers. Maybe just checking to see if the names matched up and what Luke's status was. He tapped a few more buttons and the printer beside him started to whir. He handed Zachary the printout. "There you go. You need to go around the outside of the building to the jail intake door. It's going to be locked. You'll have to press the buzzer. Takes a few times, sometimes. Don't come back and tell me they're not answering. There's nothing I can do about it. Keep buzzing until they do. Give them that paper. If your inmate is available, they'll take you through the process."

Zachary looked down at the printout. "Okay. Thanks for your help."

"Have a nice day."

## 11

Zachary retreated, following the officer's instructions to go around to the other side of the building. There was a red panel with several warnings on it and a large button. Zachary pressed it firmly and held it in for a second. He released it and waited. Having been warned by the Officer of the Day, he knew it would probably be a while. If they were routinely slow to answer, they would probably be all that much slower on a Sunday, with reduced staff.

It was only a few seconds after his second ring that the door opened, startling him.

The uniformed woman who glared out at him was short, but broad-shouldered and stout. Zachary stepped back a little, feeling crowded.

"What is it?" she snapped.

"I'm here to visit…?"

She looked at his hand and snatched the printout from him. Her eyes ran back and forth, scanning the information on the page. "The kid."

Zachary nodded. "Yeah."

She made a sideways motion with her head and stepped back, at the same time pushing the door open wider for him. Zachary entered, and she led the way through a couple more locked doors to a bare-looking reception area. There was a chute; an empty doorway with counters running down both sides of it, like the metal detector and x-ray that he was used to going through at the Roxboro police department when he went to see Kenzie, or the security check-in for an airport.

"Remove everything from your pockets," the corrections officer told him, throwing a bin onto one of the counters. "Your shoes, belt, watch, and any jewelry."

"Should I take off my coat?"

She rolled her eyes. "Yes."

Zachary proceeded to follow her instructions. When he placed his wallet in the bin, she picked it up, flipped it open to look at his identification, and compared it with the printout. She put it back in the bin. Zachary felt vulnerable after taking off his shoes and belt, as if they were somehow protective. Like a suit of armor.

"That everything?" she asked when he was finished.

Zachary nodded. She pushed a button to start the conveyor belt and the bin disappeared into an x-ray. She stared at the screen for a few seconds longer than seemed necessary. Zachary shifted anxiously. He rubbed one foot over the other, wishing she would hurry up and give him his shoes back.

"Okay. Step forward. Walk slowly through the doorway."

Zachary obeyed. His heart sank at the warning beep and the light that came on at the top of the doorway. He looked at her. She picked up a wand and started to run it around his body.

"Usually just something like the rivets in your jeans or an underwire bra for women," she assured him. She paused at his elbow as the wand beeped. She ran it around his side again, and again it beeped in the same place. "You ever break your arm?"

Zachary looked at his arm as if it belonged to someone else. Eventually, he nodded. It had been a long time ago and he didn't remember any details. Still, he vaguely remembered that arm being in a cast that had banged into everything and had driven him crazy with itchiness. "Yeah."

"Got screws in it, didn't you?"

"I haven't got a clue." Zachary looked at the wand. "I've never had it trigger a security check before."

"Yeah, this is one of the most sensitive wands on the market." She stepped back from him half a pace. "Hardly anyone gets through here without it going off."

Zachary didn't know whether he found that reassuring or disturbing.

"All right, through here." She motioned to a steel door.

Zachary looked back toward the bin that held his personal items. "Uh, do I get back…"

"You'll get your stuff when you leave. If you want, we can go through the whole business of putting it into a locker, but you're the only one here. It's more efficient to just leave it in the bin and you can get it when you leave."

Zachary hesitated, thinking about his camera in particular. Since he had turned eleven, he'd taken a camera with him everywhere he went. First, the one that Mr. Peterson had given him for his birthday, and then, after the apartment fire, a small digital camera he had purchased to use for work. Mr. Peterson had given him another analog camera for his hobby pictures. He hadn't been allowed to keep a camera with him at Bonnie Brown or other institutions that he had been in, and maybe that was what was holding him back. He didn't want to feel like he was the one incarcerated there.

"Could I take it out to my car and leave it there?"

She rolled her eyes. "No, because then we have to go through this whole thing again. Do you want to leave it in the bin or put it in a secure locker?"

"Umm… a locker, I guess. There is some sensitive equipment in there…"

Not really. An off-the-shelf phone and digital camera. Not expensive or sensitive enough to warrant his paranoia. But hopefully, she couldn't tell the difference.

It took ten minutes to get everything transferred to a locker. Zachary was allowed to set the electronic security code so he would be the only one able to open it, yet he wouldn't have a key with him when he went in to visit Luke. As if they could have effected some

47

kind of attack or escape with only a locker key. Then the CO finally took him through the steel door into a space that immediately felt like a prison. Stale air, dimmer lighting, concrete walls that looked like they had been painted over a dozen times, yet still didn't even come close to being clean. Zachary breathed slowly, concentrating on his breaths in and out. He wasn't exactly claustrophobic. But he didn't like to be locked up.

They zipped down one hall and into another. The woman indicated another door. "In here."

Zachary opened the door and found a visitor room with a table and two chairs, all bolted to the floor. The room was chilly, as if it were pulling in air directly from outside.

"Have a seat. I'll be about ten minutes."

Zachary wasn't looking forward to sitting in the stark, cold room by himself for ten minutes. But he had been through worse. He'd spent days at a time in the detention block at Bonnie Brown. He gave a brief nod and sat down in the chair that faced the door. He relaxed into it the best he could and closed his eyes. Maybe a nap. He'd had a restless night. Maybe if his brain was bored enough with the room, he could catch up on some sleep.

But his brain wasn't bored with the lack of stimulation. It decided instead to go into hyperdrive, anticipating danger.

"Just chill," Zachary breathed to himself. "Nothing is going to happen here." He took several deep breaths and tried to regulate his heart rate.

## 12

The minutes stretched out, and Zachary was pretty sure that the CO was gone significantly longer than the ten minutes promised. But that was the way things went sometimes. People didn't literally mean ten minutes when they said that. They just meant "soon." There wasn't anything wrong.

But Zachary's brain immediately began to run possible scenarios. It was jail. A lot of things could have happened to Luke. They might have found him hanging in his cell. He might have been beaten up by other inmates. He might have had an altercation with a CO. He could have died unexpectedly in custody. It happened. They had special terminology for such deaths. Excited delirium. Even if the person hadn't been excited or delirious. Zachary had been in detention at Bonnie Brown when a young autistic girl had died in the isolation cell next to his with her hands cuffed behind her back. Positional asphyxia. They hadn't had a word for it at the time. They said that she'd just died, some weird side effect of her neurodivergence. But the guards had hidden the fact that she had been handcuffed all night. By the time the medical team got there, the cuffs had been removed and she had been repositioned and covered with a blanket. The authorities who investigated it never knew what had really happened.

How would Zachary explain it to Joss if something had happened to Luke? How could he take that kind of news to her? And how could they insist on any kind of justice, knowing that Luke was basically a non-person in the eyes of the justice system? He couldn't get much lower in the eyes of society than a murderer, sex worker, and child predator. Everyone would be celebrating Luke's death.

The door thunked open, and the woman CO escorted Luke into the room. She didn't give him any instructions, but pushed him into the other chair and ran one of the chains connected to his shackles through the anchor in the table. Luke wore an orange jumpsuit that looked way too lightweight for the cool room temperature. Hopefully the cell block was kept warmer than the meeting rooms, which were not in constant use, but would heat up quickly with several bodies in them at once. Luke's feet were bare in what looked like flips flops intended for use in a locker room shower. Thin and soft, intended to protect him from fungus or other contaminants, but not warm or protective.

"You've got an hour," the CO told Zachary, then left them alone without a word to Luke.

Zachary looked Luke over. "Hey. How are you doing?"

Luke had a black eye, a nice shiner that looked about a day old. The bruising seemed to be spreading to the other eye, too. In another day, he would probably look like a raccoon. Luke was blond, his hair a little longer than Zachary thought was currently considered stylish. Even with his black eye, he was still handsome. *Really hot*, one of Madison's friends had said in describing him. He looked like someone who could have been in a boy band. A heartthrob. Clean cut, just rebellious enough to be seen as a bad boy. Just the type to lure teen girls—and boys—and coax them into a business that they never would have considered before they met him. It had clearly been at least a day since he had shaved. A fine stubble covered his jawline. More than peach fuzz, but Luke was still very young and his whiskers thin.

Luke looked away from Zachary, not answering. Zachary was silent for a few moments, waiting to see if that would draw Luke out.

"Joss called me. She is very worried about you."

Not even a shrug in response. Luke still didn't even look at him.

"She wants me to see if I can help you. Figure out what happened and how to get you out of here."

Luke stared up at the ceiling.

It would be a pretty quick interview if Zachary couldn't get any response from Luke.

"Luke. Please. Even if you don't think there is anything I can do to help, humor me. Joss wants me to do what I can. She cares about you. I do too. Other people care what happens to you. Don't just shut everyone out."

Luke lowered his eyes from the ceiling to look Zachary in the face briefly, then he looked away again. In that fleeting moment, Zachary saw pain and fear. Gone so quickly that he couldn't even be sure that he had really seen it. Maybe Zachary had just imagined it. He knew it should be there, so he had manufactured the illusion himself.

"Did you get any sleep last night? Have anything to eat?"

Luke shook his head. At least that was a response.

"Are you in a cell by yourself? Away from people who might hurt you?"

A shrug. Zachary wasn't sure whether that was confirmation or an acknowledgment that there were people there who would want to hurt him, but that he didn't care. He needed to act tough, as if he didn't care what happened to him. Zachary knew what that was like. Act vulnerable, and he opened himself up to more abuse. Act like he didn't care, and a predator wouldn't get as much of a kick out of harassing and abusing him.

"What do you need? Is there anything we could bring you?"

Zachary had no idea what the jail would or wouldn't allow, but it was just a tactic to get Luke to talk. See what he wanted, what he was thinking of, what he needed for comfort. Anything to get the ball rolling.

Luke remained silent.

"You're as quiet as Rhys," Zachary teased.

Rhys was mostly nonspeaking, and holding a conversation with him could be challenging. But at least he *tried* to communicate his thoughts, something that Luke had no intention of doing at the moment.

"What you need is a phone," Zachary suggested. The tool that Rhys used the most, outside of gestures. A few thumbed words and a gif or two usually helped Rhys get across the point he was trying to make. He didn't use sign language or an AAC, none of the systems that nonspeaking children were taught to use. It was as if Rhys couldn't use any standardized communication. As if doing so would make him too vulnerable. He had withdrawn and stopped talking when his grandfather was murdered, and it seemed that no therapy would ever help him regain what he had lost.

Luke just snorted and looked steadily away.

Zachary could feel the time slipping away from them. The CO had said that she would give them an hour. It didn't look like that was going to be enough time to get Luke's story out of him.

"Luke. Come on. Help me here. Let me do something for you. It's pretty hard to do anything if you won't say a word to me."

Luke shook his head.

"Who did you kill?" Zachary demanded, making his voice harder. Luke needed to listen. Zachary needed to be firmer with him. To insist that he respond. "Or were accused of killing? Tell me his name."

Luke's eyes flicked over to him briefly. Zachary watched him closely and saw a slight shift in his breathing pattern, a little flare to his nostrils. Readying himself. Luke cleared his throat.

"Eyler," he offered finally.

"Eyler? That was the victim's name? What's his first name?"

Luke shook his head. He clearly didn't know. Did that mean that it wasn't someone he knew well? Closely enough to know the man's last name, but not his first.

"And who is Eyler? Someone you knew from before?"

A hesitation from Luke. Tensing in readiness. Then looking away again and letting his shoulders fall slack again. Studied calm. Pretending to know nothing, to be unaffected by it all.

"So he was someone in Gordo's organization?" Zachary asked, hoping that the name of the big boss would shock Luke into reacting. Luke's eyes flew back to Zachary, then quickly away again. Good control. But then, he had been training to hide his feelings his whole life. From the time he was a little boy and no one wanted to be responsible for his care. For the years that he was in the trafficking ring and no one cared how he felt about anything, only about whether he did his job well or not. He'd had to hide his feelings if he was going to lure innocent young women and men into the organization and not give away his role until it was too late.

"Did Eyler recognize you? Come after you?"

No response.

"Were you attacked, Luke? I can see that you're hurt. Did he try to take you back?"

## 13

L uke's Adam's apple bobbed with a hard swallow. Zachary watched his face for any other indication of what he was thinking or feeling. He was good at reading facial expressions and body language, a skill he had honed growing up in an abusive home and foster care where it was essential to read the intentions of everyone around him, and a valuable skill for a PI, used to dealing with people who tried to hide things from him. Even clients tried to keep their secrets.

But Luke didn't make it easy. If anything, his expression flattened even more. He was like stone. His gaze was no longer on the ceiling or to the side. Instead, his eyes glazed and trying to meet his eyes was like looking into a mirror. There was nothing there to see.

"Luke." Zachary knew he was gone. Swallowed up in a flashback of what had happened with Eyler, or maybe in a memory further back than that, knowing Eyler in the trafficking ring or something that had happened to him when he was younger.

Or maybe there was no memory at all, but just dissociation. Luke had told him once before that it was best to just go somewhere else. Not to think about it. Not to form the memory in the first place, just to pull back and not be a part of the experience. He had learned to do it while being trafficked, just as Zachary and so many other traumatized kids had learned that there was only one way to escape when physically unable to protect themselves from the abuse.

"Luke." He touched Luke's hand, even though he knew it was probably against the rules to have any physical contact with him. There were lists of rules printed on plastic panels screwed into the wall, but Zachary hadn't bothered to read them. He'd stretched his brain enough filling out the long form at the police station.

Luke jerked back as though he'd been shocked. The chains clanked loudly, making both of them jump. Luke's jaw clenched and Zachary saw anger in his eyes for the first time. Fury at being touched or at being pulled back into the present.

"Tell me what happened," Zachary told him. "Let it out. It isn't going to help you to keep it bottled up."

"No."

"You've been accused of murder. This isn't some minor drug dealing charge. If you don't have a defense, you will go to prison for twenty years or more. Maybe for life. Is that what you want?"

Luke sat back in his chair, pulling on his chains in an effort to fold his arms into his body and get as far away from Zachary as possible. "Yes."

Zachary's brain hitched. He hadn't been expecting that answer. He thought he could talk Luke into seeing how serious the situation was. To show him that his only hope was to cooperate with Zachary, Joss, and a lawyer to figure out how to get clear of the charges, or at least to mitigate the length of the sentence.

"You want to go to prison?"

"Yes. So go home. Don't come back here. Don't bug me with your questions. Tell your sister too. I don't want anything to do with her. Not with either of you. Just leave me be."

"Why?"

Luke shook his head. He looked as confused by Zachary's question as Zachary felt about Luke saying he didn't want anything to do with Joss. Joss had been his lifesaver. The person who had been there for him for the past year, helping him to move forward and to stay out of trouble. He knew that there was a strong relationship between the two of them. An affection that ran deep. Not quite like a parent and child, but something similar. Maybe like the feelings that Zachary had for Mr. Peterson, though Luke's feelings were still seedlings, not having grown over decades like Zachary's. Still, he remembered how he had felt those first few weeks when he had been in Mr. Peterson's home, finding an unexpected ally, someone who cared about him even knowing his history. The first parental figure who really seemed to care anything about him, and the only one who had stayed a part of his life since.

"This is my life," Luke said. "Just stay out of it. Both of you."

"We don't want to stay out of it. Joss cares about you, Luke. She cares what happens to you. Let us help. Maybe you're right, maybe there isn't anything that we can do in the end, but we can at least try."

"Just back off."

Zachary shook his head slowly. "I'm not going to do that, Luke."

"It's not worth it. *I'm* not worth it."

"You are."

"I'm a rat. I'm sewer scum. Why would you want to help someone like me?"

"You're a person, and someone that I like and enjoy being around. And do you think that just anyone could live with Joss and put up with her attitude? That takes a special talent. That's someone worth defending."

Luke gave a bark of laughter. "I've never met anyone more real than your sister."

Zachary nodded. "She doesn't put a false face on for anyone," he agreed. "She calls it like she sees it. And if you don't like it... well, that's too bad. Take her as she is, opinions and all."

Luke's body language relaxed a little. His anger over Zachary touching him had faded. But the pain in his expression had not.

"Was it Eyler who hurt you? Is that how you got the black eye?"

Luke shook his head. "I don't know. I don't remember."

"Were you under the influence? Drinking? Drugs?"

"I'm clean. Not that it did me any good." His lips pressed together. "What was the point in going straight? This would have been easier if I had been high."

"Why don't you remember, then?"

THEY CAME FOR HIM

"Just don't."

Zachary tried to see past Luke's mask. Could he remember and didn't want to talk about it? Could he not remember because he had dissociated during the experience or suppressed it afterward? Was he lying about being clean and had actually been blitzed out of his mind?

"How did the police come to arrest you? How did they know it was you?"

"I was there. They could see what happened."

Zachary winced inwardly. Being caught at the scene was not a good thing. Hard to get around that. "Were there witnesses?"

"No."

"Physical evidence? Your fingerprints? Your DNA?"

Luke shrugged. "Probably."

The police wouldn't have had a chance to process everything yet. But it didn't take long to compare fingerprints. If they had caught him in the act, they didn't need fingerprints and DNA to know that he did it. But they would be used in court to prove he was the killer.

"Why haven't you gotten a lawyer? You need someone."

"There's no point." Luke stared at Zachary. "Don't you get it? Why bother? Nothing is going to help." He closed his eyes as if exhausted. "Don't waste the effort."

"Don't give up. I know you wouldn't just kill this guy without a reason. That means there was some justification. That can get you a lighter sentence, if nothing else."

"You don't know that."

"What?"

"That I wouldn't kill him without a reason."

Zachary just looked at Luke.

"You don't know anything about me, dude," Luke pointed out. "You know nothing but what I've told you, and that could all be lies. I'm good at lying. I'm a professional. It's how I survived. Why would I stop lying just because I was talking to you?"

He was right, of course. Zachary didn't have any outside verification that any of Luke's story was true. An old woman who had said that Luke's grandmother had died and then he had fallen in with bad company. That was the only thing he knew about Luke from anyone's mouth but Luke's own. Or Madison's, which was the same thing, since she only parroted what he had wanted her to believe.

But Zachary believed that he knew the truth when he heard it. That he understood enough of the pain in Luke's eyes when he talked about his childhood and early days with the cartel to know it was the truth. And Joss had been in the business. She knew what it was like and everything she had said aligned with what Luke described.

He trusted Joss to be able to see through Luke's pretenses and know what the real deal was.

He met Luke's eyes. "I know you."

Luke snorted and looked away, eyes going up to the ceiling again, chin lifted in defiance. "You don't know me, man. You don't know me at all."

Zachary straightened. He rubbed the back of his neck, stiff from slouching in the hard molded chair. "Before long, our time is going to be up and the CO will be back to take you to your cell. Do you need anything?"

Luke's mouth started to form a word, then he shook his head and pressed his lips closed again.

"I'm sure they must allow me to bring some stuff in. Books. Candy. Writing paper."

Luke shook his head again.

The decision to close his mouth appeared to be final. He wasn't going to say anything else to Zachary. The sparse answers that he'd provided were going to have to do. Zachary wasn't going to be able to get any more details out of him. Luke wasn't assisting his own defense.

"Will you talk to a lawyer if we get you one?"

Luke again shook his head.

"You don't need to throw your life away like this," Zachary said.

Luke's chains jangled as he again tried to fold his arms over his chest but was defeated by the shortness of his tether. He sat like a statue, staring past Zachary and determined not to help him.

# 14

The CO again left Zachary sitting at the table in the meeting room while she dealt with Luke. Zachary wondered if she were the only one at the jail on a Sunday morning. There couldn't be a lot to do in a small-town jail on a Sunday morning, when the court and the police station were both shut down. Maybe the jail was empty some days, without even a few drunks to keep the bunks warm.

Zachary was eager to get out of the meeting room but knew that being impatient wouldn't move along any faster. Any anxiety or impatience with the process would just make it seem longer. He reviewed the few things that Luke had told him, trying to look at them from every angle and squeeze as much information from each word and gesture as he could. Once he got back to his car, he would write down everything he could before he started to forget. And he would write down questions that he needed answered and possible avenues to pursue.

While he was still analyzing each aspect of Luke's answers, the corrections officer returned. She stood in the doorway and nodded to Zachary.

"All right. Let's get you out of here."

Zachary stood, paused for a moment to make sure he had his balance, and followed her. She was inclined to walk at a quicker pace than he was, but Zachary didn't let her rush him. Walking quickly or jogging to keep up with her would just end up with Zachary tripping and ending up flat on his face. Since the car accident that had temporarily paralyzed him, he had worked hard to learn to walk smoothly again. However, it sometimes still felt a bit awkward. Running, climbing stairs, or things like walking backward were another story. His brain seemed to remember how to do these things, but his body didn't, and Zachary would inevitably get the movements out of sync.

The CO stood at the next door, waiting impatiently for Zachary to catch up with her. When he did, she swiped her card key and entered a code in the number pad. They were back out at the front in the check-in area again. She took him to the lockers and indicated the one they had put his personal items in. Zachary was relieved that the box clicked open the first time he punched in the security code. Part of him had been certain that it wouldn't work.

"What can you tell me about Luke's arrest and the charges against him?" he asked the CO as he slowly began to remove the items from the locker and to dress himself and put the loose items back into his pockets.

The woman didn't answer for a minute. She looked at Zachary, considering. "He didn't tell you?"

"No. I think… he's pretty overwhelmed at this point. Doesn't believe that it will do him any good to talk about it."

She shrugged her rounded shoulders. "Probably wouldn't," she agreed. "It's not going to get him out of trouble."

"It could help. If there are mitigating circumstances…"

She snorted. "As far as I can see, the only mitigating circumstance is that the guy he killed was a scumbag. Removing him from the streets was a public service."

"What do you know about the victim?"

"I can't really discuss the case with a civilian. But I imagine if you read the news, you'll find out plenty about his past convictions."

THEY CAME FOR HIM

"Those are public record," Zachary agreed. "So it wouldn't be a breach of confidentiality to tell me that. I'll find out anyway from a couple of courthouse searches."

She considered this, watching Zachary buckle his belt back on. "I suppose so. Convictions for various assaults, sex trafficking, public intoxication. There are other charges that they weren't able to make stick…" She stopped, realizing that what they would like to have gotten him for probably wasn't something she should tell Zachary.

"That's about what I figured," Zachary agreed. "Any idea how far up the food chain he is? What his position in Gordo's organization is?"

Her eyes flickered at the mention of Gordo's name. Surprise that Zachary knew who he was or that it was his organization that Luke had been a member of?

Zachary wasn't even sure how rank was determined in an organization like that. Were they similar to military ranks? To the *capo* and *consigliere* in movies like *The Godfather*?

"He wasn't at the top," the CO answered slowly, carefully considering her answer. "But he wasn't a street-level hood, either. He had people under him. He had power."

But he had let someone like Luke get close enough to take him down. Arrogance? Surprise? How had Luke managed it?

"What do you know about your friend's past?" The woman nodded in the direction of the jail cells.

"That he was a displaced child, grew up without a stable family environment. He had nowhere to go when his grandmother died and spiraled out of control, ended up in the organization. Recruited there by an older boy. Became a Romeo as well as a prostitute. Seducing younger girls or boys in order to bring them into the organization."

She nodded. "Not a nice kind of guy, even if he does look like a fallen angel. Don't get it into your head that he's the victim here. He killed a man. There's no question about that. He's got a sheaf of charges and convictions a foot thick. And probably a lot of them that aren't in our file because he's gone by different names and not all of his aliases have been linked together. He's been involved with the police since he was a young child stealing from the corner store. But he's not a child anymore."

Zachary was careful not to contradict her. As long as she was giving him information, he had to be careful not to argue with anything she said. "He's been living with my sister. She got him into rehab and has been keeping him out of trouble. Until now."

Surprise flashed across the CO's face. "Your sister?"

"Yes. Older sister. They're not romantically involved," he hurried to add. "She has some experience, though; knows how the business is run and the methods they use. So she was a good person to keep an eye on Luke, to try to keep him out of trouble."

"Your sister," the CO repeated, as if trying to convince herself that it was true. "I never knew that she had any family."

Zachary was surprised she knew anything about Joss.

"We didn't grow up together. I was in a different foster home. So were our other brothers and sisters. I only just met her a year ago."

"Well, *she* has a history too."

"I know. She's open about that. But she's not in the life anymore either. It is *possible* to get out."

She didn't deny this, but didn't confirm it either.

"Do you know what evidence they have against Luke for this… killing?"

She put her hands up. "I'm just the jailer. You'll have to talk to the investigating officers about that. Not me."

She knew more than she would let on, but she believed she was doing her job by keeping the details confidential. Zachary opted to stay on her good side. He didn't know how many more times he might be coming back to see Luke if he managed to get a toehold on the case.

"I appreciate all of your help. And you being here on a Sunday. That can't be fun."

She shrugged. "A quiet Sunday means that I can get caught up on stuff that I can't during the week. It's better than days when it's a circus here and everyone wants their business dealt with imme-diately."

Zachary had all of his personal possessions back, his shoes and belt done up, and winter gear back on. But he wasn't quite ready to leave. Worry gnawed at his gut. More than just concern for what kind of sentence Luke might be facing. There were many other things to be concerned about before Luke ever made it to trial.

"Listen," he said slowly, feeling his way carefully through the conversation. "I don't know anything about your jail or usual practices, so don't take this the wrong way…"

She pursed her lips, and frown lines creased her forehead. "What?"

"Is he safe here? I know that this is where he has to be, but he's young, and he's not a big guy. Is he… he's not in the general population, with adult criminals, is he?"

"Of course not. You don't need to tell me my job. Crap like that might happen in other facilities, but no one is getting assaulted in mine. Juveniles and adults are never mixed. Not in their cells, not in any common area, visitor room, nothing."

Zachary nodded, relieved. "Good. I don't want anything to happen to him."

She looked at him under partially closed lids, like there was something she was hiding and not sure that she would reveal to him. Zachary felt an itch at the back of his neck.

"What?"

"Even if he was in gen pop at the prison, he would be protected, you know."

Zachary frowned. "By the guards? The CO's, I mean? Is that what you're talking about?"

She shook her head. "He's marked."

"Marked how?"

"You haven't seen his tattoo?"

Zachary considered. He hadn't been particularly focused on Luke's body art. He had noticed Luke's ink in passing, but hadn't paid it much attention. "He has a few tattoos."

"Yeah. Well, the one on the back of his hand, that's the one I'm talking about."

Zachary tried to picture it. A couple of interconnected letters, he thought. Stylized like the big letter at the beginning of a chapter in an old manuscript, which always made it hard for Zachary to figure out what the first letter and word were supposed to be.

"Letters, I think."

The CO nodded. "A maker's mark from the organization he is in. Identifies who his boss or owner is, so everybody knows not to damage the merchandise. And to return him if he runs away. The other inmates would recognize it."

Zachary shook his head, unable to find the words to respond to this.

"He probably has it branded on his body somewhere, too," the woman told him. "Burned in deep so it can't be removed or inked over. That's what they do with the lower-level workers. He probably didn't get the ink until he had been with them for a few years, moved up in the organization to a respected position."

Zachary was nauseated by the thought of such a scar.

"The branding is intended to hurt for a long time. To remind them who owns them and keep them compliant."

His stomach gurgled. He swallowed and tried to get his thoughts back on track. "And what about... I'm worried about his state of mind. Knowing that he's looking down the barrel of a twenty-to-life sentence..."

"Most suicides take place in the first three to seven days. We watch them pretty carefully during that period. He's got nothing in his cell that could be used for a suicide attempt. You saw how he was dressed. Jumpsuit and flip-flops. A guy's gotta be pretty inventive to attempt suicide in our cells. But we watch 'em. Newbies like him are checked every fifteen to twenty minutes around the clock. And if he gets it into his head to try something stupid like diving headfirst off of his bunk into the concrete floor, someone is going to notice. He won't get far."

She saw Zachary's shock at the statement.

"They do that. Usually don't end up with anything more than bruises or a concussion, but other facilities have had fatalities.

Someone crushes their skull, breaks their spine, or gets a bleed inside the brain. But not here. Ain't never had one of them in here."

Zachary swallowed. "Okay. Good. Thanks for looking out for him."

She nodded understandingly. "If I was him, I sure wouldn't want to wait around for my sentence. I'd be looking for the first opportunity to end it before that."

# 15

Disturbed by the CO's words, Zachary looked at his phone as he walked out of the jail and back around to the other side of the building where his car was parked, checking the time. He should make the best use of his time while he was in town, rather than having to drive back and forth or do all of his investigating remotely. He decided to go back into the police station to see what else he could discover about Luke and the crime while he was there. He had known that Luke would have a long rap sheet, but hadn't stopped to consider what else might be on it. He was, as the jail CO and Luke himself suggested, taking Luke at his own word. Of course he would show himself in the best light possible.

Luke had wanted to get out of the organization; Zachary knew that much was true. And he had admitted to committing plenty of crimes while he had been both a victim and a perpetrator in the cartel. He portrayed himself as being coerced and controlled, which was how it worked in the industry. But how much of their darkness had rubbed off onto him? He admitted to seducing other teens into the life, admitted that he had been doing it for years. What if after the first little while, he didn't have to be coerced anymore, but enjoyed the game? What if he had liked the power of moving up in the organization, the control he had over those boys and girls?

There were a lot of reasons to get out of the cartel other than the ones Luke had given. He might have known there was a sting coming. Might have disagreed with someone higher up. Maybe he wanted to branch out into his own business. He could even have stolen money, drugs, or business from someone else in the organization and needed to hide out for a while. And Zachary had provided the perfect opportunity for Luke to do so; getting him out, making the other traffickers think that he was dead, and finding him a home and a new life with Joss. Zachary couldn't assume that Luke was quite as pure and well-intentioned as he had made himself out to be.

Zachary entered the police station and saw the same young cop as before. No shift change while he had been in the jail with Luke. The cop raised his brows.

"Something else I can help you with?"

"Thanks for helping me out with that. I really appreciate it."

The cop shrugged. "That's my job. Sort of why I'm here today. You're welcome, though. I take it you got in to see him?"

"Yes." Zachary leaned on the counter, trying to look comfortable and casual. "Do you know the kid I was in to see? Hear about what happened?"

"Yeah, heard something about it. He was processed through here, but I wasn't around at the time. Some of the other guys were. I only have it second or third hand." He nodded at his screen. "And what's on the computer."

"What are all of the charges, do you know?"

The man gave him an odd look. "Murder," he said with a shrug. "First degree."

"Is that it? Nothing else related?"

"You don't need to pile them up in a case like this. One charge is all you need."

"And the arresting officers, they thought it was pretty open-and-shut?"

The cop leaned back in his chair, making it squeak and squeal as he tested its limits. "Caught him red-handed. Knife in his hand, covered in blood. What's he going to say—that he was framed? He just happened along and thought that he would pick up the murder weapon, like in some stupid cop show on TV? That isn't the way it works. In ninety-nine percent of the cases, the perp is exactly who you think it is. It's just a matter of gathering enough information to hang them."

"Which isn't too hard in Luke's case."

"I think you can see that."

"Pretty clear," Zachary said encouragingly.

"I wouldn't want to be in his shoes right now." The cop apparently thought this was funny, letting out a snort of laughter. "Hell, I wouldn't want to be in those shoes anytime. Did you see them?"

Zachary forced a chuckle, nodding. "Not quite my chosen wardrobe either," he agreed. "And I'm not particularly discerning." He looked down at his jeans and shirt and scuffed shoes and shook his head, mocking himself. "Did Luke say anything when he was arrested? Anything to explain himself? To excuse what he had done? Or a confession?"

"Nah, Carruthers said he was dead quiet. Wouldn't answer any questions about why he had done it. Must have been a fight over business, is my guess. Two pimps working the same territory. Maybe one stole business from the other. A favorite john or something." The officer shook his head. "These guys are very *sensitive*. They get into a lot of fights with each other. Lash out. Usually, it's just some scrapes and bruises, but every now and then, you end up with a mess like this."

"They were both in the life?"

"I looked at their records, both of them. Long sheets, stretching way back. Maybe your guy was trying to horn in on Eyler's territory. First time he's been arrested in this part of the state. Thought he could set up his own business. Didn't know it was already covered." The cop shrugged. "Probably."

"I thought... that Luke had gone straight."

"What? He's not straight in any sense of the word." The cop laughed. "Been out of the picture for a while, but sometimes that happens. They travel or hide from someone who is gunning for them. But then they're back. They can't keep away from it."

"Luke has been staying with my sister. I would think that she would have noticed if he was setting up business again."

"Your sister." The cop's expression was immediately masked, as if he had pulled a hood down over his face. "Your sister is…"

"Jocelyn Goldman," Zachary said.

But the cop's lips hadn't been shaping a J sound. He had intended to say something else. He stared at Zachary, something uncertain about his manner.

Both he and the corrections officer had reacted the same way. The corrections officer had known about Jocelyn's past. She had wondered whether Zachary knew about Joss's history and had been surprised to hear that she had siblings.

"What do you know about her?" Zachary asked curiously, cocking his head slightly. He thought that Joss had been open with him about her history, but there was plenty that they had never discussed. Zachary wouldn't have wanted all of the gritty details about Joss's day-to-day life of being addicted and trafficked. Joss had the right to her privacy. Her dignity. She had the right to start her life over, free of that business and from having to explain it.

"The Old Lady? We all know her around here."

## 16

Zachary put both elbows and forearms on the counter and leaned toward the cop. "*The Old Lady?*"

"I know." The cop made a waving-away gesture. "She's not that old. In any other business, she'd still be in her prime. But in prostitution? She's an old lady." His mouth moved to add something else, then he thought better of it and closed his mouth tightly, eyeing Zachary.

It was true. Jocelyn had made it clear that the reason she was no longer in the business was because no one had any use for her anymore. She looked much older than her years, aged by hard living; smoking, drinking, drugging, and all of the abuse she had put up with since they were children. She'd been old beyond her years back then, too, the oldest girl in a family with six children, expected to keep them all quiet and out of the way of their parents. An adult by the time she was into her teens.

"So you knew her before she left the business, or not until after? Was she 'The Old Lady' when she was still working?"

The cop's eyes darted to the side. "Yeah. Don't know. She's been around a lot longer than I have. Never knew about her until the past few months. But other guys around here… they go back further than that."

"And that's who calls her The Old Lady?"

He didn't answer.

"How did you find out about her the last few months if she isn't in the business anymore?"

"She makes a pest of herself." The cop looked embarrassed to be reporting this. "She's always in here complaining about things. Pimps working in her area. Drug dealers. She's lobbying for this new law or that change in legislation. And if you arrest a hooker for something…" He rolled his eyes and shook his head. "The Old Lady is on a one-person mission to completely overhaul Vermont's prostitution laws."

Zachary tried to suppress a smile. So Joss had a secret mission, did she? After telling him to stay away from the human trafficking business, to look the other way and forget about trying to save Madison and Luke from it, she'd started waging war on them herself.

"She is a pain in the neck," the cop declared. "I knew there was going to be trouble as soon as I heard that kid was one of hers. No way this thing is going to just be quietly pleaded out and disappear."

"Luke isn't actually her son."

The young cop gave Zachary an odd look. "No, I know that. But she takes kids in. Cleans them up, sets them up in places of their own, helps them find jobs and all that. And makes life… uncomfortable for anyone trying to work her area. Any suspicious characters start hanging around near her place, checking into hotels, whatever, and we hear about it." The young man motioned to his computer as if Zachary could see the number of complaints Joss had filed over the preceding months.

"I didn't even know she was doing all that. I thought… there was just Luke."

"No way. The Old Lady is like a crazy cat lady, only collecting kids instead of cats. Luckily, they're not all crammed into her house…"

"How did all of this come about? How long has she been doing this?"

"I don't know. At least a year. Something like that."

That coincided with the approximate time that Zachary had brought

Luke to Joss. Apparently, his action had triggered her social conscience and a desire to change the shape of things in the community around her. Or she'd felt the need to show Luke that there was a way to live outside of the trafficking rings. Or maybe she'd decided that the only way to keep them from seeing Luke and realizing he was still alive was to do everything she could to keep the cartels out of her neighborhood and out of Kent.

She had warned Zachary against doing anything that would raise the ire of the trafficking rings. It was a billion-dollar business and the bosses did not take kindly to anyone interfering with their profit. But apparently, that stricture didn't apply to Joss herself.

Maybe because she knew the players personally and had plenty of dirt on them, they thought it best not to do anything to hurt her. Who knew what kind of evidence she might have saved to the cloud or squirreled away in a safety deposit box that they couldn't get at, but that would come to light if she died. Maybe she had told them she had ways of reaching them and disrupting their business from beyond the grave.

"I didn't know," Zachary said, shaking his head and blowing out his breath in amazement.

The cop laughed. "You're the only one who didn't, then."

"I guess we need to have a little talk. She can bring me up to speed."

"She's a force to be reckoned with." The cop straightened some papers on the desk. "I wouldn't want to be in her crosshairs."

Zachary remembered how Joss had spoken about their father; how she had fantasized about killing him even as a child. And the way she spoke with such familiarity about guns.

The image of being in Joss's gun sights made him shudder.

---

Before long, he was on Joss's doorstep, seriously considering whether he ought to have called ahead for once instead of just showing up at her door. If she was waging war against the cartels, she might very well answer the door with a sawed-off shotgun. Or that PKM she had spoken so fondly of. He had already rung the doorbell, but he pulled out his phone, thinking maybe he'd better call her to let her know that it was him.

The door opened and Joss stood there looking down at him, her mouth a straight, thin line. But she was not cradling a machine gun in her arms, so that was a good sign. Zachary's mouth was dry. He nodded a greeting and cleared his throat.

"I've been at the jail. Thought I'd come and report to you, talk things over."

She considered for a moment, then nodded and stepped back to let him in. Zachary glanced around the small living room as he entered. There was no sign that anyone but Joss and Luke lived there. He couldn't see back into the bedrooms to see whether there were any other rescued teens sheltering there, hiding from visitors, until Joss could find another place for them to live. If there were, they hadn't left extra shoes on the mat by the door or anything else that gave away their presence to Zachary.

He followed Joss into the living room and sat down. She was watching him carefully, eyes sharp. "So?" she demanded, "What have you found out so far?"

Zachary sat on an easy chair. He didn't sit back in it, but perched on the edge, leaning forward. "Not very much yet. Luke doesn't have much to say. Wouldn't tell me what had happened. Wouldn't agree to get a lawyer. He's acting like he's resigned to going to prison for the rest of his life."

Joss nodded, her mouth twisted into a bitter shape like she had just chewed on a lemon peel.

"They, uh… they know you at the police station and jail."

She shrugged. "I'd hope so. I was just there making arrangements."

"It sounds like they've known you for longer than that, though. Like maybe… you've been waging a private war on the trafficking rings."

The hint of a smug smile replaced the bitter, puckered expression. "I told you; I know the business."

"So someone like me can't do anything to change things, to rescue people like Luke. But *you* can."

"You don't know anything. You managed to avoid ending up in the life. Lucky for you. But luckily for these kids, *I* did not. And I know where the bodies are buried."

Zachary swallowed and licked his lips. He wished she had offered him coffee. Or at least a glass of water. "Literally?" he joked, "Where the bodies are buried?"

"Sometimes."

The way she said it raised goosebumps on his arms, despite the temperature of the room.

"Why didn't you tell me any of this?"

"Why? What business is it of yours?"

"Well... maybe I could have helped you somehow. And I know it isn't any of my business, but you know I was trying to help Luke. To keep him away from the traffickers."

"You couldn't have done anything. Like I say, you don't know anything about the business or about any of the players. I do. I know what I can do, how far I can push. You won't listen to anything I tell you. You're too impulsive and you would just charge in there like a white knight, thinking you could change everything. I can't have my little brother showing up and making a mess of everything."

Zachary cleared his throat, uncomfortable. "Okay... maybe I would be too impulsive," he admitted. He knew it was one of his faults. It was the part of the ADHD package that had always gotten him in the most trouble. It had been highlighted on the very first psychological profile when he was ten and had been a problem ever since. Impulse control wasn't something that medication could give him, that he'd been able to develop through therapy, or that could be beaten out of him. Enough people had attempted it and failed. "But you could have at least told me what you were doing."

Joss just looked at him and made no further attempt to defend her position.

## 17

Zachary pulled his notebook out of his pocket and removed the pencil from where it was jammed in the coil.

"You know what happened, then. Tell me about it."

Joss raised her brows.

"With Luke," Zachary prompted. "Tell me what happened."

"I wasn't there."

"But you've been involved in this... disruption of the trafficking rings down here. So you know what it was all about. And you know the players, so fill me in on who was involved."

She gave him a wry look. "Is my little brother telling me what to do?"

"You asked me to help Luke. How can I do that if no one gives me the information?"

"Do you tell your clients what to do? They tell you what to do."

Zachary matched her smile. "Getting my clients to give me the information I need to do the job is something I do all the time. On every case. And I keep going back with more questions until I have all the information I need to do my job."

"That sounds like a threat."

"Yeah. How many times do you want me to show up here asking you more questions?"

Joss glanced over her shoulder at the blank wall. Zachary wondered what—or who—he would see if he could look through the walls. How many people was Joss trying to protect?

Joss returned her gaze to him. "Eyler. The guy Luke killed is named Eyler."

"I already got that much. Do you know his first name? Aliases? What he's been arrested for or what position he held in the organization?"

"You don't ask much, do you?"

"Just asking for the information I need to get the job done."

"Christopher. Christopher Eyler."

Zachary wrote it down, relieved to finally have some solid information. "Can you spell Eyler for me?"

"Spelling isn't my strong suit. I haven't ever seen it written out."

Zachary gave it his best guess. He was sure a few database searches would get him the right spelling. If Eyler had been involved in trafficking in Vermont for a few years, his name would be all over the place.

"And what is he in the organization? And... which organization? I don't know how they are set up. Are there rival organizations with different territories?"

"There are... smaller organizations under a bigger umbrella," Joss said, frowning as she tried to formulate an answer. "Independent operators, like franchises, controlled by someone higher up... but on a whole bunch of levels. Like a pyramid."

"With Gordo as the top boss in this part of the country."

She nodded, her eyes closing to slits. "Don't you go looking for him. You shouldn't even say his name."

"Why not?"

"Because people like that do not like to be known and named outside of their elite group. If word got out that you were sharing his name with the cops or spreading it around in your investigation, they could come after you. And you don't have any protection."

Zachary nodded and made a mental note of it. He wanted to help Luke if he could and help Joss with her cause. But he didn't want to end up being targeted because of it. He had to remember Kenzie and

Rhys and other people around him who could also be targeted if he stirred things up and said the wrong thing.

"So Eyler was…"

Joss settled back, relaxing a bit. She rubbed her chin, thinking about it. "Luke started out at street-level. He moved up the ladder a little, acting as a Romeo, recruiting for his boss's stable as well."

"Right. He told me that. He was originally recruited by…" Zachary fished for the name in his memory. A year before, he'd had been a long, confusing discussion in the middle of the adrenaline-charged night of Madison's and Luke's escape. All of them, including Rhys, had been shot at. But Zachary had processed and re-read his notes and he had read them again after Joss had called to tell him about Luke's arrest, wanting everything to be fresh in his mind. "Connor. An older boy."

"Yeah. Ancient history. At that level, people don't survive for long. Luke is long-lived, for someone who wasn't able to advance much in the organization."

"And Connor's organization was taken over by Peggy Ann. Is that right?"

"She absorbed it, yes. And several others. With each 'takeover,' she advanced higher in the organization. So, Luke was no longer owned by a low-level boss, but a high-level one." Joss considered her words and revised her statement. "A mid-level boss."

Zachary had seen Peggy Ann. Not up close and personal, but close enough that he had no intention of running into her again or interviewing her as part of his investigation into what had happened with Luke. "Right." He made a quick note to make sure he remembered the discussion. "And where does Eyler fit in?"

"He and Peggy Ann were both about the same level."

"Does that make them peers or competitors? Do people get along if they are on the same level, or do they consider each other rivals?"

"You act like people are all the same. It's different for everyone. Bosses at the same level might exchange assets, refer business to each other, combine forces to form a bigger, more powerful organization. Or they might steal from each other, kill each other off, start rumors in the organization. You don't know. Even if two bosses appear to be cooperating, one might be planning to stab the other in the back. You could put your trust in someone just to have the rug pulled out from under you. You have to always be suspicious. Always assume that even if someone is helping you now or making a deal that benefits you both… that could change tomorrow. Or five minutes from now."

"Did Luke know Eyler? If Luke was under Peggy Ann, would he ever have had contact with Eyler?"

"I don't know."

Zachary needed a better answer than that. Joss and Luke had lived together for more than a year. Surely they'd had the opportunity to discuss different people they had both known. At least a guess. Joss could at least speculate on whether Luke and Eyler had known each other when Luke had been in the life.

But she could probably only give him the answer she already had. Luke wouldn't have killed Eyler if they didn't know each other. It wasn't a chance mugging. Somehow, Luke *had* known Eyler.

"And what did you know about Eyler?"

"What do you mean?" Joss's face was smooth and expressionless.

"If you've been spending your time fighting trafficking rings in this part of the state and Eyler was killed here, by someone you know, then I assume you know what he was doing here."

She scowled at his logic. "He was hoping to get established. The trouble with killing one cockroach is that there are a hundred more waiting to take his place."

"So even though you were successful in getting rid of whoever was here before Eyler, he wanted to fill the void. Snatch up new territory while it was available."

Joss nodded her agreement.

"And how did Luke get into the middle of this?"

Joss raised her hands palms-up and shrugged. "I don't know, and that's the truth, Zachary. He wasn't supposed to be involved with anything. Eyler wasn't supposed to know about him. Luke knew that if he was seen and identified…"

"Is it possible that's exactly what did happen? Eyler recognized him somewhere and went after him? Luke had to defend himself, and…?"

"Maybe. Your guess is as good as mine. Luke never said a word to me about having seen him. I asked Luke what happened, but he wouldn't say anything."

Zachary didn't have to imagine Luke's stubborn silence. He had just experienced it himself. "Can you speculate? You might say that my guess would be as good as yours, but you lived with him, I didn't. You knew more of what was going on with him. What he might or might not do. Who he was likely to run into. You know the business and players. I don't know any of those things."

"Yes. Maybe he ran into Eyler or one of his workers. Maybe he was identified when he was out at a club or a party. Traffickers often work those places. Drop a few recruiters and see who they can scoop up. If someone recognized his face…"

"Or saw his tattoo."

Joss looked at him, chewing on her lip. "Yeah," she agreed eventually and looked away.

"Do you have one too?"

Joss pushed up the sleeve of her sweater and turned her arm to show her the ink on the inside of her forearm. Unlike the fresh, clear lines and colors of Luke's tattoo, Joss's work was faded and fuzzy around the edges, the colors dull. It served to remind him just how long she had been trafficked. Decades had passed, and Zachary had never known what she was going through.

Her tattoo was not letters, but a red velvet crown with numbers below it. The numbers were so faded that Zachary could barely read them. He swallowed, looking at it. He didn't ask whether she had been branded as well or the meaning of the numbers.

"Would someone looking at that know…" Zachary's throat closed and he couldn't finish the question.

"Who I belonged to? Not a newbie. The low-level operators haven't been around long enough to recognize it. The established bosses? People all the way up the food chain? They'd know whose mark it was." She tugged her sleeve back down to cover it. "But the symbology is common enough for someone in the business to recognize it as a trafficker's claim."

Zachary nodded numbly. He wondered if any of the girls he had known over the years had borne a similar mark. He'd been in several institutional settings. Places a teen girl might be sent if she were considered a runner or promiscuous. How many girls had he met who had been trafficked without his knowing about it?

He had known girls who hooked, escaping foster or group homes to walk the streets, offering their bodies to escape the abuse or confinement. He'd always figured if they walked into it with their eyes open, that was their choice. But how many of them had been tricked, coerced, or physically forced into the life? Just because he never saw their bosses or organizations, that didn't mean they weren't there, watching, meting out punishments if the girls didn't do what they were told. Just because the girls said they could choose the lifestyle they wanted to, it didn't mean that they had.

Zachary touched Joss's arm where the tattoo was hidden beneath her sweater sleeve. His touch was light, just barely in contact with her. "Joss… you be careful. I don't want these guys hurting you."

"I can take care of myself."

"This is a nasty business."

"Says the initiate to the master."

Zachary shrugged. Of course it was silly for him to counsel her in something that she knew far better than he did. "I don't want to lose you. Not when I've just barely gotten to know you again."

## 18

Zachary closed his eyes and rubbed his forehead for a moment, trying to get back on track. "What did the police tell you about Eyler's murder? What do you know about what happened?"

Joss took a deep breath and released it. How much did his questions and his ignorance distress her? Did she fight flashbacks when showing him her tattoo? How much of her time did she spend reliving that past?

"It was in a hotel room," she said in a clear, flat voice. "Room was registered to Eyler. Don't know what Luke was doing there. There had been shouting, fighting, quite a disturbance. The police received several calls. When they got there, it was just Luke and Eyler, and Eyler was dead. Luke's prints all over the place. In Eyler's blood. On the murder weapon."

She stopped. Zachary waited, giving her time to pick up the narrative again, but she shook her head, keeping her mouth closed. That was the full story, as much as she was going to tell him.

Considering how little the cop at the police station had been willing to tell him, he was surprised at the details Joss knew. Had the police shared them with her or had she seen? Or had she talked to someone else who had firsthand knowledge? Maybe she knew people at the hotel. People who knew she was fighting against trafficking, or just a friend who was a maid or a girl who had happened to be at the hotel at the time.

"Any sign that there had been someone else in the room?"

"There are people in an out of a room like that all the time. Who knows who might have been there in the previous twenty-four hours. Just Luke and Eyler when the police got there."

"Do you know the name of the arresting officer? Or who is investigating the homicide? I should probably talk to them."

"I might have their names."

She didn't move to check her phone or business cards in her purse.

"What was Luke doing there?" Zachary mused. "What's been going on with him? Where has he been going?"

"I told him to be careful," Joss snapped. "We talked about it over and over. How dangerous it was for him to be identified by anyone in his previous life. I did everything I could to keep him safe."

"I know."

"It's a good thing I don't have any kids. How are you supposed to take care of someone who won't listen to you?"

He knew that she included him in this complaint. As bad as he felt about any pain and frustration he had put her through as a child, he knew he couldn't have changed his choices. He had learned not to trust anyone else. Not to accept their dictates just because they claimed to care or be in charge. He'd had to be independent and protect himself. He made a sympathetic noise but didn't excuse himself or Luke. Joss knew as well as anyone that a foster kid or throwaway had to make his own choices and live his own life, no matter how bad the consequences were. As she had told Zachary when they had spoken about it, she couldn't physically force Luke to do the things she thought he should do. She couldn't stop him from going out. She couldn't control who he talked to or if he chose to go back to the people who had trafficked him. All she could do was to try to be the voice of reason and tell Luke what the consequences of his actions might be.

Just like with Zachary.

## 19

Zachary looked at the time as he left Joss's house and returned to his car. While he needed to talk to the detective on the case, he doubted that he could get anywhere with the police on a Sunday evening. There hadn't been any activity at the police station. Everyone was home with their families and wouldn't appreciate being called by a private investigator getting involved in their open-and-shut case.

And if he spent another hour or two on interviews, he wouldn't have any time with Kenzie, and they tried to keep as much of Sunday as possible as couple's time.

He started the car engine and mounted his phone on the dashboard, plugging the charging cable into it. While he waited for the car to warm up, he called Kenzie.

"Hey, Zachary. How's it been going?" She sounded relaxed. Not worn out from being called in to work, not stressed about his taking so long to get home. She seemed to be in a good place.

Was evaluating the temperature of his partner something that everyone did? Or was it something Zachary did as a response to his experience with families in foster care? Was it normal or pathological? He pushed the question to the side and focused on Kenzie.

"Good. I'm not sure how much progress I've made, but I talked to Luke and Joss. I have a few details... a starting place, anyway."

"Are you... staying to do more today?"

"No. I'm on my way back. Just warming up the car and then I'll be on my way."

"Good. Then we'll still have some time together today. That will be nice. It's been quiet around here."

"Am I that noisy?"

She laughed. "No. You don't stomp or yell. But it's just different when you have someone else in the house with you. The friendly sounds of someone else floating around, doing their thing. Being able to have a conversation just because you're in the same room or having a coffee at the same time. I like having you around the house."

Zachary was glad she couldn't see him blush with pleasure in response to this observation. But she probably knew he would react that way anyway.

He thought about the case on his way back, talking aloud to himself about what he had learned and what he speculated or had questions on. He had recently learned how to dictate notes to his phone hands-free, which came in very handy on a highway drive. He dictated several notes to himself so that he wouldn't completely forget the things he had come up with while driving. It was like having a brilliant revelation in the shower and forgetting it as soon as he was dry. Frustrating.

The highway driving went quickly. Maybe a little more quickly than it ought to have. Zachary considered staying in his car for a few extra minutes longer so that Kenzie wouldn't think that he'd sped too much.

But she was probably watching for him anyway and would just laugh at him trying to obscure how quickly he had driven by hiding out in front of the house. It wasn't like she couldn't see his car the moment he pulled up in front of the house.

He saw her eyes flick toward her phone in her hand when he walked in to greet her. Noting the time, as he had feared. But she didn't comment on it.

"Hey. Glad you made it. Pizza just got here. You want some?"

Maybe she had not been checking up on his driving time, then. If pizza had just been delivered, she couldn't have been expecting him to take another half hour to get home. Zachary could smell the spicy tomato sauce, cheese, and warm, yeasty crust. His stomach growled. Had he eaten anything else since he had left the house? "That smells really good."

They walked together into the kitchen and sat down. Zachary got a message on his phone and took a quick peek at it before dinner. Something from Rhys. A conversation with Rhys would need all of his attention, so it would have to wait until after dinner. Zachary flipped through a couple of other messages before returning his attention to the table and realizing he had just sat down and let Kenzie take care of everything else. Plates, pizza, drinks. It wasn't like he'd left her with a big job, but he had to be more aware and not do that.

"Sorry. I spaced. Can I get anything else?"

"No, I think this is it." She shrugged. "You've had a long day. I don't mind. Not like I slaved over the stove all day."

"No, but you planned it all out, and I could at least have grabbed plates."

She nodded and didn't disagree.

They each took a slice and started to eat. After the first couple of bites, Zachary sighed, beginning to relax, his body and brain happy for the fuel after a long day of looking for answers.

"So, how did it go?" Kenzie asked. "You got to see Luke, I guess?"

Zachary nodded. "The usual red tape bureaucracy and procedures to get through before I could get in to see him. Pretty quiet at the police station and jail today." He took another bite of pizza and chewed. "I should have remembered to leave everything in the car. It's been a while since I did a jail visit."

"Oh, I wouldn't have thought of that either. But it's probably more secure to leave your stuff with the security at the jail than in your glove box, isn't it?"

"Yes. But some places don't even let you do that. You're just not allowed to bring anything but your ID and one car key into the building with you. But it's not like it would have been a long walk back to the car if they'd made me leave everything there. Just around the block. At some of the prisons, you park a couple of miles away and take a shuttle up to the facility."

Kenzie nodded. "How was Luke?"

"Not great. I didn't expect him to be, of course… it wasn't like he was frantic or crying for me to get him out of there. He would hardly talk to me at all. Very distant… They have him under suicide watch."

"Poor guy," Kenzie said with feeling.

Zachary nodded. It hadn't been that long since he had been in the psych ward in the hospital, under a watch himself. But he had admitted himself voluntarily, and it wasn't the same as being in jail. He had known where he was going and that it would be safer for him than trying to tough it out at home. He knew some of the staff there, knew the rules and procedures, and knew they would do their best to look after him.

"I've never had to face that," Zachary murmured. "The likelihood of being locked up for the rest of my life. I haven't been able to see past that moment, past the dark times, but… it's not the same."

"It would be pretty tough to face," Kenzie agreed. "A long time in a miserable place."

At least when Zachary had been locked up in Bonnie Brown or another institution, he had known that it would only be for a few weeks or months. Then he would have his freedom again. And that was what Luke had faced before. Small stints in the jail for whatever they had been able to catch him for, but not facing life imprisonment.

"I'm glad they're keeping an eye on him. I wouldn't want anything to happen to him. I mean… anything worse."

"What did he have to say?" Kenzie prompted, nudging him away from a deep dive into his suicidal periods or unhappy past. "What exactly happened?"

"He wouldn't tell me anything. More or less said that it was his own fault and to just leave him alone."

Kenzie shook her head. She wiped a splotch of tomato sauce from the corner of her mouth. "But you must have been able to find out some details."

Zachary gave her a half-grin. "I *am* a private investigator."

"Exactly. So what did Sherlock manage to uncover?"

# 20

Zachary toyed with his pizza. "Not many details yet. The victim's name is Eyler. He's in the trafficking business. Higher level than Luke, who was pretty much at the bottom, even after all of the years he had worked for them. He was staying at a hotel in town. Maybe looking at expanding his territory. Because Joss has been driving the traffickers out of town." He raised one brow at her.

Kenzie looked impressed. "I knew Joss was tough, but... how was she doing that?"

"Lots of complaints to the police. And from what I can guess, blackmail. Knowing that the worst offenders can't get to her because she has dirt on them."

"Sounds like a good reason to kill her. Remove the obstruction altogether."

"I didn't ask about details, but I would guess there is a fail-safe somewhere. Documentation in a safety deposit box or stored online and set to release if something happens to her."

"Smart."

"I don't think she survived this long by being stupid," Zachary agreed.

Joss might have been victimized and an addict, but she had never been stupid. She had somehow endured her traumatic childhood and decades of trafficking and was now strong and independent.

"No," Kenzie agreed. "I don't think she's stupid. She's always struck me as having a sharp wit, despite all of the abuse she must have put her brain through as an addict."

"Yeah. And apparently, she's been helping out other kids like Luke who were looking for a way out of the business."

"Really?" Kenzie laughed and shook her head. "I have a hard time seeing tough, independent Joss being a mother hen."

"Probably more like a mother bear." Zachary thought back to those early days while the family had still been together. Joss and Heather had both been surrogate mothers, taking care of him and trying to keep him out of trouble, which was a losing prospect. Joss had been fierce. She might have employed pinches or head slaps to keep Zachary in line, but she would also have stood in the path of an oncoming train to protect her younger siblings.

Only it had been their parents, not an onrushing train, that she'd had to protect them from.

"So after Joss runs the previous traffickers out of town, this other guy shows up, ready to set up his business," Kenzie suggested, returning to the narrative.

"Right. And something happens… Luke is there, for some reason, in Eyler's hotel room, and kills him. A knife, I guess, but I don't know the details yet."

"And how did they connect him to the murder?"

"Because they caught him there in the room. Covered with blood. His prints all over everything, knife still in his hand."

"Ouch." Kenzie shook her head. "Well, I'm not sure how you get him out of something like that. Find some mitigating circumstances and get the sentence reduced… work out some kind of plea."

"That's not going to be easy. Especially not when he is not cooperating."

"What does Joss know? Had this trafficker and Luke had previous encounters? Is it possible that Eyler had recognized him and was threatening him?"

Zachary shrugged, shaking his head. "Luke was in his hotel room.

Eyler hadn't come after him. He'd obviously gone there looking for Eyler."

"Could it have been an arranged meeting? Maybe Eyler was threatening to expose him… for a payoff of some kind."

"A guy like Luke is more valuable as an asset than a blackmail target. He doesn't have much money, but he can lure and turn out new talent. Someone like him can bring in almost a million dollars a year. Eyler wouldn't get that kind of money by blackmailing him. Luke barely had any income living with Joss. He wouldn't be able to pay."

"Unless he got back in the business."

Zachary nodded. He fingered the notepad in his pocket. "If Eyler wanted something from Luke, then it was to have him working for him. Not blackmail." He was sure of himself.

Kenzie gave a nod, her eyes on Zachary's notebook, which he knew meant it was okay if he wanted to take out his notepad and write as they talked and ate. While they had decided on a rule of no phones or screens at the table during dinner in their couple's therapy, to reinforce their giving each other their undivided attention and communicating better, there were exceptions to the "no distractions" policy. One of them was that if they were talking shop, notebooks, paper files, and pictures or other files on their devices were permissible. Being able to discuss murder and forensics during dinner or a date was one of the things that had brought them together and which continued to keep them connected.

Zachary pulled his notepad out and jotted a few notes from his conversation before they could slip away from him.

"You think Eyler was probably going after Luke. To get him to work for him again," Kenzie said.

"He didn't work for him before. He worked for Peggy Ann. But Eyler must have wanted him. That had to be the reason they were together. Especially in Eyler's room. Eyler wanted to make him an offer… or to coerce him. But if there wasn't anyone else there, I don't know how he could have meant to persuade Luke."

Kenzie considered this, chewing slowly. She took another piece of pizza from the box and laid it on her plate. "You said before that Joss was worried about Luke getting back into the life. That he might be tempted because that was what he knew. It's hard work getting clean and then finding a way to support yourself."

"Yeah, that's true." He thought back to the previous conversation with Joss. "If he went to work for Eyler, he'd have money again. All the drugs he wanted. He knew his job and did it well, so he got praise and what Joss calls 'good strokes' from his bosses. He would have a social group; the other workers in Eyler's ring and the kids he brought up. I'm sure that living with Joss, he doesn't get much socialization with people who understand how he's lived, who normalize it. There are Joss and whoever she is trying to rescue from the traffickers, but he won't get approval from them like he would from people who are still in the business."

"So maybe he could be tempted. Maybe if Eyler promised him drugs, good pay, and a good position in his organization..."

"It might be enough to entice him over to Eyler's hotel room," Zachary admitted. "At least to talk it over." A feeling of heaviness accompanied the words. Luke had been working so hard. He'd done something few people would have been able to do, staying clean for a year after all of the years of addiction. But like with Tyrrell, staying clean for a year didn't mean he was cured. Both of them would fight addiction for as long as they lived.

*Had* Luke gone to Eyler, tempted by his offer? Was that why he didn't want to talk to Zachary about it? Because he had gone in a moment of weakness? Because he still craved the drugs and the approval? He needed more than Joss or anyone else straight could give him?

"I'll have to look into that further."

"How will you know if that's what happened?"

Zachary shrugged. "I'll ask questions. Start to build a picture of what happened before he killed Eyler."

"Poor Luke. After everything he has been through."

"Then it comes down to this." Zachary closed his eyes and saw Luke sitting across the table from him, gaze averted, small inside the orange jail uniform, facing the possibility of decades in prison. While it was true that Luke had victimized others, he was first and foremost a victim himself, a vulnerable child who had been twisted into something that had not been natural for him. "If that's what happened... I don't know how I'm going to be able to help. If he went there freely because he was interested in going back to work for Eyler and then killed him... How can anyone get a sentence reduced under those circumstances?"

"I don't know," Kenzie admitted. "I don't know of any defense or justification that would apply."

## 21

Zachary was feeling somewhat discouraged after dinner. Even though he had known from the time Joss called him that there wasn't much he could do to help Luke, he had still hoped to be able to find something. Something to show everyone that he had been right to help Luke get away from the traffickers in the first place, that he had a spark of human decency in him and deserved a second chance. Zachary didn't want to think that he had been conned by Luke, who had never planned to stay away from the life, or that it had been too late for Luke and he was irredeemable.

"Oh, got something from Rhys," Zachary said, sitting down on the couch and pulling out his phone while Kenzie picked up the remote to look for something they would enjoy watching together and that would hopefully distract Zachary from his funk.

He thumbed in his password and brought up Rhys's message.

It was a gif of a dog with popping eyes and the words "what's happening?"

Zachary considered his response carefully. Did Rhys know that something was going on with Luke and that Zachary had been looking into it? Or was it just a generic "What's up with you lately?"

He tapped in a non-responsive answer. *Hey, Rhys, just finished pizza with Kenzie*

Rhys sent back a big pink heart balloon. Zachary smiled.

"Rhys says hi."

Kenzie turned away from the TV screen to look at Zachary. He showed her the pink heart. Kenzie chuckled.

"Love to him too."

*Kenzie says hi. How is school?*

The dots that indicated Rhys was composing a reply started to blink at the bottom of the screen. Zachary settled into the couch, trying to get more comfortable and not aggravate his tailbone, which still hurt if he sat the wrong way. He looked at the screen to see what shows Kenzie was considering.

"*Unsolved Mysteries*? I haven't seen that in years."

"You interested? Do you like it?"

"Sure."

"It's not too much like work?"

"No. I don't have to solve these ones. Especially now that they're twenty years old."

"I like it when they have updates. That's always cool."

Zachary nodded his agreement. The phone vibrated in his hand, and Zachary looked down at it. A picture he had seen before. Luke. Cropped out of a picture Rhys had taken of Luke and Madison together. Zachary had first seen it when Madison had gone missing and Rhys had come to him for help.

His stomach tied itself in a knot. He tested the waters, not wanting to give away that something had happened to Luke if it was just a routine inquiry.

*Did Luke call you?*

Rhys quickly returned a large red X. *No.*

Zachary tried to figure out how to delicately ask what Rhys already knew. Had someone been in touch with him?

More dots appeared. Rhys composing a further response.

Another gif popped up. A toddler behind the prison bars of a playpen or baby security gate, holding on to the bars and shaking. Zachary swore to himself. Kenzie looked over.

"He knows about Luke."

"How did he find out?"

"I don't know. I thought that the two of them had broken off correspondence. The last few times I talked to Luke, he has said that Rhys isn't messaging him anymore."

Kenzie considered this. "Could he have been lying?"

"He's an accomplished liar. I can't say for sure I would know if he was. I keep wondering... about other things. The lady at the jail said that I don't really know him. Even he said so. I only know what he's told me about himself, and that could all be made up. I don't have independent verification of any of it. Except that he was in the trafficking ring and was Madison's Romeo."

"What reason would he have to make up all of the things he's said about his past?"

"To make himself look good. Make him look like more of a victim than he is."

"But as a teenager in the sex trade, he *was* a victim. There's no way around that. And they started him when he was how old? Twelve or thirteen? He doesn't have to make himself look like more of a victim than that."

"But that's what *he* told me. What if that is a lie? His age now, his age when he started out. What if he was never the victim but has always been a recruiter? Who is going to tell me anything different than he's said? There's no one to contradict him, so he can really tell whatever story he wants."

"Well..." Kenzie looked doubtful. "I suppose. But I don't know how he would keep such an elaborate lie going for a year. There haven't been any inconsistencies. Have there?"

Zachary didn't like to contradict her, but he'd been thinking about it and had to admit that there had been. "Yes... he contradicts his own story sometimes. I thought that was just... the drugs. The trauma. Dissociation. Getting confused about the timeline. It isn't hard to get mixed up when the abuse has been ongoing for so long. It all runs together and it's hard to remember what happened when and with who."

She nodded her agreement. "Yeah. Of course."

The phone vibrated again in Zachary's hand and he looked down at it. Rhys's last message was still on the screen, waiting for a response. Zachary gritted his teeth together and tapped out a brief answer.

*Saw Luke today*

A series of question marks popped up on the screen.

Zachary blew out his breath, not sure how much to tell Rhys. He didn't want to tell him too much in a text message. He should at least do that face to face. Though he dreaded the prospect. The last time he had gone to talk to Rhys about Luke, Rhys had not been happy about Zachary telling him to back off and watch out for Luke due to the danger of Luke pulling Rhys into the trafficking business as well.

And maybe that was why Luke had told Zachary that he and Rhys weren't communicating anymore. They had hatched a plan to keep him out of their business. Mollify him so that he wouldn't look too closely and see what was happening. Had there been indications that Rhys had still been in contact with Luke that Zachary should have seen? He really hadn't looked closely once Luke told him that Rhys wasn't talking to him anymore.

Had he been duped?

*He's in jail and feeling pretty down,* he texted Rhys honestly. There wasn't any point in telling Rhys that Luke was fine and would be getting out soon. Rhys would know or find out quickly that Zachary was not telling him the truth. *But he is safe. By himself, not a target. Guards watching*

It was a few minutes before he saw the blinking dots again. Kenzie pressed Play on *Unsolved Mysteries*, but Zachary didn't pay much attention to it. He kept looking at the phone, waiting for Rhys's response.

When it came through, it was succinct. *Wat happend?*

That was the big question. Zachary wished he had an answer for Rhys.

*Trying to figure it out*

*Get him out*

Zachary sighed. *Can't get him out. But trying to help. Find out what happened so we can work with his lawyer.*

*Murder? Not Luke*

In case Zachary didn't get it, Rhys sent Luke's picture again, followed by the red circle with the slash through it. Zachary knew that Rhys must be having a hard time with it. Just like Joss, even though she tried to keep on her tough mask and not show it.

*He was arrested at scene with weapon,* Zachary sent back. *He did it. But I'm trying to figure out why. What happened.*

The red circle came up on the screen again. Zachary tried to watch the TV, but kept looking down at the screen, waiting for something further from Rhys. When half an hour went by without Rhys sending anything else, Zachary switched over to message Vera Salter, Rhys's grandmother. Rhys's mother was in prison, and Vera was the one taking care of him. That gave Zachary pause, remembering what Gloria, Rhys's mother, had done and what she had tried to do. Rhys had been through enough trauma in his young life, stretching all the way back to the murder of his grandfather, which had effectively taken Rhys's voice away from him.

*Vera, it's Zachary*

It was a few minutes before there was any sign of Vera composing a response. She knew how to use the messaging apps, since that was one of the primary ways Rhys communicated. Still, there was no guarantee that she would have her phone within reach or notice that Zachary had sent her a message if she and Rhys were in the house together and she didn't need to keep her eye on the phone.

*Zachary, is everything all right?*

*There's been trouble. Luke arrested for murder.*

The dots started flashing immediately.

*What? No! He's too young.*

*visited him in jail today. worried about Rhys. Keep eye on him?*

*Of course. Should I tell him?*

*He already knows. Was messaging me about it*

*How?*

*Don't know. Maybe still in touch with Luke?*

Vera responded with a word Zachary knew she wouldn't use if they were having a spoken conversation, shocking him slightly.

*I didn't think they were,* Zachary typed, *but maybe they lied*

*Yes,* Vera agreed succinctly. And then there were no more messages from her either.

Zachary looked up at the TV and tried to get back into the flow of the mystery they were discussing. He was confused and thought they might have switched cases while he'd been focused on texting with Rhys and Vera. He kept looking back down at his phone, waiting for one of them to message him back. Rhys angry at him because Zachary had messaged Vera, or Vera letting him know that Rhys was okay. Or not okay.

But his phone did not vibrate again.

# 22

The next day, Zachary got up determined to get more information. He only had the bare bones of what had happened and he needed to know more. He started with a few internet searches, but word of the murder had apparently not made it to any of the news networks yet.

It was Monday, so Kenzie was back to work at the regular time and would be occupied all day, possibly even late. That gave Zachary plenty of time to get back to Kent to get some boots-on-the-ground investigating done.

There weren't a lot of hotels in Kent, so he knew it wouldn't take him too long to figure out which of them had been the scene of a recent murder and all of the drama that would have surrounded the arrest and investigation. The registration clerk at the Best Western directed him immediately to the non-chain hotel across the street, the International Rest Easy Suites. Zachary thanked the young man and crossed over to the other side. He didn't go to the registration desk there, but did a quick circle around the common areas on the main floor initially, then approached the front desk from the area of the elevators, which would give them the impression that he was a hotel guest.

"Excuse me... I was wondering where I would find the maids that cleaned the rooms over the weekend... Friday, actually. Friday night or Saturday morning...?"

There were three employees at the desk, and they looked at each other before the taller of the two men elected himself to answer the question.

"Is there some problem I could help with, sir?"

"No. No, not a problem. It's just that... my girlfriend, she put her rings down on the edge of the sink. I don't know why girls do that. And now she can't find them. I don't think anyone stole them," he hastened to add, holding up a hand. "But they might have gotten mixed in with the washcloth and towels..."

"If anyone had found them, they would have turned them in to the lost and found." The tall man turned and looked at the other two. "Any new rings in the lost and found?" he asked, as if it were not *his* job to know what was in there.

"Nothing like *that* found over the weekend," the young woman said, shaking her head. She smoothed her blazer in a nervous gesture. She gave the other two a significant look. Acknowledging that there had been *other* things of interest going on over the weekend. Zachary was sure it would have made a big impression on everyone. Even if the murder didn't make it to the news, it would undoubtedly be the talk of all of the hotel employees.

"I just wonder if I could talk to the maids and see where the towels and everything end up. My girlfriend is really upset, and even though it's her own fault for putting them on the side of the sink, I want to do what I can to help her."

"They probably went down the drain," the younger of the men suggested.

Zachary refrained from rolling his eyes. It wasn't nearly as easy to lose a ring down a hotel bathroom drain as it was to lose something like small stud earrings. Rings couldn't usually get under the edge of the stopper or through the strainer.

"I sure hope not. Or I'll be calling you to get a plumber to take apart the trap," he said with a laugh. "And the maids are..." He pointed randomly toward the elevators.

"We'll have to find out who did your room and speak with her," the tall clerk said unctuously. "You can't just go walking into the service areas and question the staff."

Which was exactly what Zachary wanted to do. "Oh, okay," he said. "Room 605. If you could find out for me."

He turned and walked back to the elevators as if to go back to his room. But when the elevator doors closed, he hit the basement level, not the sixth floor. Despite the man's response, all three of them had given away the location of the maid's service area, looking down or at the elevator, and then to the left. The left when he was facing the elevator was right when he got off, so he turned down the right corridor and headed toward the voices he could hear in the distance.

After passing several closed doors and branching service corridors, Zachary arrived at a break room where several uniformed maids were talking. They stopped when they saw him in the doorway.

"Hi. My name is Zachary Goldman, and I'm investigating the murder Friday night? Saturday morning? I'm sure you all heard about it…"

They looked at each other uncertainly, but there were several automatic nods of agreement.

"We've already told that other cop that we didn't see anything," a redhead complained. "None of us did. So just let us get back to our work."

Even though they had been standing around on a break talking. *Now* she had to get back to work.

"Yeah, sorry about that. We always end up going over the same ground half a dozen times. You wouldn't believe how often something is missed the first time. Or stories change, or people remember things later. We don't want to cause anyone any trouble, but I would appreciate your cooperation."

He didn't say he was a cop. That was their own assumption, based on the fact that he said he was investigating it and was dressed as they imagined a plainclothes police detective might be dressed. He wasn't going to disabuse them of the idea.

"Who was in charge of cleaning room…" Zachary pulled out his notebook and started flipping pages. "Hang on a sec… room…"

"Room 412," one of them provided impatiently.

"Right. Room 412. I see that." He flipped to a blank page in his notepad instead. "Who was supposed to be cleaning that room?"

"They had a sign on the doorknob," a Hispanic maid said. "No maid service. If people don't want their room cleaned while they are here, they put out a sign. Room 412 had a sign, kept it on the whole time they were here. So no one cleaned it."

"I see. What about now? I assume it has been cleaned now?"

"Not yet! Have to rip out the carpet and replace it. And sand and repaint walls. We don't clean until *after* all the work is done. Otherwise, we do it twice."

Blood soaked into the carpet and sprayed or cast off on the walls. Zachary imagined it was pretty gruesome. But he wasn't going to leave it up to imagination.

"Could one of you let me into the room?" Zachary patted his pockets. "I think that one of the detectives was given a card key to get in and out, but I didn't bring it with me…"

The maids exchanged aggravated glances, but an older woman seemed eager to get a look at the notorious crime scene. She stepped toward Zachary, nodding. "I will do it," she said in a long-suffering tone for the benefit of her colleagues. But her eyes were bright, excited to be involved. "Follow me."

The woman's name was Mildred, and she had introduced herself and filled Zachary in on all of the details of her husband, children, and two young grandchildren by the time they finished taking the elevator to the fourth floor. She then fell silent, the gravity of the situation entering her consciousness.

23

---

Mildred led the way to the hotel room and paused there for a moment as if she might be having second thoughts. Zachary wasn't surprised. It was one thing to imagine the excitement of what might have happened in that room, a ghoulish interest in death and murder and all of the rumors that had been circulating through the hotel. But it was another thing for her to actually see it herself, to be walking in there with an investigator to see what had really happened.

"If you could just let me in," Zachary said. "You should probably not come in. We don't want to destroy any evidence."

She looked relieved and disappointed at the same time. "Well, yes, I suppose. I don't want to cause any problems with the investigation."

Zachary nodded. There was no sign or tape sealing off the hotel room, which meant that the police were finished with it. They had already collected any evidence that they were going to and had released the scene. The hotel could have it cleaned and sanitized and rented out already, if they had wanted to. If they'd been able to clean up all of the blood.

Mildred inserted her card key and pulled it out. The green light turned on, and she turned sideways to allow Zachary past her. He

103

turned the handle before the lock could re-engage and pushed the door open.

"Thank you very much for your help."

Mildred murmured something about being happy to help and arched her neck in an effort to catch a glimpse of the mayhem inside the room. Zachary let the door shut behind him and then walked in.

Nothing had been visible from the door, so Mildred was out of luck in seeing something she could brag to her friends or gossip with her coworkers about. Although that probably wouldn't stop her. She could just make something up. A hall ran past the bathroom and then into an open sitting room space. It was littered with food wrappers and other detritus that Zachary didn't want to look at too closely to begin with. There was a doorway to the right and a kitchenette to the left. As far as Zachary could see, there were no obvious signs of the murder in the kitchenette. He opened the door to the bedroom and reached around the wall to turn on the light.

He could smell the blood even before he turned on the light. He squinted his eyes in preparation, knowing that the scene was going to be shocking.

There was, of course, no body. The victim's body had been removed Saturday morning. They had taken the blankets from the bed as well, so that only the bare mattress remained, soaked in blood, now a dull, rusty brown. There was cast-off blood from the knife on the headboard and wall, indicating that Eyler had been stabbed more than once. It was not a single stab wound or a slit throat. Zachary pictured Luke there with an older man. Bigger, maybe a bit pudgy around the middle, losing control and stabbing multiple times.

Why? Being stabbed in the bed made it doubtful that it had been a business meeting. An assignation? Had Eyler baited or insulted? If he was trying to get Luke back into the business, then there had probably been threats, an attempt at intimidation. He would have done better by bribing Luke, offering him drugs and the other things that the lowlifes used to lure young people into the fold.

Zachary entered the bedroom and walked around it slowly, looking at the window, the wall, the surfaces of the dresser, and around the bottom of the bed. The bedside units were not side tables with drawers, but open shelves, which guests would be less likely to leave things behind in. There had definitely been drugs in the room. There were wrappers and caps from syringes and a sort of burnt plastic smell still in the air despite the amount of time that had passed. There was a strap that might have come from a piece of luggage or might have been used as a tourniquet to raise the user's veins to make it easier to inject.

There were also long strings of condom packets on the bedside shelves and floor, some of them intact and others torn open and used. There were no used condoms on the floor or in the garbage cans, so Zachary assumed the police had taken them as evidence, along with the used needles. He studied the pattern of the cast-off blood and pulled out his camera to take pictures of it, then moved on to photograph the rest of the room. There wasn't a lot for him to go on, but it helped to get a feeling for the room and how things must have gone down.

There was another bathroom attached to the bedroom. Not a tiny one, but spacious with a jetted tub. Even though it was a fairly nice hotel, everything felt grimy and oppressive. The fingerprint powder smudging many of the surfaces in the bedroom and bathroom probably contributed to the feeling of everything being dirty. Red-brown handprints on the wall and sink in the bedroom gave Zachary pause.

Any personal possessions had already been removed by the police. Still, Zachary could see discarded makeup applicators and wipes and other personal products in the wastepaper bin, along with more long, skinny syringe wrappers. There were towels and washcloths missing, which he assumed had been removed by the police, since the maids had not yet done anything with the room.

There was no under-sink cabinet or medicine cabinet on the wall, all places where guests might accidentally leave something. The hotel's soaps and shampoos had been left in a basket on the counter, but the discarded bottles and wrappers were on the edge of the tub or in the garbage. The "no maid service" sign had been on the door for several days, so the amenities had not been restocked.

Zachary lifted the lid from the toilet tank for a quick check inside, but saw nothing out of the ordinary. He took the toilet paper roll off its holder, took apart the two sides of the springed cylinder, and found a cache of pills that the police had missed. He took pictures of everything and put them back.

He walked once more around the bedroom, looking for anything else that would give him some insight into what had happened there. He looked again at the messy living room and the apparently unused kitchenette. Lots of fast food and junk food wrappers and containers in the garbage cans and on the floor of the living room. Nothing that indicated the presence of salads or fresh produce, though he checked the fridge just in case anything had been left behind. It was empty. He checked through the drawers of the kitchen methodically, taking a picture of the contents of each one. There were only the bare essentials that someone might need if he took it into his head to cook. Maybe not even that.

Zachary looked through everything one more time, snapping a few more pictures, and then left the suite, headed once more for the front desk.

# 24

When he returned to the front desk, the tall man who had previously taken charge looked at him with a scowl of suspicion. This time, Zachary focused on his name tag, which gave only his first name. Arthur.

"Who are you really? You're not a guest here," Arthur accused.

Zachary nodded. "I'm investigating the death of your guest here the other day. Mr. Eyler."

"We already talked to the police about that."

"And I'm sure you answered all of their questions the best you could. But new things have come to light. Some things need follow-up."

"A couple of the maids said that you went down there. Interrogated them and talked Mildred into letting you into the room."

Zachary was lucky to have avoided security. But he'd figured it would take a while for them to figure out what was going on. By the time they got someone to the room to check up on him, he could be in and out. And he'd been right.

"I asked a few questions," he asked. "And yes, Mildred was kind enough to let me into the room when I asked."

"There's nothing there. The police have already investigated and taken all of the evidence. You didn't have any right to be in that room. It's burglary."

Zachary smiled cooperatively. "It isn't burglary when you let me in."

"I didn't let you in. A maid let you in. Because you lied to her." His mouth was an ugly red slash across his face. "You told them you were a cop, but you're not one of the police detectives investigating the murder."

"I didn't say I was a police detective."

"Whether you did or not, that's what you made them think. You intentionally misled them. Just like you lied and misled me with that rigmarole about your girlfriend losing her rings. Just who are you and what game are you playing here? Are you some reporter or thrill-seeking paparazzi?"

"I'm a private investigator," Zachary told him calmly. He reached into his pocket and brought out a stack of business cards. He separated one out and handed it to Arthur. "As I said, I am investigating the death of Mr. Eyler."

"Investigating it. But you're not police."

"No. I'm a *private* investigator."

"You can't be in here."

"I'll leave," Zachary agreed. He cocked his head slightly. "After you tell me why you're letting sex traffickers operate out of this hotel."

"What the—?" Arthur exploded. His face grew beet red. "What are you talking about? Just who do you think you are, throwing around accusations like that? We would never allow something like that!"

"You have been. Who knows how long this has been going on. Eyler was in town for a while. I don't know whether his predecessor used this hotel as well. I guess I'd have to talk to the staff to find that out."

"There's nothing like that going on here!"

"I just saw that hotel room. I can assure you, there definitely is."

"If there was, there was no way for any of us to know about it. How would we know something like that?"

"There are signs. He gets a room in the back overlooking the parking lot. He brings in a lot of young girls with fancy clothes or phones, but they never talk. Only he talks, and he pays in cash or with a preloaded credit card for a week or two at a time. There are noise complaints, music playing, people coming and going all the time, a lot of them men. Sound familiar?"

The other two hotel workers were crowding close, their eyes wide, listening intently to every word. Arthur's face, previously flushed, was quickly draining of color. Zachary tried to see over the high counter to see if there were a chair for Arthur to sit down on if he started to feel faint.

"The maids said that he keeps the 'no maid service' sign on the door all the time. So they don't get in there to clean." Zachary paused, watching him, examining his face for any tells. "You knew all this, didn't you? Maybe you weren't sure what was going on, but you had your suspicions."

"It's not my responsibility to know what guests are doing. What they do behind closed doors is their own business. It's the job of the police, not me."

"You cared enough to find out what I was doing."

"You're not a guest," Arthur said mulishly.

"You thought I was. And who do you think is supposed to report suspicious activities to the police?"

The other man leaned forward, inserting himself into the conversation. "I thought maybe they were models," he offered. "You know, real skinny with fancy clothes?"

Zachary studied him. "And you thought he was doing headshots out of a hotel room in small-town Vermont?"

"Well…" The younger man reddened almost as much as Arthur had. They had guessed. Of course they had. But they had kept out of it. Maybe because they were told to by management. Maybe because they didn't want anything to do with the police. Sometimes people learned from experience. One report to the police that came to bite them, and they would be far more likely to exercise caution the next time.

"It's disgusting," the young woman piped up. "I can't believe they would do that here. Gross."

"It happens all over," Zachary said. "Not just here. Not just this hotel. But we can't fight it if people keep looking the other way."

# 25

They all stood there uncomfortably, knowing that they hadn't said anything, but unable to justify it. This was good because then they would be more likely to help Zachary to make up for it.

"He was here for two weeks?" he guessed. Long enough for Joss and Luke to know he was there.

"Not quite, I don't think…" Arthur tapped the keyboard in front of him. "Oh. Longer, actually about two and a half."

"How many girls?"

Arthur looked trapped. He looked at the others. "I didn't really notice. Maybe three or four. Not at the same time; it was usually only one at a time. But three or four in rotation. I just thought… he was fooling around."

"None of the girls were ever together?"

"Well, just once or twice. It did happen. But not very often."

"So you knew that the girls knew each other. They weren't just girlfriends he was keeping from finding out about each other."

"Well…" Arthur scratched his ear. "I guess not."

"Could the three of you describe the girls that he brought in rotation?"

They looked at each other.

"There were two blondes," the woman said. "And that redhead. And a smaller woman who was Chinese or something."

"Is that it?" Zachary asked. "No brunettes? Other ethnic groups? Boys?"

"There was a Black girl." Arthur remembered. "She wasn't here very often. Tall. And skinny. All of them were skinny."

Zachary walked them through descriptions of each of the girls, getting as many details as he could. He didn't know whether it would be of any help to him in the end, but he didn't want those girls to be invisible. They had been ignored by the people who should have noticed them, should have reported suspected trafficking out of the hotel. They had been overlooked as if they were not real people.

Aside from the five regulars, the clerks thought that there had been a few others off and on, brought in for an hour or two and never seen again. And there had been other women who didn't have the same look as the "models." Older, hard-looking women who did not act submissive like the girls. Women who had worked their way up in the organization and now had stables of their own, probably. Peers of Eyler or maybe even over his head, there for business meetings rather than turning tricks. At least, that was what Zachary assumed. Some women stayed in the business for a long time, like Joss, but they were less likely to be working out of a hotel room, supervised by a handler. Zachary didn't know for sure what Joss had done as she got older. He hadn't asked her the details and didn't really want to know.

There had been a lot of men in and out and, while there had probably been some repeat customers, the employees couldn't describe any. They had seen the girls regularly, and the men mainly were let in a fire door from the parking lot; they didn't walk past the front desk.

Eventually, Zachary felt like he had probably gotten everything he could from them. Arthur and his coworkers had turned out to be a valuable source of information once he had gained their cooperation. Then he remembered one more thing. He pulled out his phone and went through his recent messages. He tapped on the picture Rhys had sent him of Luke to expand it to fill the screen and turned the phone to show to them.

"How about this guy? Have you seen him around?"

"Is he the one?" the woman asked in a hushed tone. "You know, the one that killed *him*?" Her eyes rolled up toward Eyler's room.

Zachary shrugged. There would undoubtedly be pictures in the paper and internet news by the time Luke got to trial. And his name and aliases. "Have you seen him?"

"I'm sure I've seen him around here," Arthur said with a nod.

"When? Can you remember?"

He shook his head slowly. "Anything other than the last day or two is just a jumble. I couldn't tell you which day."

"Friday? Were you on shift in the evening?"

"No, I was on during the day. And I don't think that's when it was. I'm sure it was longer ago than that."

"Days? Weeks?"

Arthur frowned, looking down at the picture, his forehead wrinkling. "I just can't be sure. I would say… last week, but it is so hard to be sure. I'll say something happened a month ago and then realize it's been a whole year."

"A week or longer?"

Arthur moved his head back and forth, thinking about it, then nodded. "Yeah. I would say so."

"And you?" Zachary looked at the other two employees. "Do you think you saw him?"

"He looks familiar," the younger man said and shrugged. "But I couldn't say that it was from here. Could have been here, or at a party, or on TV. I'm really not very good at faces."

"Do you think it might have been somewhere else?" Zachary prompted, pushing back on the suggestion. "What was he doing? Who was he with?"

The man closed his eyes, thinking about it. "I think… I don't think it was here. I can see him drinking or doing karaoke or something like that. Out with friends. Having a good time." He shook his head. "Not here."

"Do they ever do karaoke night here?" Zachary asked, with a nod toward the lounge.

"Yes, but I've never gone to it here. It's lame." He sent an apologetic glance at Arthur, who might be his boss or maybe just more experienced.

"There was another boy," the woman said. She looked at Arthur as if needing his permission to go on. "I kind of thought that he was the man's son. He came in with him a few times when he didn't have one of the girls with him." She swallowed. "I just thought he was his son. Right?"

Zachary shook his head. "Probably not. Can you describe him?"

"Oh…" She looked at the ceiling, thinking back. "I just thought… that's what made sense at the time. He was just a young kid, maybe thirteen. Um… dirty blond. About this tall…" She held her hand out beside her, at about her shoulder level. A reasonable height for a thirteen-year-old boy. Not too malnourished. "He would… have his arm around him, you know. I thought he got visitation some days or picked the kid up from karate because his mom couldn't that day. Something like that, you know?"

"And how did the boy seem?"

"I don't know." She shook her head. "What do you mean?"

"Was he… playing with a handheld game or his phone? Was he cheerful and bouncy with his 'dad' or sullen or pouty? Did he talk to him? Ask him for things or suggest things they could do while he was visiting?"

"No. No, none of that. He seemed… sleepy usually. Like he'd gotten out of bed too early or was tired after a long day. He never said anything. He'd just be there, under his dad's arm." She gulped and corrected herself. "Under that man's arm. Kind of… cuddling." She shook her head and nearly whispered. "I didn't know."

When he had all of the information he could get from them, Zachary pulled out a couple more business cards and handed them out.

"Please let me know if you think of anything else. Or if you see any of these people again."

# 26

Zachary checked his messages when he got out of the hotel. He had kept his phone on "do not disturb" while he'd been conducting his investigation at the hotel so that he wouldn't be distracted by any calls or messages. There were no personal calls, but there was one number with no ID and a voicemail message. Zachary played that and found a testy message from a cop who identified himself as Detective Richards. He wanted to talk to Zachary as soon as possible and didn't sound too pleased about it.

Zachary decided to try the police station and see whether he could see Richards face-to-face rather than talking over the phone. It was harder to just blast someone and refuse to listen to anything they said. Much harder to "hang up" on someone standing there in front of you.

He was at the police station in a few minutes, greeted by a different Officer of the Day from the one who had been there Sunday morning. Rhodes, by his name badge.

"I was wondering whether Detective Richards is in," Zachary inquired politely.

"Do you have an appointment?"

"I don't, but he was trying to reach me earlier. He left a message on my phone."

Rhodes pursed his lips, considering. Apparently, he hadn't had to make the judgment as to whether to screen someone Richards was trying to reach before. He was used to the appointment/no appointment dichotomy, which was easy to manage. "Uh... if you'll give me a minute, I'll see if he is available."

He took a few steps away from the service counter toward one of the desks, then turned around, looking embarrassed. "Uh... I didn't get your name. I guess I'm going to need that."

"Zachary Goldman. It's on the Eyler homicide."

The officer's eyes widened slightly at that. Zachary saw him give a tiny nod of affirmation to himself. Yes, he was doing the right thing. Rhodes was going to want to talk with a witness on the Eyler case. Zachary imagined they probably did not get a lot of homicides. And the ones that they did get were probably mainly domestic disputes or drunks. Not sex trafficking.

He walked over to his desk and picked up the desk phone. With his back to Zachary and his voice low, he dialed an extension and had a short conversation. He hung up the phone and returned to the service counter.

"Detective Richards will be right out. You could have a seat while you're waiting..." Rhodes motioned in the direction of the single row of chairs lined up under the window in case Zachary had missed them.

Zachary walked over to the window and looked out at the street, watching the traffic and pedestrians passing by outside. He would probably be spending more time than he would like in a hard plastic or metal chair; he would avoid sitting until he had to.

Detective Richards didn't take long to come through the locked security door. He was an older man with a military bearing and a slight gut. A formidable, no-nonsense kind of guy.

"Goldman?"

Zachary nodded. "That's me."

"This way."

Zachary followed him through the security door and down the hall to an interview room. Zachary was glad not to be chained to the table as Luke had been. Not so happy to see that he had been correct about the hard metal chair that would not conform to his body shape and ease his healing tailbone.

Zachary sighed and sat down anyway. Might as well not start off the interview appearing uncooperative. He tried to sit with his weight on one side rather than balanced in the middle. He should have brought one of his special pillows with him, but that would have been embarrassing. He'd rather be physically uncomfortable than mocked by the big policeman.

"You have some identification?" Richards demanded.

Zachary had to get back up to work his wallet out of his back pocket. He opened the flap to show his driver's license and handed it to the detective.

Richards barely gave it a glance before handing it back. Just ensuring that he wasn't dealing with a kook, Zachary supposed. Or that if he was dealing with a kook, he would at least be sure that he knew who he was talking to, rather than trusting that Zachary hadn't given him an alias.

Zachary sat back down and again tried to make himself as comfortable as the metal chair would allow. Richards didn't sit immediately.

"Why don't you explain to me your interest in the Eyler homicide," he suggested.

No hint as to what he already knew. Keeping his questions open-ended.

"I know Luke," he explained. At Richards's blank look, he elaborated. "Your… suspect. Uh…" He felt for his notebook to double-check the name Joss had given him. "Joseph Daniel—"

Richards waved Zachary's fumbling answer aside. "Bryant. I doubt that is the name he was born with any more than Luke. So, okay, Luke. How do you know Luke?"

"I know him from a previous case that I was involved with. I can't give you the details, but that's when I met Luke for the first time. Joss called me to let me know that he'd been arrested and to see if I could find out anything that might help him."

"Who is Joss?"

"Jocelyn Goldman."

Unlike the others, Richards didn't make any sign that the name meant anything to him. Either he wasn't plugged in to the grapevine, or he had a much better poker face than the jail CO or the cop that Zachary had talked to on Sunday.

"Luke has been staying with her. She has a history... and was helping Luke to stay clean. Helping him to start a new life."

"You know about his history."

"Yes... I know what he told me about it, anyway."

Richards studied him, frowning, then nodded. "Exactly right. You have no idea whether the stories he tells are true. Chances are, they aren't. They're just stories he made up or heard somewhere else. Thought he'd recycle them for his own use. He's a con man, been in trouble ever since he could walk."

Zachary was silent on this point. He shifted his position slightly and tried to change the direction of the conversation.

"I was hoping you could give me some of the details of the case against Luke. Well, not details, of course. Just the general gist of the case. Anything more than what has appeared in the news?"

"If it hasn't been in the news, then we didn't release it to the public. You're not here so that I can share my investigation with you."

"No, of course not," Zachary agreed. It wasn't like he'd ever had police cooperate with him or feed him information. Or at least, very rarely. He wasn't expecting it to be that easy.

"I have some information that you should probably know," Zachary told him, extending an olive branch. "Things that may be important to the case."

"You haven't figured anything out that we haven't already covered," Richards dismissed. As if Joe Public never managed to figure things out before the police. Zachary had been involved in too many other cases that the police had given up on or been wrong about to believe that for a second.

He just sat there, waiting for Richards's curiosity to get the better of him.

Show up at a police station and start bragging about how he knew things that the police didn't or how he figured something out, and they would write him off as a kook, like he was one of those psychics who called in with tips, insisting that they knew the whereabouts of a murdered or missing child. But hold back, act as if he didn't care to tell the police anything, and sooner or later…

"What information?" Richards asked grumpily. "And just so you know, I've already heard about your antics at the hotel. Impersonating a police officer is against the law, you know."

"I didn't tell anyone that I was a police officer. I said I was investigating the case. If anyone asked whether I am a cop, I let them know that I was a private investigator."

"You intended them to believe you were a cop, no matter what you said."

Zachary shrugged.

# 27

Richards stared at him, trying to intimidate him. But Zachary just waited it out. The silence again worked in his favor.

"What do you know?" Richards asked again. "Or think you know?"

"I know that Eyler was trafficking girls out of that hotel room. I'm sure you already figured that much out, but I did get descriptions of some of the girls he has been taking there. Maybe that would be helpful in finding out what happened around the time that Eyler was killed. There may be witnesses that haven't come forward."

"I see. Is that it, then? Descriptions of some hookers?"

"Trafficking victims," Zachary corrected. "Vulnerable minors. Not criminals."

"I didn't say they were criminals."

"I wonder how many DNA profiles you are going to get from the condoms and needles that you recovered at the scene."

Richards rolled his eyes. "At least a dozen, I'm sure. But all of that is beside the point. We already know who killed Eyler. Your friend Luke. All of the rest of this is just distraction. I don't need more witnesses. I don't need more DNA profiles to identify all of the johns and every other piece of filth that has been in that hotel room while

Eyler has been pimping out of there. We'll process it all because this is a homicide case and they'll want everything they can get to shore up the case, but we don't need it. Your boy was caught red-handed, Mr. Goldman. Smoking gun in his hand."

Zachary must have frowned at that, because Richards backed up and clarified.

"I mean that figuratively. I meant the knife. Which was *literally* still in his hand when he was caught. And his bloody prints all over that hotel room."

"Mmm." Zachary nodded. "That's something I was wondering about."

"What?"

"If you had just killed someone and had their blood all over you, why would you go around the room touching everything? And why would you still be holding the knife in your hand while you did it? I mean... was this a fetish? Was he confused or hallucinating? If he was actually doing something... like trying to cover up what he had done or searching for something, then wouldn't he put down the knife? He wouldn't be walking around the suite holding on to it."

"That's what happened. Don't ask me why your psycho friend did what he did. Because there's something wrong with his head, obviously."

"Ah. Right."

"He has a history. Trauma. Head injuries. Overdoses. All of that stuff does a number on your brain. I wouldn't expect him to behave logically, like you or me. Criminals like him do all kinds of crazy stuff. Laying down and going to sleep in the middle of a robbery. Trying on the woman's panties. Ordering pizza. You would think that people would just run after doing something like that. That they would wash their hands and leave the knife there and sneak off before the authorities could get there. But the guy is not right in the head. That's just the way it is."

Zachary had to admit that he'd heard stories like that. It was true that criminals often did crazy, illogical things. Especially if they were on drugs. But he knew Luke, and Luke had not struck him as being that kind of person. He had been an addict, so it was entirely possible that he'd been on something and had a complete break from reality, hallucinating or paranoid.

"Was he high when you arrested him?"

Richards shrugged. "He tested clean. But who knows? He could be on some new designer drug that we don't test for yet. Or, like I said, brain damage from previous episodes. The kid's drug history goes back years."

"He seemed fine when I talked to him. And when I've seen him before. He doesn't act like he has brain damage."

"You can't always tell. Someone could be able to carry on a perfectly normal conversation like we're doing now, but not have any judgment, or flip out and go schizo on you thirty seconds later. You go to some of these mental hospitals, and you think the person you're talking to is a nurse or orderly, and then find out they're one of the patients. Who knows what delusions this kid could have?"

Zachary shifted uncomfortably. He did not like the way that Richards was talking about mentally ill patients. Zachary understood that Richards was just speaking of his own experience. But Zachary had been in the psych ward himself and wished Richards wouldn't be quite so cavalier and dismissive.

"Are you having Luke examined by a psychiatrist, then?"

"That's not my job. That will be up to the lawyers."

"He's in your jail. Isn't it your responsibility to make sure that's the appropriate place for him? If he should be in a psych ward…"

"No. Again, that's a job for the lawyers. The kid is safe in the jail. Nothing is going to happen to him there. If he needs a psychiatrist or medication or therapy, his lawyer can worry about that."

"He doesn't have a lawyer yet."

Richards shrugged. "Still not my concern. I arrested him, which means he goes to jail. That's the way the system works."

Zachary could argue it. A cop could certainly invoke Title 18 and have Luke evaluated. But Richards had no interest in doing so. He wasn't concerned about Luke's mental state, only about making sure he was off the street.

"So… are you interested in any of the information I learned at the hotel today?"

Richards scowled. "I really oughta arrest you for impersonating a police officer."

Zachary waited a few seconds. "So you're not interested?"

Richards sat down in the other chair. Zachary didn't know whether this was because psychologically, the cop was now putting him on the level of a peer rather than someone he was trying to show authority over, or if his feet were just tired from standing.

"Fine. What did you discover at the hotel? Besides the obvious, I mean. We already removed all of the forensic evidence, so it isn't like there was much left there for you to find."

"If I was you, I would do a more thorough search of the suite."

Richards's face got a shade redder and he looked ready to explode. Zachary set his phone on the table, unlocked it, and tapped the screen. He found the pictures of the pills he had found in the bathroom and showed them to Richards.

"In the toilet paper holder."

Richards swore, a single, angry syllable. Zachary couldn't help shifting back slightly, instinct telling him that Richards was going to take a swing at him. But Richards kept himself under control. He picked up Zachary's phone and swiped through pictures in both directions, checking out all of the photos of the hotel, before handing it back.

"Is that all?"

"I didn't do a thorough search. Just looked around. I was only there for a few minutes. I wouldn't be surprised if there is more to find. I'm not confident that the site review was as... rigorous as it should have been."

"Uh-huh. It isn't like we didn't have all the evidence we needed against your friend. I'm not sure what the probative value of some pills in the bathroom is. We already knew the place was full of drugs. You're not saying that these pills belonged to your friend, are you?"

"Well, no. But I like to have a full picture of the situation, not just how things looked at first glance."

"Even when that first glance was of a kid holding a bloody knife over a bloody corpse?"

Zachary shrugged. He hadn't found anything that would exonerate Luke or would give him an argument for a lighter sentence. But it was early days. It would be months before Luke's case went to trial. As urgent as it felt to get him out of that jail and back home, that wasn't the way things were going to work out. He was going to be in jail for a long time and, after conviction, in prison for even longer. He wasn't going to be going home to Joss.

"What about the descriptions of the sex trafficking victims that were working out of that suite?"

Richards sighed. "I don't see what the point is, but yes, give me the descriptions, if you have them."

"I imagine there is security camera video too. You can probably find each of them on the video if you look."

"You think so? This guy was a pro, not just some hick hiring out his girlfriend. They use doors that don't have security cameras. If there is a camera in an elevator or hallway that they don't want to be caught on, it's easy to spray or smash it. They wear hats or hoods and keep their faces turned away from cameras. They know how to avoid video cameras."

"Maybe some of the nearby businesses, then. They wouldn't have been worrying about those. There was a car lot nearby. Some convenience stores. I'm sure they all have video."

Richards made a motion for Zachary to get on with it. He flipped through his notepad to give Richards the descriptions of the prostitutes that the hotel workers had taken note of.

"They could be witnesses. You don't know if Eyler was alone when Luke... was there. One of these people may have seen something important. Something that throws an entirely different light on what happened."

"It's not a matter of throwing a different light on it. We know what happened. A hooker's perspective is not going to change the facts of the case."

Zachary bit the inside of his cheek, trying to keep himself from reacting to Richards's disdainful words. "It could."

"And do you really think that we'll be able to find these girls?" Richards motioned to the notes he had just written down, transcribing from Zachary's notebook. "They are going to be long gone.

They will have left town. Maybe even the state. Whoever is taking over from Eyler, they'll have those girls out of reach by now."

Of course they would. Why would they keep them around to talk to the cops? They had plenty of experience moving people around the country. Zachary sighed. Those girls would never be heard from again.

# 28

S o, you think that Luke killed Eyler *why?*" Zachary asked.

"Because he was caught red-handed."

"No, I mean… why would he do that? Why would he kill Eyler? What was his motive?"

"We don't need a motive when we catch him red-handed. This isn't some detective show on TV where you have to figure out everyone's motivations. The fact is that ninety-nine percent of the time, the person who killed the victim is exactly who you think it would be. The challenge is in gathering enough evidence for them to be arrested and convicted. Trying to figure out who is the murderer is just for dramas. Cheap novels and TV detectives."

"But don't you want to know? Don't you want to understand what happened? For the jury, at least?"

"I'm not the one who has to present it to a jury. I'm just the one who needs to charge him and coordinate getting the evidence. It goes to the prosecutor and he takes over. We have a lot of forensic evidence to be processed, which will take months, but I already know exactly what it's going to show. It's going to show that Luke killed Eyler. The rest is just extraneous and unimportant."

Zachary shook his head. The circumstances of the case mattered.

Richards might be satisfied with "we know he did it because he did it," but Zachary was not. He needed to understand what had happened. Once he could put it all together in his head in a way that made sense, he would be done with it. Until then, he would keep asking questions.

"Look," Richards said, "there's not that much to understand. Criminals kill each other all the time. It saves us a lot of paperwork and the taxpayers all of the money it would have taken to keep Eyler in prison for thirty years. That's a good thing. We're grateful to him for that. But there's no great mystery here. You can ask 'why' a hundred times, but in the end, it doesn't matter."

"You think it was a business deal gone wrong."

"Of course I do. They were both in the business. Prostitute kills pimp. Usually, it's the other way around, but we'd rather the pimp was the victim. It doesn't matter whether it was because the kid wanted to set up shop on his own and Eyler wasn't going to let it happen. It doesn't matter if it was over Eyler withholding pay or drugs or trying to get the kid to do something he didn't want to. It doesn't even matter if it was jealousy because Eyler favored another hooker over him. Luke confronts Eyler, they yell and scream and Eyler ends up getting stuck. By the time we get there, it's all over and all that's left to do is take Luke into custody and Eyler to the morgue."

"Luke wasn't working for Eyler."

"I don't think you can know that. He could have been."

"He wasn't," Zachary said, with more certainty than he felt.

"Then he was trying to branch off on his own. Not a good idea when there is another boss in the area, but the kid thinks he's got a chance. Eyler sends for him, and either the kid is stupid enough to go confront him face to face on his own, or Eyler sends out the goon squad to bring him in."

Zachary raised one finger, objecting. "If Eyler's men brought Luke, then where were they when Luke killed Eyler? Standing by watching?"

"I'm sure they didn't think that he was a danger. Unarmed kid, been in the business for years, he knows how to behave."

"And that doesn't bother you?"

"Eyler was a big guy. Capable of looking after himself. Overconfident, maybe. I'm sure he didn't think Luke was any danger to him."

"It just doesn't make any sense," Zachary insisted.

Richards shrugged. "It doesn't have to."

---

It was clear that Zachary wasn't going to get anywhere with Richards. Each was sure of his own position. Richards knew that Luke had done it and that no one had been able to see it coming. Zachary was equally sure that Luke would not have put himself in that hotel room without a very good reason.

After ending their interview, Zachary wanted to see Luke again. Maybe now, knowing more of the details of the case, Zachary would be able to get something out of him. If Zachary could only identify mitigating circumstances around the murder, at least it would be a start. He would have something to go to Joss with.

Since Zachary had already filled out the required forms on Sunday, the officer at the front desk told him he could go around to the jail and they would let him visit Luke. Zachary found the door locked as he had the previous day. He had thought that it might be open on a weekday. But then, it was a jail. He should have expected it to be locked up tight.

They were, at least, faster to answer the door buzzer than they had been on a Sunday. Zachary had left as many of his personal items as possible in the car this time so that he didn't have to give much more than his shoes and key to the male CO who checked him in.

"You're here to see the kid?" the hulking man questioned, looking down at the clipboard in his hand after ensuring that Zachary was not bringing any contraband into the jail.

"Yes. That's right."

"Come with me."

Zachary followed him to a visiting room that was pretty much the same as the one he had been in on Sunday. Zachary decided to stay on his feet until Luke got there, to save him having to sit for so long on the uncomfortable chairs. The one at the police station had been bad enough.

The CO had been turning to leave, but he paused, looking back at Zachary. Zachary didn't move, waiting to see if he wanted something. The CO turned back around.

"Siddown."

"I just thought I would stand while I'm waiting. Been sitting all day…"

The man shook his head. "Sit."

"Okay." Zachary gingerly lowered himself into the chair .

"If there's going to be trouble with you not following the rules, you will not be allowed to visit."

"I didn't know it was a rule. Sorry."

The CO pointed to one of the plastic panels bolted into the wall with its long list of rules that must be followed during visits. Zachary hadn't read it and didn't plan to, but he pointed his nose toward it anyway. The CO waited another moment, then nodded and withdrew, shutting the door behind him. Zachary sighed and waited. He was going to be pretty sore by the time he got home.

It seemed like a long time before the CO brought Luke in. Half an hour or even forty-five minutes. Zachary didn't wear a watch—and wouldn't have been able to wear it into the visiting room—and he didn't have his phone with him, so he didn't have any way to verify his feeling about how much time had passed. He knew from past experience that his ADHD or meds could cause a sense of time distortion.

The door opened and the CO walked Luke in, one big hand holding on to Luke's arm in what looked like a painful grip. "Sit," he ordered, while at the same time shoving the slight teenager into the other chair, not waiting for compliance. A puff of sound escaped from Luke when he hit the chair, but he didn't voice any complaint. He waited patiently for the CO to anchor his shackles to the table. The CO walked back out and stationed himself outside the door, occasionally looking in the narrow window with wire mesh crisscrossing through it.

Zachary forced a smile. "Hey, Luke. How's it going?"

The bruises seemed to have set in darker in the twenty-four hours since Zachary had seen him. The oversize orange uniform made him seem small and insubstantial. Zachary worried again how Luke would be treated while he was in jail, and later, after he was convicted, in prison. The CO said they would keep him safe, but things happened sometimes. Security holes. Things that the COs were aware of and let slide. A series of mistakes that left a vulnerable teen at the mercy of bigger, more violent men.

Luke picked at a scab on his arm, not looking at Zachary.

"Rhys was asking after you."

That got Luke's attention. He looked up. Clearly, this was not what he had been expecting Zachary to say.

"Yeah?" he asked. "How is Rhys?"

"He seems fine. Very concerned about what's happening to you."

"Well, you can tell him I'm fine. Gonna be a long time before we can see each other again."

That was one positive aspect of Luke's arrest, at least. Zachary didn't have to worry about Luke luring Rhys into the trafficking business.

"I thought you told me that Rhys wasn't answering your messages. That you weren't in contact with each other anymore."

"Yeah, I did."

"Was that just a lie?"

Luke shrugged and didn't answer, leaving Zachary to wonder. Someone had told Rhys about Luke being arrested. Was it possible that person had been Luke himself? Joss had said he hadn't called anyone, but she might not have known. Or had someone else filled Rhys in?

"I went and had a look at the hotel," he told Luke.

"Nice place, hey?"

"It *was* nice," Zachary admitted. "But what was being done out of there was not."

"That's just the business. Gonna happen whether it's a nice place or a dive."

"Every hotel? You think every hotel is being used for trafficking?"

"Most of them."

Zachary didn't think that could be the case. But that had been Luke's life experience. Probably circulated from one hotel to another for a couple of years until he was trusted enough to be out on the street unsupervised to do the dirty work of bringing new talent into Peggy Ann's stable. Or Connor's, if he had still been around then.

"Well, anyway… I saw the room. Why don't you tell me what you remember about it?"

"About the room? Nothing special. Big. Fancy tub. Nice surroundings; johns like that. Makes them feel like they're not down in the sewers like they are."

"I meant what do you remember about the murder? About Eyler."

"Fat slob hadn't changed. Lives in a pigsty. Hardly ever washes. Treats his assets like crap."

"You knew him when you were working with Peggy Ann? Or before that, with Connor?"

Luke gave him a sharp look. "Why?" he snapped.

"I'm trying to get a picture of what happened. How you knew each other. Your history. What led up to him being killed."

"You don't need to know anything that happened. All you need to know is that I stuck the pig. Did the world a favor by taking him out. Should have done it years ago."

"Why didn't you? What pushed you into it now?"

"He was just the same. Nothing changes, just the names of his victims. Made me sick."

"Seeing that he was still trafficking?"

"I knew he would still be trafficking. No one gets out of that voluntarily. Not someone in his position, making money hand over fist. Why would he quit a good thing?"

"Why did you go to Eyler's hotel room?"

"To kill him."

Luke's answer was just a bit too quick.

"How did you know where he was staying?"

Luke hesitated. He shrugged, but Zachary could see him trying to come up with an explanation. "I still… hear things. If you know the business, you see and hear things that other people wouldn't. I knew he was in town. It wasn't hard to find out where."

"How did you know he was in town? Did you run into him?"

"What difference does it make?" Luke objected again. "I killed him. I don't need a deal or a softer sentence. I don't care about that. I always knew I'd end up in prison sooner or later. It's pretty amazing that I made it this long without any long stints."

"So, knowing he was in town, what made you find out where he was staying and to go kill him? Why wouldn't you keep your head down so that no one would recognize you? You blew all of that work you did on starting fresh. Let everybody know who you are. You seemed like you were doing really well with Joss. That you had... a new direction. Were excited about it."

"Excited? No. It was kind of... novel to have this new life, not to have to do any of the things I used to to survive. And your sister is great. But it wasn't the way I wanted to live the rest of my life."

"I didn't know that Joss has been rescuing other kids."

"So what? You don't own her. She doesn't have to tell you everything she's doing."

"I didn't say she did."

Luke jerked on his chains, making them clang loudly against the anchor. "Why are you even here?" he demanded, raising his voice. "I didn't ask for anyone's help. I don't want your help or help from any do-gooder! Just stay out of my life." Luke swore, standing up abruptly.

Zachary jumped back, even though he knew Luke's chains would keep him on the other side of the table. It was a reflex reaction, that instinct to protect himself.

The door opened and the CO strode in. He grabbed Luke by the shoulder and shoved him down, dumping him back into his chair. "Stay there!" he barked, reaching for the chains to untether him. "You keep your hands still, or you'll meet the business end of my taser."

Luke continued to swear and cuss. Zachary wasn't sure whether he or the CO was the target of Luke's words. The CO unlocked the chains from the anchor and pulled Luke back to his feet. He looked at Zachary as he started to push Luke toward the door. "Don't bother to come back, got it? Don't need people who are going to rile the prisoners up."

"I didn't—"

"Stay there. Until someone comes back for you."

Then he pushed Luke through the door and let it close behind him.

## 29

When he eventually got back to his car, Zachary tried to ignore the off-balance feeling that the encounter with Luke had left him with. If he thought about it too much, he would end up getting anxious and emotional. He hoped that by ignoring his body's visceral reaction to Luke's explosion, he could keep forging ahead and the uncomfortable, off-balance feeling would right itself. Just like riding a bike. If he tried to stay still or go too slowly, he would wobble all over. But if he just bore down and sped ahead, staying upright was easy.

But emotional confrontations were not like riding a bike.

Zachary pulled out his phone and checked for new messages. There was a voicemail from a number that he didn't recognize. He played it back and was quickly distracted from the meeting at the jail.

A soft woman's voice. "Mr. Goldman, I hope you don't mind me calling. You said that if I found out anything else about the... the unfortunate death we suffered recently, I should let you know, so I thought I should. It's Mildred, from the hotel. The maid service. I was the one who took you up to the room...? I guess you know that. Your memory is probably better than mine. One of the other maids here, she was on the floor when they were fighting. You know, *them*; before the police came. Okay, so call me back or stop by. Thanks. Bye."

Zachary gathered that she was trying not to use inflammatory words like "murder." They probably had strict instructions from management that they should not mention Mr. Eyler's untimely death anywhere they might be overheard by guests.

He drove back to the hotel rather than calling Mildred back. He was going to need to see the other maid's face and body language and didn't want to be trying to coax her to talk over the phone. Especially if, like Mildred, she had to be circumspect with hotel guests nearby.

He texted Mildred's number when he got there.

*It's Zachary. I'm here at the hotel. Where you want to meet?*

It was a while before Mildred was able to text Zachary back, which was not a surprise.

*There is a coffee shop down the street. By the car lot. Meet us there.*

Zachary sent a thumbs-up back and got out of this car. He could walk the block to the coffee shop. He had been spending way too much time on chairs that aggravated his tailbone. It was time to stand up for a while and, hopefully, it would stop throbbing.

He waited outside, watching the foot traffic on the street, paying attention to what stores and facilities were close to the hotel. When he eventually saw the two women in maid's uniforms walking down the street toward him, he went into the coffee shop.

It was mid-afternoon, and the coffee shop was not too busy. There were plenty of tables open, and the chairs looked much more inviting than the ones at the police station and jail. Zachary joined the short line at the cash register and, as he got to the front, the two maids entered. Mildred led her friend up to Zachary, looking anxious and awkward.

"Hi!" Zachary gave them both a warm smile. "What can I get you?"

"Oh, nothing..." the smaller maid said, shaking her head. "I don't need anything."

"Well, if we're going to sit down and talk in a coffee shop, we should at least pay for our time. I'm going to have a coffee, but if you want a muffin or some juice..." Zachary motioned to the display case and notice board. "Whatever you feel like. But you should have something."

"Well... okay."

Mildred gave Zachary a smile and nod of approval. He ordered both women what they wanted, and they took a corner table where Zachary could see anyone coming in or going out of the cafe.

"I am Rosetta," the smaller woman offered, nodding to Zachary a little shyly.

"Nice to meet you, Rosetta. You can call me Zachary. Mildred said that you were around before the mur—before Eyler died. and maybe you might have heard some of what was going on."

Rosetta nodded. She dropped her eyes to her tea and thought about it.

"I understand there was an argument. Quite a disturbance. Several people called the police about it."

"Yes. They were very loud, lots of yelling and screaming, not trying to stay quiet so that other people would not hear them. You could hear them several doors down." Rosetta shook her head. "I was cleaning a room just across the hallway. I was very frightened. Worried that they might come out and find me listening to them. They were... very violent people. I could tell. I did not want to be in the middle of things."

"No," Zachary agreed. After being shaken just by Luke's sudden change in mood, he could well imagine how a loud altercation would feel threatening to the small, vulnerable maid cleaning the room across the hallway. "That must have been really disturbing."

"Yes."

"Can you tell me about what you heard?"

She played with her teabag, not looking at him. "I hear... the big man shouting. There is always music playing," she told Zachary. "All the time. We get complaints about it sometimes. But he pays for a week or two, in cash, and I think..." She trailed off and looked at her companion uncertainly. "I think maybe he pays extra for the complaints to go away."

Zachary sighed, thinking about Arthur and the other staff members at the front desk. And there would be other people there on the other shifts. A little bit of extra cash spread around to ensure things went smoothly for Eyler and his business. He made fistfuls of money as long as he was operating. There was plenty for expenses like paying the hotel staff to look the other way and pretend not to know that something illegal was going on in that room.

"You're probably right," he told Rosetta. "He probably did."

She looked reassured by this. Mildred didn't say anything to contradict her or tell her that she should not be talking out of school.

"Because of the music, you cannot usually tell what is going on in there. It is covered up. But the big man..."

"Eyler."

"Mr. Eyler... he is very loud when he is angry. He is easy to hear over the music."

"Could you tell who he was angry at? Who was in the room with him?"

She shook her head. "They were too quiet to hear over the music and Mr. Eyler's shouting. I know there is someone else there... but I cannot hear."

Zachary nodded. "Could you tell what Eyler was yelling about? What had upset him?"

"He was yelling about... 'I take care of you,' and 'You owe me. You do what I say.'" She shrugged, looking down at her tea and fishing the teabag out. She took a small sip but didn't look as if she even tasted it. "So, I thought maybe... a girlfriend or a child." Her eyes swam with tears. "He was very loud, very angry."

# 30

How long did the fight last?"

"I don't know. A long time. I was trying to get the room done and to move to the next one... but I didn't want to be in the hallway if one of them came out. I didn't want them to see my work cart, so I pulled it into the room. And I waited." She dabbed at her eyes, her hand shaking. Reliving the trauma, adrenaline pumping again, fearing for her own safety and whoever was on the receiving end of the abuse.

"It's okay," he assured her. "You're safe here. Whatever happened, no one is going to come after you. No one knows what you heard or that you are talking to me. Eyler is dead and his people have pulled out. They'll want to fly under the radar for a while now, not attract police attention."

She nodded gratefully and used her napkin to soak up the tears that were leaking from her eyes.

"You are very brave to step forward like this. I appreciate you telling the truth, even when you are scared. Someone needs to hear what happened."

It was a few minutes before she seemed to get herself back under control. She swallowed and nodded and patted Zachary's hand. "You are a very nice boy."

Zachary's ears got hot. He rolled his eyes up to the ceiling, trying to control his reaction, but it clearly didn't work; Rosetta and Mildred both laughed at his red ears and face.

"Uh, thank you. Did you see anyone come into or leave the hotel room? Or were you in the other room the whole time?"

"I did not see then. Other times, I saw people come and go. They were very busy."

"Did you ever see a young man go in there?"

"With the big man, yes."

Zachary hesitated. "Which one? There was a younger one, maybe thirteen, and an older one who looked... nineteen or early twenties."

"Oh..." She looked surprised at this. "I only remember the young one. I thought... his son. It must have been his son, I think."

Zachary didn't correct her misperception. Like the clerk at the front desk, she had jumped to the easiest, most comfortable solution. People didn't think of boys being prostitutes, of young boys being trafficked just like girls. So they saw a different relationship. An affectionate arm around the shoulder, a whisper directed in the boy's ear, and they saw Eyler as a father figure rather than a predator. Just as the hotel clerks had preferred to think of the girls as models rather than trafficking victims.

Zachary nodded. He found Luke's picture on his phone again and showed it to her. "Did you ever see this one?"

"In the lobby maybe, or on the elevator... before the shouting. He didn't go into Mr. Eyler's room when I started my cleaning. But I thought he would."

"Why?"

"That is the room people were coming and going to. Other suites on the floor were rented to families. Older couples. They tried not to put too many people on the floor because of the noise and complaints. I see him again... when the police were there. When they found Mr. Eyler dead. The boy was there, and they arrested him. I was peeking around the door..."

"Yeah. That's who was arrested. But I'm trying to figure out what happened. If there is a way to get him off with a lighter sentence. Was Eyler making threats? You were afraid of him. Do you think there was reason for Luke to be afraid of him too, in the room with him?"

Her eyes got wide. "Yes, yes, of course. They were fighting. Mr. Eyler was shouting. I'm sure he was afraid."

"Was there anyone else there? Any of the men that you had seen go into Eyler's room before?"

"I don't know. I don't think so, or they would have been there when the police came. I did not see anyone else come out with the police."

Zachary nodded. "I really appreciate you taking the time to talk to me about this. It's helpful to get some inside information on what actually happened that day. There's nothing of note in the papers and, of course, the police won't tell me anything."

"You're working for the young man?"

"Sort of. But he won't tell me anything either. It makes it pretty difficult to find anything out."

"Well... I'm sorry for him. I hope you can do something to help him. He looks like a nice boy, but that Eyler—he was not."

---

Zachary wrote additional notes in his notebook as he thought through Rosetta's story. He had decided to go for a walk while he worked things through. As well as his tailbone being sore, he was also restless and anxious, his ADHD making him feel like he might explode if he had to sit any longer. He considered taking one of his ADHD pills, but they were extended release and it was too late in the day to take one without it interfering with his sleep. A brisk walk would help. And if he couldn't think of anything else to do while in town, highway driving always soothed his need for constant motion and helped him focus his thoughts.

He stopped every block and so and jot down another note, then walked off briskly again. He was out of shape. His shoes pinched and rubbed uncomfortably and his legs tired long before he expected them to. He needed to get more regular exercise. He could at least think about walking places around town instead of automatically hopping in the car whenever he needed something.

His mind roved back and forth over the case. What Joss had told him. Rosetta's story, the bits he had learned from Richards, and Luke's reactions to his questions. It wasn't a lot to cobble the whole story from. He had an overview of the crime and what had happened that day, but none of the details. None of the events that had led up to Luke's meeting with Eyler in his hotel room that day.

Rosetta had been able to provide some details, and Zachary couldn't shake the feeling that the other staff at the hotel could fill in more. They had seen the comings and goings of Eyler and his guests. Had Luke been there before? Had he gone to the hotel with the specific plan to kill Eyler? Or had it been for something else and things had gone sideways?

Zachary was sure that Luke hadn't intended to work for Eyler. And he hadn't planned on going into business and competing with Eyler. Those were two things he was absolutely certain of.

As much as he could be.

Zachary flipped through his notebook to find the information he needed. He called the hotel and asked for Kurt, the younger man who had been on shift with Arthur and the young woman when Zachary had questioned them. He was put on hold for a moment, then heard the man's cheerful greeting.

"This is Kurt. How can I help you?"

"Kurt, it's Zachary Goldman. The private investigator."

"Oh," Kurt's enthusiasm dulled. "Hi."

"I was wondering if you had remembered anything else about Luke. Where you might have seen him before."

"Yeah. I was planning to call you. But now is not a good time."

"When are you off?"

"Another hour."

"Can I take you out for dinner? Coffee? A drink?"

"Huh. You might not want to do that, if you don't want to tarnish your reputation."

"Oh?" Zachary was taken aback. "I'm not sure what you mean. Is there somewhere we could meet that you could talk freely?"

"I don't know."

"Your place?" Zachary offered, hoping that would make Kurt more comfortable. "Wherever you want."

"No. Maybe… there's a bar where we might happen to run into each other. Do you know the town? It's O'Callaghan's, near the highway."

"I'm sure I can find it. You'll be there in a little over an hour?"

"Yeah. That should work."

"I'll see you there."

# 31

Zachary waited a while, hoping that Kurt would already be at the bar so that Zachary wouldn't attract attention to himself, a stranger in town hanging around waiting for someone. Kurt had sounded pretty jumpy about the two of them getting together. Still, he had picked a public place to meet. Somewhere they might be seen. Whatever he was worried about, it didn't seem to be that one of Eyler's men would show up and teach both of them a lesson.

He walked into the bar and waited for a moment, blinking, for his eyes to adjust to the dimness of the interior. He spotted Kurt at the bar, looking as if he were just there to drink alone. No glance toward the door to see if Zachary had arrived yet. Not obviously waiting for someone else to join him before placing his drink order. Just a young man out for some refreshment after a long day at work. And Zachary imagined their shifts were probably quite long and tedious, dealing with complaints and travel-weary guests all day.

Zachary walked up to the bar and took a stool two down from Kurt. "A Coke," he told the bartender. "And... I don't know... nachos?"

"Loaded?"

"Yeah, sounds good."

Zachary didn't look at Kurt, waiting for him to take the initiative. Kurt sipped his beer, not looking at him. Zachary was willing to wait and let him pick his timing.

The bartender placed a tall glass of Coke in front of Zachary and, a minute later, handed him a large plate piled high with nacho chips, cheese, and toppings. Zachary eyed it dubiously.

"That looks good," Kurt commented.

Zachary slid it toward him. "Help yourself. There's no way I'm going to eat all of this. I was thinking of an appetizer, not a full meal!"

Kurt snagged a few chips and munched on them.

"Zachary Goldman," Zachary introduced himself. "Just passing through town."

"I didn't think I'd seen you here before. Kurt."

Zachary nodded. "Nice to meet you."

After a moment, Kurt slid over to the bar stool next to Zachary and helped himself to some more chips. He made small talk with Zachary for a couple of minutes, his eyes jumping from the bartender to the other patrons, to the door, and back to Zachary's face. He started to relax eventually, his beer glass refilled and half of the chips eaten.

"We have to be careful," he explained to Zachary. "I didn't want people to think that we were dating."

Zachary raised his brows. "Oh?"

Kurt shrugged and nodded. "They know at work that I'm gay. But that doesn't make it okay to talk about it at the hotel. I'd get in real trouble if I started talking about bar hopping and parties and *that kind* of behavior."

Zachary nodded. He'd been in gay bars before, working cases that necessitated it, and he knew that, despite the relaxation of anti-gay legislation, there was still a lot of anti-gay sentiment alive and well in Vermont. And probably all over the country. It was not comfortable being targeted by bigots. More than that, it could be dangerous. Zachary had landed in the hospital the last time, working the Jose Flores missing person case.

"I think we're safe here. For now."

Kurt nodded. He took a couple more nacho chips. "I didn't run into Luke at karaoke."

"Okay. You want to tell me about it?"

"He was out… socializing. Not drinking. He said he didn't want to have to go through detox again. But he wanted to be out and to meet people his age who shared his interests."

"He was lonely."

Kurt agreed. "Isolated. He couldn't just stay home with that old lady all day. He would go stir crazy."

"What did she think about that?"

"She didn't like him going out. Figured he was going to get himself into trouble again. But she couldn't control his life. He has to *have* a life, not just be locked up inside all day."

Kurt broke off, and they were both silent for a few moments, realizing that Luke was now locked up inside all day and likely would be for years to come.

"He was going out to bars and other entertainment spots looking for company."

Kurt nodded. "Nothing wrong with that. It's practically a national pastime. When you're gay or bi, it's a little more complicated. Feeling people out. Trying to make contact with the right people. People who will be interested, not disgusted or violent."

Zachary nodded.

"Last thing you need is some guy waiting for your outside of the bar," Kurt said, "just waiting for you to show your face."

"Yeah. I get it."

Kurt studied him, forehead creasing. "Are you—? I didn't get that vibe from you."

"No. I'm more than happy with my girlfriend. But I was on a case. Trying to get a lead on a guy in a gay bar. And a group of neo-Nazis followed me when they saw me leave. Decided to teach me a lesson."

Kurt's face went white. "Are you kidding me? And you were there by yourself?"

"I was. I didn't think anything would happen to me outside.

Once I left the bar, I thought I was home free. Walk to my car, go on to the next place."

Kurt shook his head back and forth slowly. He swore. "You gotta look out, man. Go with friends. Get a cab or ride share right outside the door. Don't walk away from a place like that alone."

Zachary shrugged. A little late for that advice now. Though he had been warned at the time. "I guess I learned my lesson. Not the one they wanted to teach me, maybe, but I'll be a lot more careful the next time."

"How bad was it?"

"They were interrupted by a good Samaritan. I went to the hospital, but didn't stay over. No broken bones or ruptured kidneys." Zachary said it lightly, though he hadn't been laughing about it at the time.

"Don't joke about it, man. You're lucky. Not everyone survives a stomping like that."

"I know. I was lucky for the passerby who decided to do something about it."

"Really lucky."

They were both quiet for a time, nibbling on the nacho chips and sipping their drinks.

"Luke was good people. Charming. I enjoyed being with him. Hanging out, dancing, whatever. We weren't serious. Just friends. He wasn't looking for a commitment. I got that."

Zachary nodded. "He's always seemed like a good guy to me."

He realized after saying it that it wasn't entirely true. In fact, the first time he had met Luke, he had seen him as a monster. Someone who was taking advantage of a young girl. Holding her hostage and pimping her out. There hadn't been anything he could do at the time but call the police, and Madison refused to leave Luke, so there was nothing the police could do either. But then Luke had reached out. Had sent a message to Zachary under Madison's name, saying he wanted out. And from there...

"Heart of gold," Kurt agreed.

"Did he tell you about his past? His history?"

"No. He didn't talk about it. I knew there had been some bad stuff in his past. Stuff that he didn't open up about, but I was okay with living in the present. Everyone has stuff in the past that they would rather not talk about. Nobody lives a blameless life with nothing to be ashamed of."

"True."

Kurt rotated his glass on the bar, turning it around and around as he contemplated the time he had shared with Luke. "I did know… that there was a lot of stuff he didn't want to talk about. I knew he'd drank and used a lot; that was why he wouldn't touch anything with alcohol in it. And if we were out somewhere and the drugs came out, he would suggest leaving. He didn't want to stay around it, be tempted. I figured that was probably where most of his shame came from. But I also knew… addicts, out on the street, no family to look after them… a lot of them end up turning tricks to get drug money. Especially if they're queer. One vice feeds the other."

"But he didn't tell you about that?"

"No. He kept that door closed, and I was happy to comply. We were having a fun time together. Didn't need to spoil that with a lot of sordid details."

"But then… something happened," Zachary suggested.

"Yeah."

# 32

Somebody recognized him?" Zachary guessed.

Kurt looked surprised. He nodded and took a sip of his beer. He wiped his mouth with the back of his hand. While his voice was cool, it looked as though he were trying to hold back tears. Anger or grief or pain? Zachary couldn't tell.

"Yeah, we were out passing the time, getting some moves on. Actually, there *was* karaoke." Kurt laughed. "I'd actually forgotten that. But we weren't singing. Just cheering on the people who were. Or making fun of them."

"I'm not the type to get up in front of an audience," Zachary confided.

"I need a few drinks under my belt before I will. So we were just listening, enjoying the show, and then this guy is in front of Luke, stepping between him and the stage, getting in his face. Luke was ticked. But this guy keeps banging the drum. Saying he knows him. Calling him Noah. Grabbed Luke by the arm and held him, looking at his hand, saying that he had to come back."

"How did Luke respond?"

"Said the guy was crazy; he didn't know what he was talking about. But the dude kept hanging on to him, tapping the tat on the back of his hand, saying things like he's owned. He's bought and paid for. That he has to go back again."

Zachary nodded, waiting for the rest of the story.

"Luke said it was just a tat he'd picked out of a book. That it didn't mean whatever the dude thought it did."

"Was he convinced?"

"No. No way. Luke pulls away from him, threatening to make a big scene and have the guy arrested if he doesn't keep his hands to himself. The guy lets him go but immediately starts making phone calls. Luke was really freaked out. He said he had to go. Had to disappear before the goon squad showed up. Didn't want to be taken back there. Wherever *there* was." Kurt sighed and shook his head. "Was it with Eyler? Is that who had owned him?"

"No. But he knew Eyler from before. His boss and Eyler knew each other. Did he say anything about Eyler? His name? Did this guy who came up to him know who he had worked for? Was he one of Eyler's men?"

"Whoa, whoa," Kurt held up his hands. "Stop there, man. I don't know. I don't know anything. He didn't tell me who he had worked for or who the other dude worked for or anything like that. I told you; he didn't want to talk about that part of his life, and I didn't want to know. You think I wanted to go over all of that negative stuff and sit around being miserable with him? No, we were there to have a good time. To put everything else behind us and just enjoy being together."

Zachary nodded and tried to slow his brain down. He needed to know those things, but Kurt wasn't going to be able to provide them. He had been happy to be kept in the dark about all of the murkier stuff in Luke's past. Zachary needed to look beyond those logistics and just get the best picture he could of what had happened.

"Okay. What happened? Did he get out before the goon squad showed up?"

"Yeah. He ran. We both ditched the place. Went in different directions, then met up again somewhere else. He said that he'd lost the guy and everything was fine."

"Was he worried about running into him again? That he wasn't safe here anymore?"

"No. He said he'd need to stay away from that bar for a few days, until he was sure that no one would be there looking for him. That's all. He didn't act like he was worried about anything. He never mentioned *Eyler*."

"What did the guy who confronted him look like?"

"Tall, black hair, medium brown skin. Maybe Hispanic, I don't know; I didn't hear an accent. But some of those guys speak better than we do."

He didn't match any of the descriptions that Zachary had been given so far. "Did Luke call him by name?"

"No. I don't think so."

"And did this guy ever show up at the hotel? One of Eyler's guests?"

"Nnno."

Zachary heard his hesitation. "What? You think you know where I could find him?"

"No. It's not that. I did think that I saw him at the hotel once. But I'm not sure it was the same guy. I was drunk that night. I'm not a good witness. I couldn't swear that it was the same guy."

"People don't look the same when they're out in the open under good lights as they do dressed for the nightlife, with dance lights flashing, in the dimness of a bar."

Kurt tipped his glass toward Zachary. "You got it. Exactly. I just couldn't be sure whether it was the same guy, or just a nightmare, or a trick of the light. We didn't talk about him afterward. Pretended like it had never happened."

"And this guy that you saw at the hotel, was *he* associated with Eyler?"

"I'm not sure. He came in from the back. Went up the elevator. He could have been going to see Eyler. Or he could have been going anywhere else in the building."

"Well… your story confirms one thing, and that is that someone recognized Luke. Someone knew that he was here and knew that he belonged to one of the trafficking rings, even though it wasn't Eyler. Eyler might have seen it as an opportunity to acquire a good asset."

Kurt looked like he had something else to say. Zachary looked at him, waiting.

"That wasn't the end of it," Kurt said.

"Oh?"

"I heard that Luke was in a fight in another bar a few nights later. I wasn't there, so I don't know who it was or what happened. But something was going on. Maybe the guy found him again, tried to take him away, and wouldn't be put off this time. Maybe he decided he didn't care if the police got called, that he could force Luke to go with him before the cops would get there."

"You don't know who it was, though."

"No."

"How did you hear about it?"

"Just through the grapevine. People talking about it. Whenever there is something interesting going on, it gets spread far and wide through the clubs. Even faster in the LGBT community. It's a way to protect ourselves, make sure everyone knows what is going on."

"But it doesn't sound like you got a lot of details."

"No. Wish I could tell you more."

"Which club was this at?"

"Oh. Maybe you could find something out there. Maybe someone over there saw."

Zachary nodded impatiently.

"It was the Duck and Dog." Kurt shrugged and rolled his eyes at the name. "It's usually pretty safe there. They got good security. If it had been somewhere else… who knows what would have happened."

Kurt pushed his empty glass toward the bartender, who exchanged it for a full one. He tapped his fingers on the edge of the bar before picking it up to drink it.

"I didn't know," he said. He flicked a glance at Zachary and then away again. "I really didn't. I knew Eyler was up to something shady but, like I said, I thought they were models or something. That he was just operating an unregistered business out of the hotel. Ducking taxes. Something like that. I didn't know he was trafficking those girls. I would have said something."

Zachary nodded and didn't contradict Kurt, but wondered whether it were really the truth. It seemed like it should have been pretty obvious what was going on in that hotel room.

"And with this guy and Luke... I didn't think it was that serious. We kind of laughed about it. Mocked the guy. Said that he was crazy if he thought that one person could belong to another, like a slave. Wasn't there a war fought for that? You know. Just being kind of silly about it. I never thought that... I never thought there was something serious behind it. That someone wanted Luke that badly, that they thought they owned him and had the right to dictate what he could do. I thought it was all just drama. Some loony. And when I saw him at the hotel. I didn't know for sure it was him. It could have just been someone with a resemblance."

That was a lot of excuses for not seeing the evidence of human trafficking right in front of him. But there were a lot of people who didn't think that human trafficking existed in the United States. Or that if it did, it was only illegal aliens, or that it only happened in the big cities. They didn't want to believe it was happening right in front of them.

"I'll follow up with the Duck and Dog. Maybe they can tell me what happened with Luke. What this altercation was that he was involved in."

Kurt nodded. He rubbed at his eyes with the heels of his hands as if he had just woken up. "Thanks. I feel horrible that I missed all of this. I just thought... Luke had done drugs in the past. Maybe this guy had too, and it scrambled his brain. I didn't take any of it seriously."

## 33

Zachary could see that he was going to be quite late getting back to Kenzie in Roxboro. He had tried to pack too much into one day. But he didn't want to go back home without seeing what he could find out at the Duck and Dog and to have to return to Kent just to do that. The bar wouldn't be open in the morning, so he would have to return in the evening another day. He would have to be late getting home to Kenzie two nights instead of just one. Better to get it over with, even if he was tired after the long day.

The bar was open when he got there. Initially, he just sat down with another Coke and watched the early patrons arriving. He knew he should probably have something more to eat, but the nachos with Kurt had killed his appetite and nothing else sounded good.

He nodded to the bartender, who was puttering around behind the bar trying to look busy until the bar filled up.

"I hear you had some excitement here the other day," he commented.

"Excitement?" the bartender raised his brows. "What excitement?"

"Some kind of altercation. Between a young guy I know who lives in town and some... outsider."

The bartender studied Zachary and shook his head. "You don't live around here either. I haven't seen you here before."

"No, I'm from Roxboro. Just here for a visit. But… my pal is in trouble, and I'm just nosing around, trying to get a bit more information about what happened. Because what else am I going to do? Just let him rot away in jail?"

"In jail? If I'm thinking of the same night as you are, no one was arrested. It was over quick, mostly verbal, and the two of them just got bounced." The man shrugged. "Hardly something to write home about."

"Yeah, unless he got into another fight with the same guy later on. Then… things might have escalated."

The bartender looked interested. "I hadn't heard about that. Really? Again that night?"

"No, a few nights later. So now he's sitting in a jail cell." Zachary shook his head. "He's a nice guy. It really wasn't his fault."

The bartender leaned on the counter. "Luke, right? That's the guy?"

"Yeah." Zachary smiled. "You know him?"

"Sure. He's been around here a bit the last few months. You get to know the regulars. He'd never made any trouble before. It surprised me."

"How much did you see?"

"Well, I don't have the best vantage point here. I was busy with my job, so I didn't see how it started. Just a brief scuffle, and then it was all over and they were both tossed out." The bartender's eyes scanned the bar patrons. "Now, if Cathy is around…"

Zachary looked around as well, though, of course, he had no chance of identifying Cathy, whoever she was. There were not a lot of women in the bar. But the evening had just begun. There would be more later as they finished their dinners and trickled in.

"There," the bartender said, pointing across the room at a young woman in what seemed to be a combination of punk and goth. She looked in his direction, maybe sensing that someone was watching her or talking about her. The bartender made a jerk with his chin, inviting her over to join them.

THEY CAME FOR HIM

Cathy made her way over to them and looked Zachary over. She looked at the bartender. "What's up? He's not exactly my type."

Zachary felt his face getting red and hoped it wasn't too obvious in the dim lighting of the bar. The bartender snorted.

"The other night. A week ago, or whatever it was. When Luke and that other guy mixed it up…"

She nodded. "Yeah."

"You were here, right? Did you get it?"

Cathy nodded again and studied a chip in the black nail polish on her thumb. "Sure. Of course."

The bartender spoke to Zachary. "Cathy, here is our aspiring videographer. Always got her phone or camera out, capturing anything interesting that happens while she's here. Has made some good promo cuts for us. She hypes the bar. We endorse her videos. It's a good arrangement."

Zachary looked at Cathy, impressed. "And you got footage of the fight between Luke and the other guy?"

"Yeah. Sure. Most interesting thing that has happened here in a few weeks. Fights always get people's attention." She adjusted a large shoulder bag, pulling it from her side to her front. She dug around in it, muttering. She pulled out a tablet and set it up in a display position on the bar. Zachary watched her tap through a few screens and scroll through a long list of videos. She tapped one, and Zachary bent closer, his eyes focused on the shot of Luke and another man he didn't recognize, facing off against each other. Squaring up to each other, fists clenched, ready.

Luke's face was white and hard. Unbruised. The other man was not Eyler, whose face Zachary knew from the sparse news articles reporting his demise. The man didn't have his build, either. Eyler was frequently referred to as a big man or as fat. The man on the screen was older than Luke, but he had a fighter's build. Narrow hips, broad shoulders, biceps that were well-defined but not bulging. He had a dark goatee, hair buzzed as short as Zachary's, and an expression so hard it looked like his face had been chiseled out of rock.

At first, it was impossible to tell what the two men were saying, with the music and conversations going on throughout the bar. But as people noticed what was going on, they stopped talking, watching to see what would happen.

The older man reached for Luke, grabbing him by the arm and twisting it to look at the tattoo on his hand.

"…think you can set up business here?" he demanded, shouting to be heard. "You're out of your depth, kid! This isn't your territory and you ain't got the cred to run anything."

"This *is* my territory," Luke argued, jerking his arm away and giving the other man a retaliatory push. "Mine, not his. He's been in town what, two weeks? I was here way ahead of him, and he's not setting up on *my* territory."

"You've got no assets. A few washed-out girls you picked up and think you can turn? You got no experience running a business like this. Being able to bring them into the business isn't the same as being able to run it yourself," he sneered.

Luke didn't argue the point. "You tell your boss that this is my territory, and if he doesn't get out, I'll take him out myself!"

Zachary went cold at the words.

On the screen, the drama continued. The older man laughed in Luke's face at the threat, taking a step closer to him. He shoved Luke. Luke swung back with a hard fist, and the two of them engaged for a few blows, falling back away from each other before the bouncers pushed their way through the crowd to put a stop to it. A bouncer grabbed each of them and hustled them toward the door. The men did not fight against the bouncers, who were two or three times Luke's size.

Zachary could hear Luke still shouting at the other man. "You tell him if he doesn't get out of Kent, I am going to kill him!"

Then they were removed from the scene and pushed out the door. Zachary hoped that the bouncers followed them out the door to ensure they didn't kill each other on the sidewalk outside.

But they hadn't killed each other outside. Luke had killed Eyler in his hotel room.

"Well." Zachary stared at the image frozen on the screen when the video was over. "That was certainly better than trying to get bystander accounts."

THEY CAME FOR HIM

Cathy grinned at him. "Good video, right? It's made a lot of views."

Zachary looked at the screen and started to take in a few other details that he hadn't noticed before, too focused on the video itself.

"This is online?"

"Sure."

"It's public?"

She nodded. "That's the best way to get people to see it," she pointed out dryly.

If the police conducted their investigation thoroughly, they would find it. And that would be the final nail in Luke's coffin. A public threat against Eyler. A demonstration that he was prepared for physical violence, if that was what it took.

Zachary had no idea how he was going to spin that.

## 34

Zachary needed to talk to Luke. To really talk to him, with Luke actually involving himself in the conversation and answering Zachary's questions. Zachary's list of questions was growing.

But the jail would not be open to visitors so late in the day. And Zachary might have problems getting back in to see Luke. Luke's angry outburst at the end of their last conversation had resulted in the CO telling Zachary not to return. At that time, he hadn't thought much about it. He hadn't planned to go back so soon and figured that they would forget any trouble by the time he returned.

He sat in the car, thinking. After a few minutes, he tapped Kenzie's name on the phone and waited for her to pick up.

"Late night tonight," Kenzie observed as soon as she picked up. Zachary felt bad for not getting in touch with her sooner, but he had been right in the middle of the investigation. Everything seemed urgent and he didn't feel like he could take the time.

"It is. And I'm trying to decide what to do now. I've made progress today, but I need to talk to Luke again tomorrow. See if I can get some answers now that I know a little bit more about what happened before the murder."

"And you don't want to come all the way back here, just to turn around and go back in the morning."

"I can if you want me to. We could still spend some time together tonight and have breakfast together in the morning."

"But it's a waste of time and gas. And I assume you're not getting paid for this job."

"I wouldn't ask Joss to pay for this. I'm the one who brought Luke to her in the first place. In a way, I started this whole thing."

"Well, not intentionally." Kenzie gave a short laugh. "You certainly didn't do anything wrong by helping Luke to get away from the trafficking ring and finding him a new home with Joss. None of us could know how things would turn out."

"I wish I could... go back and change things."

"What would you change?"

"I don't know." Zachary thought about it. He had done the best that he could. Would taking Luke somewhere else have been any better? Another family or friend who could take him in? A rehabilitation program? He knew that there were organizations that helped sex workers get off the street and start a new life, but he didn't know if they dealt with young men as well as women, or if Luke would have been open to going through a program like that.

Even knowing what would happen down the road, Zachary couldn't see any path other than the one he had taken. He didn't know how things could have worked out any differently. Luke had been trying...

But when he thought about the Luke he had seen on the video Cathy had recorded, he had a chill. Luke saying that it was his territory. Luke threatening to kill Eyler if he didn't get out of town. All along, Zachary had been telling himself that Luke would never get back into the business, and he certainly wouldn't decide to start turning girls out on his own. He knew what Luke had gone through, how much he had wanted to escape that life when he had grown so attached to Madison.

Or at least, he knew what Luke had told him. Maybe none of it was true. Zachary didn't know those things for himself. He only knew what Luke had told him and what he had believed from his interactions with Luke. He had never actually seen any of it.

Had Luke just been stringing him along the whole time? Was he just as warped and twisted as the man he had killed and, rather than protecting himself, had just been trying to take over the territory himself?

"Zachary?"

"Sorry." Zachary tried to focus on Kenzie. "I don't know. The more I find out, the less I think I know Luke and what I'm talking about. I thought I knew what I was doing. I thought I knew what kind of a kid he was. But all of this has made me wonder."

"I was really concerned when he came to the hospital with Joss while you were there. And he was there at the same time as Rhys. I couldn't understand why he would come back here when he knew how dangerous it would be if one of the people he knew in the past was to see him and recognize him there. Why would he take that chance? And I was worried for Rhys, of course. I always worry that Luke could lead him into a relationship that wasn't good for him. That boy has been through enough trauma in his life."

"Yeah." Zachary's heart thumped hard in his chest when he thought about Luke exposing himself and maybe putting Rhys at risk as well. But Luke was in jail now, and he wouldn't be getting out any time soon. Rhys was safe from him. From that one danger, at least. "Did you know... that they were still in contact?"

"I thought Rhys stopped responding to Luke's messages."

"So did I."

"They were still talking?"

"Looks that way. Or there was an intermediary that was passing messages back and forth between them."

Kenzie made a noise of disgust. "I can't believe them! I suppose you just can't believe anything teenagers say. They go through this period where they are so rebellious and secretive, wanting to try everything out for themselves..."

Zachary remembered Joss's complaint that he wouldn't listen to anything she said, but would make up his own mind and disregard her warnings, even when he knew that she was more knowledgeable than he was. Had he ever grown past that "seeking independence" stage? Or was he stuck emotionally and had never matured?

"I remember… lying and hiding a lot of things from my foster families or group home leaders. Not listening if I wanted something and someone told me no." He grimaced. "Incorrigible, just like my mother said."

"Don't go down that path. You know that what your mother did and said was unfair. You never talk like that to a child. And you don't abandon them and say that you don't feel like taking care of them anymore, either. *Don't* judge yourself by what your mother said."

"She's not the only one. There were plenty of others who couldn't manage me. Who wouldn't keep me because I wouldn't behave and do the things they said to. Even with the Petersons, when I would go back to visit Mr. Peterson to get his help in developing my film, they would say—his wife especially—would tell me to call and set something up instead of just showing up on their doorstep." Zachary paused, swallowing. "But I never did. Right up to the time that they separated and Mr. Peterson wasn't there anymore. I just showed up and expected him to be there and able to work with me." Kenzie made a noise, starting to respond to him, but Zachary went on. "And then when I found out he wasn't there and got his new address, then I went over to his new place and showed up on *his* doorstep."

Kenzie laughed. Zachary wasn't sure what was funny about it. It was painful, looking back and seeing how disrespectful he had been. That despite how kind and accommodating Mr. Peterson had always been, Zachary just hadn't seen the need to do what they asked. If he had called ahead, they could tell him no. If he just showed up, they would have to let him in. Mr. Peterson had never turned him away.

"I can just see you doing that," Kenzie said, still chuckling. "But you have changed since then. *Now* you call them ahead to set up visits."

"Usually." There had been a couple of times when Zachary had not called ahead, too emotionally overwrought. And Mr. Peterson and Pat were always accommodating and said he was welcome to drop in any time. "I mean… I'm an adult now, so I have to behave like one. Or I should, anyway. But I still feel like that. Like that little boy or teenager… that… I just want what I want, and I don't think of anyone else's feelings."

"I don't think you do that very often. Sometimes you get overexcited or you know what needs to be done and just do it. But I'm not sure I can think of anyone around here who thinks of other people *more* than you do."

Zachary scratched his head, trying to reconcile the way he saw himself and the way Kenzie saw him. He sighed. "Do you want me to come back tonight? Or should I stay here?"

"You sound done-in. I think you should stay there. Get yourself a hotel room and relax. Have a good sleep tonight. I don't think you need to drive all the way back here and then back out in the morning. I'm going to head to bed before too long anyway. Call me in the morning, and we can video chat for breakfast."

Zachary felt the smile spread across his face. He liked that idea. They could still have their morning routine. He could still talk to Kenzie before work and see her smiling face. "But I thought phones were not allowed at the table," he teased.

"This is an exception. Do it. We'll have virtual breakfast together."

"Okay. I will."

"Good. And call me tonight after you get situated. Just so I know you're settled for the night. If you want, you can tell me about what you found out today. But if you're not up to it, we'll just say goodnight."

"Okay." Zachary nodded. "I will."

## 35

Zachary had to admit to being anxious about going to the jail again in the morning. He kept remembering the rough CO, how he had shoved Luke around and threatened him. He had told Zachary not to come back again. What if he were on duty again? What if he were the one in charge of inmate visits and told Zachary that he was banned from the jail and wasn't allowed to talk to Luke anymore?

But there was no guarantee that the same staff would be on every day or even every weekday. They might take other shifts. They might be rotated regularly. It could be the woman CO who had helped him on Sunday or someone he hadn't met yet. And it wasn't like they had a wall of shame where they displayed the pictures of everyone who wasn't allowed to visit the jail. He doubted if they even had a list on the computer with the names of everyone they wanted banned from visiting.

Or maybe they did.

And if they did, had his name been added to the list? Or was it just an empty threat?

He eventually decided that the CO was probably just blowing hot air. He had a quick temper and a job that allowed him to push people around physically. He probably couldn't be bothered to deal with administrative lists. Chances were he had forgotten all about his sharp remark toward Zachary. Inmates got into arguments with visitors all the time. That was why they had CO's watching the visitor room in the first place and so many rules written on the wall. Luke's meltdown had been minor, probably forgotten by the CO as soon as Luke was back in his cell.

Zachary was getting used to the security check at the jail. Having to be wanded every time, and the CO performing the check asking him whether he had ever broken his arm. Try as he might, he couldn't remember how he had broken it or whether he had known that they had put screws in it. He only vaguely remembered how annoying the cast had been. But then, all casts were annoying, and he'd had enough of them to know that.

His heart fell when he saw that the same CO brought Luke to the visitor room as had brought him the previous day. He pushed Luke down hard into the seat, making him wince. "There'd better be no more nonsense like yesterday," he warned. "You want to end the conversation; you just give a wave. Don't need to act like a spoiled two-year-old." He looked at Zachary and favored him with a glare. "Didn't I tell you yesterday not to come back here?"

Zachary shrugged. "I don't know, did you? There was a lot of yelling going on. I might not have heard you."

The CO gave a short bark of a laugh and, despite his objection, let Zachary stay there and stepped back out of the room after anchoring Luke to the table.

Luke was glassy-eyed. Tired? Or had they drugged him after his outburst of the day before? Some facilities were very free with chemical aids, with a doctor on staff who happily wrote out scripts for whatever the security staff said they needed to keep the population quiet and compliant.

"Hey," Zachary greeted. "How are you doing today?"

Luke shrugged. His head wobbled slightly, but Zachary didn't know whether it was intended as a head shake or was just an involuntary movement.

"I made some good progress yesterday. Trying to find out exactly what happened with you and Eyler on Friday and in the days before."

"You're not a lawyer. Don't need you."

"You want to just rot in prison? I would think you would welcome the help."

Luke shook his head. "I didn't ask for you to be here. Just tell Joss… no. Leave me alone here and just focus on the others. This experiment didn't work." He raised his eyes and looked into Zachary's for a moment. "Did you ever think that it would?"

Zachary tried to read Luke. Was he basically a good kid, like Zachary had thought, who had been victimized and coerced into doing something that was against his nature? Or was he predatory and just making up lies to make Zachary feel sorry for him?

He knew that Luke was charming and a good liar, and still, looking into his face, could not see the guile. He knew what Luke had done, how he had victimized other teens, but he couldn't see the darkness in him.

Was Luke *that* good of a liar?

"How long have you known Eyler?"

"I didn't know him."

"You did. You knew who he was and what he was doing. Why would you kill him otherwise? You went there specifically to confront him."

"Why would I do that?"

"I don't know. I can't figure it out. At the Duck and Dog, you said you wanted Eyler out of your territory."

Luke was definitely surprised by Zachary's knowledge of what had happened at the bar. His eyes widened slightly and his jaw clenched. He shifted his gaze so that it was over Zachary's shoulder at some invisible point beyond him, keeping his face blank. "The Duck and Dog?"

"You got into a fight with one of Eyler's men, and you told him to tell Eyler to get out of your territory or you were going to kill him."

"Then why are you still asking questions?"

"I want to hear your story."

Luke shook his head. "No."

"You talked to me before about your past. When we were trying to get Madison way from Peggy Ann and the rest of them."

"Did I?" Luke's voice was far away and unconcerned.

"Do you remember telling me about Connor?"

Luke's eyes went back to Zachary's face. He licked his lips. "Who?"

"You told me about how Connor was the one who seduced you and brought you into the cartel. How he lured you and turned you out like you did with other kids later."

Luke didn't answer. Zachary looked for any tells. A small nostril flare. Constricting of his pupils. Anything else that would give him more information about how Luke was feeling. He worked his way into the conversation slowly, trying not to cause a blow-up like the day before.

"You remember Connor, don't you?" he asked gently.

Luke's mouth formed the beginning of a denial. Then he closed it, pressing his lips tightly together to keep any words from escaping. Zachary waited.

"You fell in love with him," he prompted.

"Yeah," Luke admitted finally, unable to deny his feelings toward Connor. "He looked after me. Said all the right things. Did all the right things to pull me in. Gave me drugs. Protected me. Of course I fell for it. Just like any of the kids I turned out."

"Because when you take a kid that no one cares about and lavish attention on him, that's the natural reaction."

Luke nodded his agreement. "Works every time, even on someone like Madison, who had two loving parents. But they lived separate lives. She was by herself a lot or hanging with her friends. Lonely people make good targets."

Zachary took a deep breath. "What happened to Connor?"

# 36

The muscles in Luke's jaw jumped. He looked away again, trying to maintain his impassive expression. "Told you. He died years ago."

"How?"

"What does it matter? Everybody dies."

"Was it drugs? Something to do with the trafficking? Cops?"

Luke's gaze shifted to his hands, and he studied them as if evaluating a manicure job.

"Was there a connection?"

Luke looked at him, forehead creased. "Connection between what?"

"Between Eyler and Connor."

He hadn't liked Luke's previous reaction to this question. It stuck in his head, and he wanted to figure out why. What had his brain caught on to that he hadn't recognized consciously?

Luke's eyes looked like they would burn right through Zachary. Zachary had been right; this was a sensitive line of questioning. One that he had to handle very carefully.

"What was the connection?" he asked gently.

"I don't know." Luke's shoulders rose in an annoyed shrug, then stayed high, making him look hunched and protective.

"You're not fooling me. I can see there's something there."

Luke was silent, staring back down at his hands again. Zachary tried not to look at the CO standing on the other side of the door and wonder how much time they had left to visit. He could try to wait Luke out, but he wasn't sure that was the right way to get Luke to talk.

"Why won't you tell me? If you cared about him, don't you want to talk about him? About how much he meant to you and what happened to him?"

"Connor has nothing to do with this case. I told you he died years ago."

"I know. But I think there is still a connection between him and Eyler. What is it?"

Luke shifted and leaned back in his chair, slouching dramatically, trying to make it look as if he were not tense or upset by Zachary's words. "Connor once... belonged to Eyler."

Zachary felt a small thrill at the confirmation. His instinct had been correct. Even though no one had identified a connection between Connor and Eyler, Zachary had just felt like whatever was between Eyler and Luke had not started when Eyler had moved into town and started up the business but had been festering for many years. Way back to Connor. Zachary nodded slowly and thought about Luke's answer, trying to sort it out.

"He once belonged to Eyler? But then what happened?" Zachary didn't exactly know how transactions were managed or hierarchies shifted in the trafficking business. Was it like a pro sports team? Was it a rigid structure and discrete transactions? Or was it a flow, constantly shifting and changing in a liquid state?

"When I met Connor, he was with Peggy Ann."

Zachary nodded. He had seen Peggy Ann, so he had a picture in his mind of the severe, angry-looking woman. Women who rose up in the ranks in the trafficking business were hard. Harder than the men.

"But he told me about how he had originally been with Eyler."

"Did Eyler bring him in? Or did someone else under Eyler bring him in?"

"Don't know. But it wasn't like it was with me. Eyler had Romeos turning new kids. But he also did grabs."

Zachary shuddered. "Is that what it sounds like?"

Luke nodded. "At least with what I did... I could say that it was their own choice. Maybe I lured and seduced them, but deciding to turn tricks was always their own choice. I never forced anyone into it." He closed his eyes, those long, almost feminine eyelashes contrasting with his pale skin. He swallowed and looked back up at Zachary. "But I never grabbed anyone off the street. Eyler, he would go out in a van with a couple of goons, and they would look for someone out walking by herself, on a lonely street. Pull over, grab her —or him—and drive off."

Zachary imagined the terror, dramatized on TV many times over, of being grabbed by strangers, thrown to the floor of a van, bound and gagged, and spirited away. The victim's family would never know what had happened to him.

He licked his lips, shaking his head. "That's awful. Is that what happened to Connor?"

"Yeah." Luke's eyes flitted around the room. "He was on the street, homeless, had been kicked out by his folks. You know." He shrugged with one shoulder as if he didn't care. "Like lots of kids. It happens. But when there are guys like Eyler around..."

"It's not safe. But when you met him, Connor wasn't being held captive anymore. He wasn't being forced to stay."

"There are different ways of forcing people to stay. You don't need chains and shackles." Luke rattled his chains against the anchor. "There are plenty of better ways. Eyler got him hooked. Crack, proba- bly. And Eyler was a real sadist about controlling the supply. Liked to see his assets suffer. They'd be going nuts in withdrawal. Would do anything to get more product. They would do whatever he wanted for the next hit."

Zachary shook his head in sympathy. "Those kids' lives are ruined just because they walked down a street alone."

Luke nodded. "Wasn't the only thing he did, either. Like I said, he was a sadist. The slightest infraction, just looking at him the wrong way or taking too long to answer. Being sick. A bad report from a john. And he'd take it out on them. Beat 'em bad. If they refused a job, he'd torture them. Do whatever it took to make sure they did. Between jonesing for the next hit and bein' messed up... they'd do the job."

That was more how Zachary had pictured the human trafficking industry before he had learned about the psychological conditioning that was used by Romeos like Luke.

"You might think that they would run the first chance they got," Luke said. "As soon as they were free and out of sight of an overseer... but that's not the way it works. If you're living in fear and craving your next hit, you don't run. You stick to what's safe and will get you more product. Doing exactly what you're told. Doing everything you can to show your boss that you're loyal. Do what you're told. Report on others. Ingratiate yourself."

"And that's the kind of life Connor had been living. So when he targeted new kids by giving them love and attention, he saw it as doing them a favor. Saving them from having to go through that kind of torture."

Luke considered this, gazing up at the ceiling. He nodded slowly. "Yeah. I guess. That's probably how he felt."

"How did Connor go from belonging to Eyler to belonging to Peggy Ann? How does that happen? Is it just... like a sale of a product?"

"Sometimes. Different bosses might do swaps or sales. Keep moving kids around to make it harder for the cops to track them. Get rid of someone who isn't a good fit for their business. Or a trouble-maker. With Connor... it was a little different."

Zachary waited for the story. Luke was clearly finding it easier to talk now, with the conversation focused on Connor instead of him. Maybe he'd never been able to tell this to anyone before. Never been allowed to talk about the person who had brought him into the life, to grieve him when he died. It was important for people to be able to talk about loss. Or so Zachary had been told by Dr. B.

"What happened?" he prompted when Luke didn't continue immediately.

Luke tried to scratch his neck, but the chains wouldn't let him move his hands that much. Instead, he stretched and rolled his shoulders, thinking about it before jumping into the story.

"Connor wasn't doing real well with Eyler. Maybe if he'd taken the softer approach, it would have worked. But Connor was always in trouble with him. Resisting, rolling his eyes and dissing Eyler, passed out when he was supposed to be working a job. I don't know what the last straw was. Connor never really said. Maybe he didn't even know. Something happened and Eyler and his thugs beat the life out of Connor. Dumped him somewhere in the alley or a sewer. Left him for dead."

Zachary's eyes widened at this description. Eyler must really have been at the end of his rope with Connor to dispose of him like that. With the cash that each asset brought in, getting rid of a kid was blowing hundreds of thousands of dollars per year.

# 37

"But things obviously didn't work out like Eyler had expected," Zachary said. "Connor survived."

"Yeah. Imagine that was a pretty big shock to him." Luke snorted. "Someone found him still alive and Peggy Ann decided to see if she could save him. Big risk. I don't know why she did it. She would have known that he was a pain in the neck. That Eyler had intentionally dumped Connor. To put any time and effort into saving him and seeing if she could still use him once he recovered… she must have seen something in him that Eyler hadn't."

"Different perspective. Maybe she thought he'd respond better to other methods. That he'd be grateful to her for saving him. She must have figured that he could bring in some money, or she wouldn't have done it."

"Yeah. The bosses, they don't do anything out of compassion or any human feelings. Not that I ever saw. This was all before my time, so I only heard about it. She nursed him back to health. But then she had to deal with her bosses about whether that made him hers or not."

Zachary frowned. "If Eyler left him for dead, and she was the one who put all of the effort into helping him, then why wouldn't she be his new 'owner'?"

Luke shrugged. "If you saw a car pulled over to the side of the road with its flashers on and no one around, and you decided to tow it to your place and fix it up, does that make it yours?"

Zachary tilted his head, acknowledging the point. "Okay, yeah. I guess it wouldn't. But I figured that legal title and... moral title in a criminal organization would probably be a little different."

"Yeah. That's why they had a big discussion about it. Whether Connor was still Eyler's property even though he'd thrown him away, or Peggy Ann's because he would have died if she hadn't picked him up. It's not the kind of thing that happens very often in an organization like this."

Zachary didn't imagine it did.

"So... that's how he went from being Eyler's asset to being Peggy Ann's," Luke said with a shrug.

"He must have been grateful to Peggy Ann for saving his life."

Luke fixed Zachary with a stare. "You think so?"

Zachary had to reconsider, thinking about what kind of a life Peggy Ann had saved him for. Turning tricks for her instead of Eyler. Recruiting other young people. While Peggy Ann might not be as violent as Eyler, she wasn't exactly a mother hen. She had to be just as tough as any of the men in the business. Tougher. It wouldn't have been a picnic. Maybe Connor would have preferred that he had just died.

"He would tell me not to complain," Luke said. "If I got talkative and said how much I hated Peggy Ann or what kind of a boss she was... he'd remind me that it could be a lot worse. She would punish me if I screwed up, but her punishments didn't compare to Eyler's. And she was a lot more careful with the drugs. She didn't give as much as Eyler did or withhold it as long, so we didn't have the big spikes and crashes we would have if we'd been working for him. Still enough to hurt if you didn't get your next fix, enough to convince you to just shut up and do what she told you to. But not curled up on the floor screaming."

It wasn't the first time that Zachary had counted his blessings that he hadn't gotten hooked on drugs coming up through foster care. There had been plenty of opportunities. Plenty of his foster siblings or group home inmates knew where to buy and had stashes hidden in the house. There had been enough offers of something to take the edge off by apparently well-meaning friends. But he had managed to avoid them.

"What happened to Connor? Did he overdose? Or was it something related to his injuries?"

If Connor had died "years ago" as Luke had claimed, then he probably hadn't been with Peggy Ann long. Perhaps Connor had never fully recovered from the beatdown.

Luke shook his head. "Come on, man…"

"You don't want to talk about it. I know. But you'll feel better if you can share it with someone." Zachary hoped that was true, and it didn't just traumatize Luke more to have to relive it. "I think it's important. All of this feeds into what happened when you went to confront Eyler in his hotel room."

Luke raised his eyes to meet Zachary's for a moment. He had said from the start that he had killed Eyler and didn't want any help from Joss or Zachary. He had accepted spending the next few decades in prison. Maybe the rest of his life. There was just the tiniest glimmer of hope in his eyes when he looked at Zachary, and Zachary hoped that what he had said was true and it would be helpful to show mitigation. Maybe Connor's death had nothing to do with Eyler or the confrontation in his hotel room. But surely how Eyler had treated Connor, whom Luke had loved, had something to do with how he had reacted. Maybe there was some mitigation. Something that would make a prosecutor or jury consider a lighter sentence.

"Eyler always resented Connor and anyone associated with him. Guess he was jealous, seeing how profitable Connor was for Peggy Ann after Eyler had discarded him. He resented the bosses deciding that Peggy Ann was his new owner and didn't have to give him back or pay anything for taking him."

Zachary nodded, making a noise of agreement. It made sense. Eyler felt like Peggy Ann had stolen something from him and shown him up. Zachary could understand why he would resent her.

"Because Connor brought me in, Eyler always treated me like trash too. Whenever he or his men saw one of us—Connor or one of his stable—they always harassed us. Goading, threatening, sometimes getting physical. Nothing serious, because then Eyler would get sanctioned. Just little stuff that they could get away with. Trying to make our lives miserable."

"He and Peggy Ann worked closely together?"

Luke shrugged. "Yeah... both worked the same territory. Competed for business. Didn't usually deal with one another, but sometimes. We saw each other, had to deal with both of them operating in the same area."

"That must have been difficult."

"Our lives were difficult, with or without Eyler. Bosses, cops, johns, addiction, being assaulted. Eyler was just one more thing. Just one more... predator to look out for."

His voice had gone flat. If he were anything like Zachary, that note in his voice meant that he had shut down his emotions. They were becoming too much, and he couldn't deal with them. He had talked before about dissociating, separating himself from his experiences. Zachary suspected he was now looking at everything from the outside. His time with the cartel, dealing with Eyler, talking to Zachary; he was no longer part of it, but watching it all from a distance where he didn't have to feel the pain and emotions.

"So... what happened to Connor? What did Eyler do?"

It had to have been Eyler. Luke wouldn't have talked about how Eyler was bullying and harassing them otherwise. It wouldn't have been part of the story. Had the supposedly mild physical abuse become more? Eyler had let his resentment of Connor take over?

Luke stared off into the distance. A thousand-yard stare, like Zachary wasn't even there. Like they weren't confined to the visiting room but were out on the highway, looking far down the road.

"Eyler hired him for a side job. A special assignment."

"Could he do that? Wouldn't he have to get Peggy Ann's permission?"

"Yeah, of course. But he didn't. It was a secret; Connor couldn't tell anyone about it. Eyler offered him a fortune. Thousands; I don't know. We didn't make that kind of money. Just enough to survive, with the rest of it going to our bosses. But he offered Connor some outrageous amount for this special one-time deal. All he had to do was keep it a secret and, of course, Connor would if he wanted the money."

"But you knew about it?"

"He didn't tell Peggy Ann or anyone who might report back to her. But him and me were... I told him not to take it. We both knew what kind of guy Eyler was, and if he was offering money like that, there was risk involved. Big-time risk."

"You mean risk of being found out? By the cops or Peggy Ann?"

"No. Physical risk. Some high rollers, they'll pay a lot to have their special fantasy fulfilled, but that's routine. The boss will make all of the arrangements and take all the money. The asset only gets the usual rates. If the boss is offering more... it's because no one else wants to take the risk with this guy. That it's worth the beating they'll get for refusing the job."

"Why would anyone consider it, then?"

"Because... for Connor, the money meant... the possibility of getting out of the business. Having enough to go somewhere far away and start a new life. Free and clear, with a new identity, somewhere the organization would never be able to find him."

"He wanted to get away from Peggy Ann?"

"From her, and all of it. He'd nearly been killed. And when he recovered, it was to the same life. Just a different personality. It was better, but it was the same."

Zachary nodded slowly. Maybe it was something like going from one foster family to another. Things could get better, but other things could get worse. And some things stayed the same no matter what family he went to. He never felt like he belonged in the families he went to. He would always be the outsider. The new kid. New at the home, new in school, never staying in one place long enough to form a real relationship with anyone. He knew he would never become part of a forever family. That everywhere he laid his head, it was temporary. That wherever he went, there would be predators, but he wouldn't know who they were until they revealed their true colors, and then escape was impossible.

"He took this job, even though it was risky, thinking that he would be able to escape the life."

Luke nodded.

Zachary's stomach was in knots. He knew he needed to continue the questioning, but he knew he would be horrified when he found out what had happened to Connor. He knew it would be heart-breaking and awful and that he wouldn't ever be able to forget it once Luke told him. He couldn't bring himself to prompt Luke to go on with the story. There were a few minutes of silence, and then Luke went on anyway. Maybe, as Zachary had said, he needed to tell the story.

"He didn't know who the john was. I don't think Eyler ever told him. Not before he left that day. Maybe right before they met... but I doubt that Eyler would have risked Connor backing out once he got there."

Luke drew a circle on the table with his finger, going around and around, trying to stay in that far-off place he had gone to and tell his story.

# 38

This john... he was bad news. He had messed up hookers before. Did some real damage. As a boss, it's not worth servicing a dude like that, no matter how much money the payoff is. If you lose an asset, or they're in the hospital for months, it's tens of thousands of dollars."

"But if it's not your asset..."

"Yeah." Luke's face was flat, unflinching. "If it's not your asset, then it's worth the risk."

"He'd put... assets... into the hospital for that long before?" Zachary tried to imagine the kind of damage Luke must be talking about that would sideline someone for that long. Or to be written off as a complete loss.

"People said he'd done more than that. I don't know where all of the stories came from, how many of them were true. But if they were... some of the kids he'd hooked up with... they never came back."

Zachary shuddered, flashing back to Archuro. Zachary had been bound and shot up with drugs, unable to move, while the sadist told him all of the things that he planned to do to Zachary both before and after his death. All of the little rituals that he enjoyed and how long it would take. That the torture would last for days before

Zachary's body finally gave out. And even then, Archuro would not stop.

Luke's eyes had focused on Zachary. Zachary's reaction to the revelation must have surprised him. He had expected an exclamation from Zachary, shock and dismay, not this silence. Zachary gulped. He wished that the jail would have let him bring a water bottle in with him. He felt so parched he could hardly speak. And it was not just a side effect of his meds.

"He was embargoed," Luke advised, continuing with the narrative when he knew that Zachary was still following him. "That means that none of the bosses would supply him. They had all agreed to freeze him out. Force him to go somewhere else for satisfaction."

Zachary nodded silently.

"Connor never came back," Luke said without inflection.

"Did they... ever find his body? Do you know for sure that he's dead? That Connor didn't just take the money and go?"

Luke took a deep breath and let it out. "Yes. They found him. The cops. Eyler must have dumped his body once it was all over. Left him in some farmer's field so he wouldn't be associated with Eyler. Cleaned him up to try to hide his involvement. Cops said it didn't matter. They could still tell that he'd been bound and drugged. Some special cocktail the john cooked up to incapacitate him."

Zachary felt cold. Nauseated. He looked at the door and at the CO standing on the other side, wondering if he should signal him. If he were going to be sick.

"He was cut up," Luke went on. "Like, this guy was a psycho. Something seriously wrong with him." He shook his head. "And there's something seriously wrong with the psycho who feeds him another victim. Eyler knew what he was. Everyone did." Luke swallowed hard. "Eyler intended for Connor to die. I know it."

And Luke had finally avenged Connor's death of years before. Eyler was lucky that the vengeance hadn't been well-planned-out and executed. That he hadn't been made to suffer the way the Connor had. For him, death had come quickly. Much more quickly than he had deserved.

It was a long time before Zachary could force himself to speak.

Luke didn't seem to notice the silence. He just sat there, lost in his memories or trying not to be drowned in them.

"What did Peggy Ann do when she found out?" Zachary finally asked. "There must be... you said that the bosses got together to decide whether she was Connor's owner or not. There must be some kind of consequence for someone who... poaches another's boss's asset and ends up getting him killed."

"Yeah, sure," Luke agreed. "They put restrictions on his business. Sort of... put him on probation. Wouldn't let him advance or grow his base. Kept him back for a few years. That let Peggy Ann get ahead of him. But now... Well, you found out, right? He's expanding. He's taking on new territory, adding to his stable, setting up shop in *my town*. After all he did, he's operating like nothing ever happened. He got his revenge on Connor and on Peggy Ann. And on anyone who was close to Connor. He deserved to be punished. Really. Not just a temporary setback, but really punished."

"Killed?" Zachary questioned.

"Yes. I'd kill him twenty times over if I could. The only thing I regret is that I couldn't torture him like that john tortured Connor."

---

The CO returned to take Luke back to his cell. He looked back and forth at Zachary and Luke, both silent, and raised his eyebrows, but he didn't ask any questions. Probably he was just pleased that Luke hadn't exploded again. Luke waited, his body slack, while the CO unlocked the chain that anchored him to the table and stood and walked like a sleepwalker when the CO ordered him back to his cell. The CO took one last glance at Zachary and walked away without saying anything.

Another CO took him back to the reception area of the jail and gave him his belt, shoes, and key back. Zachary walked back out to his car and sat in it for a few minutes, his whole body shaking, fighting all of the images of Archuro and trying to discount the similarities between the two attacks. Was that how Archuro had started out before moving to kidnapping immigrant men to fulfill his horrible fantasies? Or had he been doing both at the same time? Zachary couldn't imagine that two men had been operating in Vermont simultaneously, doing what Archuro had done. When the cartels had refused to supply him with any more victims, he had gone out hunting on his own.

Eventually, Zachary put his key in the ignition and started the car. Warmth flooded through his body that was more than just the car heater kicking in. The sound of the engine meant freedom. The ability to get away, to go wherever he pleased, away from anyone who wanted to harm him. And it meant that in just a few minutes, he would be speeding down the highway, his brain calming and body relaxing. And then he would be home with Kenzie.

# 39

He hadn't taken into account the fact that he had gone to the jail to see Luke as soon as visiting hours began. While the interview felt like it had lasted forever, it had not, and the day was still young when he hit the Roxboro town limits. Kenzie was still at work and would be for hours. There would be no one waiting for him at home.

That left him feeling rudderless.

He went home to an empty house. He remembered to disarm and reset the burglar alarm, despite his anxiety. He went into the living room and opened his computer to check his email. He looked at the date and the calendar to determine whether he had anything scheduled. If it were Wednesday, he had therapy with Dr. B. And it would be a good day for a therapy session; she could help him break out of the dark abyss he found himself in. But it was not. Zachary cast around for someone else to call.

He thought of Rhys, but he would still be at school. Mr. Peterson was his go-to for someone to talk to and ground himself and was almost always available. Still, Zachary couldn't talk to him about anything to do with Archuro. Archuro was too closely connected with Mr. Peterson and Pat, and Zachary wouldn't take the chance of sending Pat back into that same dark hole as Zachary was struggling to get out of.

There was plenty on his task list and his email inbox was undoubtedly overflowing, since he had been so focused on Luke's case for the last few days. He wasn't even sure when he had checked it last. But Heather had taken it upon herself to monitor his email while he had been in the hospital, and that had worked out so well that he had asked her to keep an eye on it going forward, to make sure that he didn't lose track of things. She was very organized and had become his right hand in Goldman Investigations.

Heather.

Few people in his life could actually understand what he had been through with Archuro. She had been assaulted when she was a teenager and, having no emotional support at that time, had been forced to go on as if nothing had happened and hadn't been able to actually deal with the pain and find the strength to deal with it until just a year ago when she had learned of Archuro's attack on Zachary. It was hearing about his experience that had drawn her to him.

Of course, Joss had probably had to deal with assaults just as bad or worse, but he had a pretty good idea that if he went whining to her, she would just tell him to lock it in the vault and quit being such a baby.

Zachary found his phone in his hand and Heather's name up on the screen before he was even aware that he had decided to call her. He tapped her picture and listened to the ringtone. He hoped that she wouldn't be out shopping or doing some work for her husband. Zachary didn't pay her full-time wages or give her enough work to occupy all of her time; she wasn't waiting at his beck and call.

"Zachy," Heather greeted cheerfully. "Hi. How are you?"

"Feathers." Zachary smiled, comforted already just by hearing her voice and their childhood nicknames.

"What's up? I haven't heard from you for a while, and you sound… like you're somewhere else."

"I just needed…" Zachary's voice cracked. He wasn't sure what he wanted to say to her. He didn't really want to tell her the dreadful tale of what had happened to Connor. He didn't want to burden her with Luke's case and the meager chance that he would ever get out of prison after what he had done. Instead of finding mitigation in what Luke had done, Zachary had instead managed to establish that there were preexisting bad feelings between Luke and Eyler and a clear motive to kill him. Not exactly what Joss had been hoping for. "I just wanted to hear your voice."

"Aw. Rough day?"

Zachary found himself nodding. "Yeah. It kind of has been."

"What can I do? Anything I can help out with?"

"No. Tell me what's going on that I need to do. I haven't even looked at my email."

"I noticed! It's okay, there hasn't been anything really urgent, or I would have called you. There's employment screening stuff for you to look at. I did the basics, but you need to do the deeper background. And there are a few insurance surveillance jobs, if you want to take one of those on today."

"Surveillance. Yeah, that sounds good." Watching to see whether accident victims were walking, running, or lifting grandkids or groceries when they were supposed to be disabled by a car or work-place accident; that was something he could easily spend a few hours on, but it wouldn't take a lot of thought. He could sit in his car, listen to some music on the radio, and just watch someone else's life instead of thinking about his own.

"Okay. I think we've got three. I'll send them to you, and you can see if they are at home."

"Or out playing tennis."

"Right," Heather agreed with a laugh. "Will that help? Are you sure you don't need anything else? I've got time to talk, if you want."

"Um… yeah." Zachary let out his breath slowly and tried to relax his shoulders. "I don't want… you don't need to hear the details, but… just something that's brought it all back up. The assault. Archuro."

She swore, which made Zachary chuckle to himself. Too often, he saw Heather as a timid little housewife, an empty nester who would never say a bad word to anyone. He sometimes forgot the little firecracker she had been when they had both been small or how fierce she had been when finally confronting her own attacker. She was no little church mouse, his Feathers.

"Point me at whoever triggered you and I'll let them have it," Heather threatened.

"It wasn't intentional," Zachary said, "and I was kind of forcing him to talk about something that he didn't want to, so it's my own fault. I didn't expect it to..." He swallowed and cleared his throat. "I didn't think it would be... so similar to what happened to me."

"Are you okay? Do you want me to come there? We could go out on surveillance together; you can show me how it's done."

Zachary was taken aback. "Really?"

"Sure, why not? I don't have anything that *has* to be done for the rest of the day. It won't take me that long to get there. You can have some lunch and relax for a bit. Take a look at those backgrounds if you need something to occupy yourself with, and then we can go out together."

The idea of spending the afternoon with his big sister was very attractive. Instead of just stewing by himself, waiting for Kenzie to get home and rehashing the conversation with Luke over and over again in his head, he could talk with Heather. Show her how to conduct surveillance, find out how she was doing, talk about the mischief they had gotten into together when they were kids and Heather was supposed to be keeping him out of trouble but sometimes instigated it herself. He found her easy to talk to and she would know to avoid the subject of Archuro unless he brought it up himself.

"Zachary?"

"Yeah. That would be really good, actually."

"Okay. I'll hit the road here. See you after lunch."

Zachary said goodbye and she disconnected. He looked at the phone for a moment and thought about checking his email and social networks, but decided against it. Heather had reminded him that he had to eat. He'd had only the bare minimum for breakfast, the food he had to eat to ensure he was not taking his meds on an empty stomach. If he got distracted by his email, he would forget to eat lunch, and Heather would definitely give him a lecture when she arrived. He opened the freezer door to see what microwavable meals he and Kenzie had stocked.

# 40

Heather gave him the first address, and Zachary didn't need the GPS to find it. He was familiar with the Montpelier community and quickly found the quiet street the subject lived on. He pointed out various places that they could park to watch the house, and detailed the positives and negatives of each.

"We might have to use a few of them. Move around a few times so that people don't see the same car sitting there for a couple of hours. This car blends in really well, but if someone goes out shopping and sees us sitting here, and then they get back from shopping and we're still here, they might get suspicious."

Heather nodded. "Yeah. I notice that kind of thing, and it makes me nervous. Not like it used to; I used to be really paranoid about it, because of..." She trailed off.

Because she hadn't known who her attacker had been and had always been afraid that he would return one day to hurt her or one of her children. Now that she knew he was behind bars, her life had changed.

"We'll take a quick look behind the house too. See if there's a car in the garage, anything suspicious in the garbage, what the back exit looks like. There are no stairs in the front, so it's easy to access if he really is injured, but it can be a big tip-off if he has to use stairs to get to his car and there's no lift. According to the medical report lodged with the insurer, he can't get around without a walker or wheelchair."

He drove down the block and navigated to the alley, driving slowly until he identified the same house from the back. There were no stairs, but he hadn't expected there to be. It didn't appear to be built on a hill, so if the front was flat, the back probably was too. But sometimes there were surprises behind.

There was not a garage, but a gravel parking pad. The car parked there matched the description of the one registered to the subject's wife. The subject's car had been damaged badly enough in the accident to be written off and, since the insurance company had not yet paid the claim, he probably had not had enough money in savings to buy something new. Or he wasn't able to leave the house, so they no longer needed a second vehicle. Zachary pointed each observation out to Heather so she would know what sorts of things to look for.

"Do we really need to check the garbage?" Heather asked, looking at the bins.

"We're not going to do a detailed comb-through. Just have a quick look to see if he's bought a home gym lately or something else that would indicate he is able to do more than what he says."

"But how would we know who it was for? His wife could buy a home gym."

"If there is one, we'll have to see whether we can see it through the windows and see who is using it."

"You can do that without being seen?"

"Easiest way is one of these…" Zachary opened the glove box and pulled out a tiny camera. "It's very unobtrusive. Stick it to the window when they are out of the room, and it broadcasts a signal to my phone. I can see what's going on without having to be peering in the window with my camera. I can leave it there for a few days until I'm sure one way or the other, then remove it again when I'm done."

"Have you ever gotten caught?"

"With one of these? No. Caught surveilling a subject…?" He shrugged. "Yeah. It happens."

"What do you do?"

"Bluff. Get to my car and take off. If worse comes to worst and they call the cops, then I have a PI license, can show them that I was there on legitimate business and not just a stalker or a burglar casing the place out."

Of course, that line did not work if he were actually watching someone for personal reasons and was caught out. If the subject was his ex-wife, for instance.

Before getting out of the car, Zachary picked up another small electronic device from the glove box. Heather opened her door and also got out.

"What's that?"

"Tracker." Zachary glanced up and down the back alley, then crouched down and placed it on the inside edge of the car's back bumper. He felt it click on the metal and tried to wiggle the tracker. It wouldn't move. The powerful magnet held it firmly in place. "You want to put it where you can retrieve it again quickly, but it isn't visible to anyone just casually looking at or under the car. Hopefully, the subject doesn't have an oil change scheduled or some other car maintenance, because if they put it up on a lift, it's a lot easier to see."

"If this is his wife's car, why do you need to track it?"

"It appears to be their only car. That means that if he goes out, whether his wife takes him to a doctor's appointment or he goes out to play golf, he'll be in this vehicle. If he's in that much pain, he isn't going to take the bus or walk far. He could take an Uber, but if someone has a car available, they'll use it. We don't know if we might need to come back here to do a detailed garbage search or something else when they are both out. If we can track their usual daily schedule and tell when they are farther away from the house, it's much safer. Today we came in blind, not knowing whether he would be here or not." Zachary looked at the house. It was impossible to tell whether both husband and wife were home or not. "Once we've watched them and seen who is using the car when, it will be much easier."

Heather nodded. She was looking around nervously, not wanting to get caught.

"Don't look like you're not supposed to be here. Act calm and casual, like you live here or are visiting your friend. If you look anxious, people will want to know what you're up to. If you act like you're supposed to be here, you'll be invisible, unless they have other reasons to be suspicious."

Heather took a deep breath and forced herself to stop moving and looking all around. "Okay. Sorry. I'm not used to fieldwork."

"You'll catch on. After you've sat on your butt for six or eight hours, you stop worrying so much about getting caught. You get to the point where you would prefer to get caught…"

Heather laughed. Zachary walked over to the garbage and recycling bins. He opened the garbage bin lid. "I'll check this one, you see if there is anything interesting in the recycling."

The contents of the garbage bin were all in black bags. While Zachary appreciated not having to sift through loose garbage, he much preferred it when they used the clear bags. He pulled each bag out and put them down on the ground, then quickly opened them, shifted the contents around for anything large or suspicious, then popped them back into the bin. Heather rummaged around in the cardboard and plastic containers in the recycling bin.

"I don't see much here. Mostly just grocery packaging."

"Anything medical?"

"No, not that I've seen. But they'd need to put that into the garbage or medical waste, wouldn't they?"

"Not the outside packaging. Anything sports related?"

"No hockey sticks."

Zachary laughed. "Okay." He put the last garbage bag back into the bin. "Nothing obvious at this point. We'll go back out front. There were some good parking spaces there. If they come out, it will probably be through the back door to the car. From where we are parked in front of the house, we can see the back door if it opens because it is on the side of the house. Then we watch the tracker to see where they go and fall in behind them once they're a few blocks away."

"Aye-aye, sir."

## 41

Zachary looked at the time on his phone as he shifted restlessly, trying to find a more comfortable position. They had changed parking locations a few times and had each taken a walk around to stretch their legs and take a look around the neighborhood. But Heather wasn't used to surveillance and, even though he was enjoying their time together, Zachary's tailbone was also signaling that he had been sitting in one place for long enough. He tapped his screen to log his time, then called Kenzie at the medical examiner's office.

"Hey, how are you doing?" Kenzie greeted. "Are you going to be home tonight?"

"Can I have a friend over for supper?"

Kenzie laughed. "Well, I suppose so, if you promise you'll get your homework done."

Zachary chuckled, happy that she didn't seem to be stressed by the suggestion that he bring someone home with him. "I'm with Heather."

"Oh, great! Yes, I'd love to have Heather over for supper. We can talk about you."

"Hey, that wasn't what I was planning!"

"Too bad. Once you put us together, it's out of your control. Are you at her place, then?"

"No, she and I went to Montpelier for some surveillance. Spent the afternoon together."

"You were done with Luke pretty quickly, then?"

Zachary felt his smile disappear as she reminded him of the interview with Luke and what had happened to Connor. "Yeah. And I wanted to get home. I'll… I guess I'll tell you about it later."

"Sure. You okay?"

"I'm fine. We've been keeping ourselves occupied. Do you want me to pick something up on the way home? Then you don't have to make anything or wait for delivery."

"Sure. Get whatever you guys like. You know what I like."

"Okay. See you in a couple hours."

"Take care. See you soon."

He hung up and realized that he hadn't asked her how her day was or whether she would be off in good time. Since she had agreed to dinner but hadn't told him to hold it until later, he had to assume that she would be home in good time to share a meal with them.

"All set?" Heather stretched and rolled her shoulders. "I'm glad you decided it was time. My muscles are getting really cramped."

"You have to build your way up to longer stakeouts. This wasn't too bad, but I can't sit for much longer."

Zachary started the car and pulled away from the curb, giving the house one last look before they left. He was always sure that something would happen right after he left. While surveillance jobs could be hard, he had a difficult time breaking away sometimes, wanting to stay for just five more minutes in case something happened.

They got out to the highway in a few minutes. Heather didn't make any comment about Zachary's driving speed.

"What about Tyrrell?" she asked. "Do you want to invite him over for dinner too? That would be fun."

"Uh… well…"

She looked at him, evaluating his reluctance. "We don't have to if you don't want. It was just a suggestion."

"It's just… I know that when he's around me, it makes him think about when we were kids, and all of the crap that went on… and the problems he has with his kids… and if I end up talking about this case with Luke, and I have flashbacks, then he feels like he has to be the strong one… I just don't want to put all of that on him. I want him to have the chance to recover and get back to a normal life."

Heather nodded. "You don't have to explain, you know. It's okay to just say no. I'll accept that."

Zachary thought about that. He'd lived in too many places where a flat "no" would earn him a punishment. Sometimes just a loss of privileges, but often a physical "reminder" to watch his mouth and his attitude, or even being slapped into isolation at Bonnie Brown or locked in a room or a closet at a group home. He had learned to be pretty careful how he answered, never saying no if he could help it.

"That still… doesn't feel safe," he confessed. "It's not you. I know you would never do anything to hurt me. But…"

"As long as you know I'm fine with it. If it doesn't feel okay, then do what does. But you don't have to be afraid that I'll be upset or won't let you make your own choices. You're allowed."

Zachary nodded. "Thanks."

He stared at the road and the cars ahead of him, letting himself slide into the meditative driving state that soothed his anxiety.

---

Kenzie liked Thai and Heather said that she did too, so Zachary bought several of their favorite dishes at the local Thai restaurant. Zachary wasn't sure what time Kenzie would be home and hoped that the Styrofoam dishes would keep everything warm and fresh until she did. But he supposed they could be microwaved if they got cold.

Heather sat on the couch beside him when he opened his email inbox. He had her emails to him filtered into a special folder because he had found that she was really good at keeping him organized and on top of the email requests that came in from clients. He read through the summaries and notes that she had made for him before starting the rest of the email.

"You need a better way to track your tasks," she told him as she watched him sift through the emails and add a couple of items to his task list. "If you use an app where you can send stuff to it directly from email to your task list, labeled with the client name and the type of task it is, you don't have to keep all of the details in your head or search for them in your inbox."

Zachary rubbed the back of his head. "Yeah… I suppose that would be good."

"You'd be able to see immediately what stuff you had to do on the computer, what calls you had to make, what errands you had to run and surveillance you had to do. And it would all be tied back to the original email so you could just click once to re-read the details."

"Do you have an app that does that?"

"Look." She pulled out her phone and started to show him through her task management app. "And you can set dates and alarms so that you only have to see what to do today, and if you get side-tracked, there are reminders. My son always had to have alarms."

"Yeah. I've been doing that with the calendar. Trying to remember to put all of my appointments into it with alarms so that I have enough time to get places even if I forgot about it. It's good… if I remember to put everything in it."

"It works for tasks too. Why don't I set up an account for you? I can set up the projects and contexts, and I can add tasks and notes to it directly instead of emailing you about them. Because we're duplicating the work if I email you what needs to be done, and then you add it into the app. I'll show you how to send emails to it and label everything, and then you can add tasks directly to it as well."

Zachary shrugged. He was glad that she was offering to set it up and organize it. If the structure were already set up and she just told him what to do, it wouldn't be so overwhelming. He tended to put off big projects that were tedious and required a lot of organizational effort. Then he ended up forgetting things or hurrying to do them at the last minute. "Sure. That sounds good, if you really want to set it all up."

She smiled. "I like organizing things. It's like solving a puzzle."

"You know what else is like solving a puzzle? Being a PI," Zachary deadpanned.

Heather laughed.

Zachary heard the garage door opening. "And there's Kenz. Good. Everything should still be warm."

## 42

Zachary stood up and walked into the kitchen to greet Kenzie and start opening the food containers. Kenzie stopped him when he gave her a kiss, holding his face still for a moment to look into his eyes.

"You're okay?"

He nodded. "For now."

"The talk with Luke didn't go well?"

"I'll tell you about it."

Heather joined them in the kitchen, and they worked together to set the table and spread out the delicious-smelling food so everyone could help themselves. Zachary's stomach growled. He had gone for so many years on medications that suppressed his appetite or made him nauseated that it always surprised him when he felt hungry. He put his hand over his stomach, immediately wondering whether he had remembered to take all of his meds that morning. But it was too late to worry about it now. He might as well just enjoy the meal.

They all sat down.

"So... how was your day today?" Zachary figured he'd better make up for not asking her when they had talked on the phone. "I suppose that when we have company, we're not allowed to talk about dead bodies at the table."

"Only in the most very general terms," Kenzie agreed, giving Heather a wink. "I did have dead bodies today, yes."

"Did you do an autopsy? Or just… test samples and administrative stuff?"

"Did an autopsy this afternoon. But it went quickly, as you can tell, since I'm home in good time. It was pretty routine. A doctor who wanted to know how an experimental protocol had worked."

Zachary took a bite of noodles and chewed them slowly. "I assume since the patient was dead, the experimental protocol was a failure."

"Well, not necessarily. It wasn't the protocol that killed him. And the doctor will have to check our x-rays and measurements against what he did at the last check-up to see any growth or shrinkage. But the patient died of pneumonia, not directly from the disease or treatment."

"And you don't think that the pneumonia was a side effect of the treatment?"

"Not directly. But either the disease or the protocol could have weakened his system and made him more susceptible. Or made it so that he couldn't fight it off."

Zachary nodded. If they had been alone, he would have asked her for more details. They both enjoyed talking about the clues that she found while performing her job, and anything that Zachary might be able to ask her about the forensics in a case he was working on. Kenzie was always careful not to give him any names or identifying facts.

Heather and Kenzie discussed non-medical things for a few minutes, catching up on each other's lives and running through the usual gamut of weather and other routine small talk. Zachary was focused on the food on his plate, not really following their conversation, but he felt Kenzie's gaze when she turned to him. He swallowed the food in his mouth without chewing and it went down in a lump. He chased it with a couple of gulps of water.

"And things didn't go well with Luke today? Or is it something else?"

"It's both, I guess." Zachary took a smaller sip of water, irrigating his suddenly dry mouth. "Things didn't go the way that I had hoped with his case. Instead of finding anything that would help him, the details that I've found out just make it worse. More nails in the coffin. And also... a personal connection." He took a deep breath and tried to decide how to explain it and how much he wanted to say in front of Heather. It wasn't that he minded her hearing anything about his assault so much as his not wanting to say anything that would bring back what she had suffered when she had been attacked as a teenager.

"You think that Luke planned to kill that guy?" Kenzie asked. "Is that what you mean?"

"He went to Eyler's hotel room, knowing that Eyler had caused Connor's death. Connor and Luke were really close. I can't see any reason Luke would go to Eyler's room other than to take revenge. He'd uttered threats in public. Said that if Eyler didn't get out of town, Luke was going to kill him."

"Ouch." Kenzie nodded. "That looks pretty bad for Luke."

"Maybe he just went there to see if Eyler had left," Heather suggested. "Or to... encourage him to go."

Zachary shook his head. "Luke didn't have any way to convince Eyler to go. He could threaten, but he didn't hold anything over him. He didn't have any leverage, and Eyler was bigger and more powerful than he was."

"Then how could he have thought that he could kill him?"

Zachary frowned, thinking about it. He took another bite of the food. It was good, but he could barely taste it, too focused on Luke's case and all the loose threads that the story still presented. "Well, he did, so obviously he could. But I don't know where all of Eyler's men were. He should have had some security around him. I don't know how Luke could have caught Eyler off guard."

"Well, I suppose if Luke is a good enough shot, then he didn't have to get too close," Kenzie offered.

Zachary shook his head, holding up a finger to refute this. "He wasn't shot. He was stabbed."

"Stabbed." Kenzie's lips pressed together. "Well, that is up close and personal, unless he's a knife thrower."

"No. Don't think so. He's a street rat, not a circus performer. The detective didn't give me any details of the injuries. And it's an active investigation, so a request for information wouldn't go anywhere. But it was obvious from the blood spatter that he was stabbed more than once."

"Maybe he's really skilled with a knife and Eyler didn't know it," Heather suggested. "Maybe he didn't know that Luke carried one and didn't think Luke would attack because he was smaller...?" Heather didn't know any of the background of the case, but she had obviously picked up what she needed from the little Zachary had said. Maybe knowing less helped her see clearly, instead of being impeded by all the relevant and irrelevant facts that Zachary knew.

He was thinking, running through pictures in his head. Trying to remember everything he had learned in his brief visit to the crime scene. A crime scene from which all of the evidence had already been removed. No body, no murder weapon, none of the things they thought were relevant or might have trace evidence on them.

"What are you thinking?" Heather asked after a moment.

"That... he wasn't carrying a knife."

"How would you know that?" Kenzie asked. "Is that what he told you? You know that he could be lying about any of the details."

"Oh, I know he's not telling me all of the facts," Zachary assured her. "He won't tell me anything about what happened. Just that he killed Eyler."

"He *didn't* tell you that he wasn't carrying the knife?" Kenzie persisted, not having gotten a clear answer from him.

"No, he didn't."

"Then how could you know?" Heather asked. "The police? Was it in the news?"

"No. It was in the drawer."

He looked up from his plate. Both of the women looked baffled by his statement. Zachary tried to backtrack to give them the information they were missing.

"It was a suite with a kitchen. Just a small one. I took pictures of all of the drawers." He pulled out his phone and navigated to the cloud storage where he had saved the pictures from the kitchen. He flicked through them, looking at the photos of the drawers in particular. "There is a cutting board. But no knife."

They all exchanged looks.

"Well…" Heather considered. "You know how hotel kitchens are. They're never fully stocked. They're always missing something that you need. In my experience. When we vacationed with the kids, we used to like to book hotel rooms with a kitchen so that we could make food there instead of paying for fast food all the time. And they were always missing a pot or pan, or a pancake turner, or oven mitts. The knife might have disappeared weeks or months before and never been replaced."

"Maybe," Zachary admitted. "But if Luke went there unarmed…" His brow furrowed and he shook his head, trying to figure it out.

"What?" Kenzie asked.

"Why would he go see Eyler unarmed? If he intended to kill him, then, of course, he would take a weapon."

"Then he probably did. Heather's right. The kitchen knife has probably been missing for a while."

"Maybe. But it would have made more sense for him to get a gun. A way to kill Eyler from across the room. Not having to get within arm's reach of him."

Zachary had another bite of the Thai food, then pushed his plate away from him an inch. He wasn't going to be able to get any more of it down.

"What *did* Luke tell you?" Kenzie asked. "Or don't you want to talk about it?"

"He told me about Connor."

"Oh, right. You did say that. And Eyler killed Connor?"

"Yeah, indirectly. Supplied him to a john that he knew was dangerous. Who had assaulted and possibly killed other prostitutes."

Heather shuddered. "How horrible."

Zachary was glad that he had decided to stop eating. Talking about Connor brought back the rest of the emotions he had been trying not to deal with and made his stomach tie into a tight knot.

"The thing is… what Luke told me about it…" He looked at

Kenzie, trying to anchor to her and keep his voice steady. "It sounded like Archuro."

Kenzie gazed at him for a moment, unblinking, as she tried to make sense of this. "You think… that the john who killed Connor might have been Archuro?"

Zachary nodded. Kenzie did not ask for all of the details of the similarities between the two cases. She knew better than to ask for the details of what Archuro had done and said. Zachary had never been able to voice them to her or to anyone else. But she had seen his scars and she knew some of what Archuro had done to the other men he had killed. Zachary had been trying to think of how to convince her without explaining the parallels to her, but Kenzie seemed to accept it at face value. He was the one who would know.

"It could be, couldn't it?" he asked Kenzie. "Archuro didn't live that far away. He could easily have… hunted there. There's nothing that says because he picked up his own victims some of the time, he couldn't have hired from a trafficker at others."

Kenzie nodded. "It's not unusual for a serial killer to have hired and possibly killed prostitutes in the past. Sometimes it's people in that community who recognize it and clue the police in."

Like with Jose and the other men who had disappeared from Archuro's hunting area.

Heather touched Zachary's arm. "But he's in prison now. He's not going to hurt anyone else."

Zachary swallowed and nodded. That was, of course, aside from the damage that he'd already done. Zachary would probably suffer from his encounter with Archuro for the rest of his life.

## 43

Zachary already had his phone in his hand from looking at the pictures he had taken at the hotel so, when it vibrated, he looked down at it, even though their usual rule was no phones at the table. A notification that he'd received a message from Rhys flashed across the top of the screen. Zachary looked at his plate and the rest of the food on the table.

"Do you mind if I take this? It's Rhys. I'm kind of... finished with eating, and..."

"And with talking?" Kenzie suggested.

Zachary nodded. He needed some time to himself. Heather had helped him to hold things together until Kenzie got home, and he'd been able to tell them the bare bones of what he had learned from Luke, and now he needed space. Kenzie knew him well.

"Go ahead," Kenzie agreed, waving him away. "Heather and I will catch up on all of the gossip."

He thought they had already done that, but she was giving him an "out," and he would take it. He picked up his plate to scrape it into the garbage and put it in the dishwasher. "You can leave the cleaning up for me. Just... remind me in an hour if I forget."

"Heather and I can manage it. It isn't like there are any pots and pans to scrub."

"Okay... well..." he shrugged, looking at the food and dishes left on the table, "just let me know if you need a hand."

Kenzie nodded and again motioned him away. Zachary retreated to the bedroom, where he could chat with Rhys without being distracted by the conversation between Kenzie and Heather.

He stretched out on the bed and brought up the messaging app to see what Rhys had sent.

A picture of Adele with the word "hello" superimposed on it.

*Hi. How are you doing?* Zachary tapped back.

He hoped that it would just be a conversation about Rhys and what he was doing at home or school. Not about Luke and what was going on with his case.

Of course, that hope was immediately dashed when a picture of Luke appeared on his screen.

*First, how are you?* Zachary insisted.

He waited for the dots to appear on the screen, indicating that Rhys was composing an answer. Was he doing something else while holding the conversation? His homework or talking with Vera? Or was it taking that long for Rhys to identify his feelings and start to formulate a response?

Eventually, a picture of a basset hound appeared on the screen, its droopy mouth and wrinkles making it look sad. Very similar to how Rhys's mouth naturally fell into an unhappy frown. Zachary waited for a minute to see if there were any words to go along with the picture, but apparently, Rhys wasn't able to formulate anything verbal.

*Sorry you're feeling bad. It must be very hard for you.*

Luke's picture appeared on the screen again. Zachary sighed heavily.

*I'm still working on finding a way to help him. He's in a bad situation.*

Then finally, Rhys's first words. *u help him*

*I'm doing my best. Trying to come up with answers. But he is not talking to me.*

There was no immediate response. Zachary closed his eyes and rubbed his forehead and the space between his eyebrows. He hadn't noticed the headache until then. He was tired and frustrated, irritated at not being able to help Luke and angry at him for refusing to help in his own defense. Also stretched thin by his flashbacks to Archuro and the assault.

The phone vibrated. Zachary opened his eyes and looked down at it.

There was a picture of a flower. A daisy, he thought, except it was purple and he didn't know if daisies came in colors other than white. What did that mean? Rhys was sending him a peace offering? He was mourning?

Zachary hit the question mark and sent it, asking for more details.

But the answer back from Rhys was just as cryptic.

*Aster*

Zachary blinked and tried to think of what Rhys was trying to tell him. The word didn't connect up to anything he could think of. He got up and went back to the kitchen to talk to Kenzie. The two women paused in their conversation and looked at him.

Did that mean they had been talking about him?

Probably.

They were his partner and his sister. While they each had their own interests and were friendly with each other, the primary connection between them was Zachary. And he provided them with lots of material to discuss.

He handed the phone to Kenzie. "Can you make sense of that?"

Kenzie looked at it. "Aster?" She looked back at Zachary questioningly.

He shrugged, at a loss.

Heather looked interested. "An aster is a flower," she said. "I learned that living with the Astors all those years. Even though that's not where their name came from."

"Do they look like purple daisies?" Zachary asked.

"Yeah. Or it can be a girl's name. I can't think of anything else off the top of my head." She looked curiously toward the phone. "How is it used?"

"Just by itself. But it *could* be a girl's name." Zachary took the phone back from Kenzie, nodding. "I'll try that."

He returned to the bedroom.

Sitting down on the bed, he tried to figure out what to say to Rhys.

*Is Aster a girl?*

Rhys responded with a picture of a girl floating several inches off the floor. Was that significant, or Rhys's form of *well, duh*?

*I don't know Aster*

It was a few minutes before Rhys responded with a picture. This time, a selfie taken by Luke, with him and a young woman in the frame, their faces close together so that he could capture both of them.

Aster.

Zachary felt a thrill go through him at this new bit of information. Exactly who was Aster and what did she have to do with anything? She was clearly a friend of Luke's. In the background was a blur of lights and moving bodies. A bar or nightclub. While Luke looked old enough to drink legally, even though he was a teenager, the girl looked younger. Maybe sixteen. Her face was a little round. Cherubic. Just enough baby fat to make her look like a mischievous little angel. She smiled into the camera, enjoying her time with Luke.

If they were close, why hadn't Luke mentioned her? Because he wanted to keep his relationships private? He must have known that Zachary didn't want him and Rhys to be friends, or he wouldn't have lied to Zachary, saying that they weren't communicating with each other anymore when they were. Maybe he figured Zachary would try to take Aster away from him too. And he was right. Zachary wouldn't want that angel-faced young woman to be pulled into the trafficking world either.

He tapped another message to Rhys. *Luke didn't mention her. Are they BF/GF?*

Considering Rhys's attraction to Luke, it was probably insensitive to ask him if Luke and Aster were boyfriend and girlfriend. But where else was Zachary going to get that information? Joss hadn't mentioned

Luke having a special girl, so Zachary had to assume she didn't know about Aster.

*friends,* Rhys texted back succinctly.

But would he know? They only communicated by electronic messages, so Luke could get away with not telling Rhys they were intimate partners.

*Where is she? Where does she live?*

He received back an animated gif of a dog that looked like Scooby-Doo shrugging. *I don't know.*

*Do you know how to contact her?*

*No answer*

Aster was not answering Rhys's messages. Did that mean that something had happened to her? Or was she in danger? Hiding? If she was close to Luke, she might be too scared to come forward, to share what information she knew about what had happened.

*Do you know anyone else who might know?*

Rhys sent the picture of Luke and Aster again. Luke knew. That wasn't terribly helpful when Luke was not talking to Zachary. But maybe if Luke thought Aster was in danger, he would. Zachary drummed his fingers, thinking.

*Can we talk? Can I come over?* he eventually typed in.

A bobble-headed dog nodding gave him the affirmative.

## 44

Rhys was apparently watching for Zachary. When he pulled up to the curb, Rhys opened the door of the house and stood waiting for him. Zachary walked up the sidewalk and fist-bumped with him as he entered. Vera was reading in the living room. She looked up long enough to welcome Zachary, but apparently figured it was best for her to just stay out of the way for now and give the two of them room.

Rhys led Zachary into the kitchen. He stuck his head in the fridge and rummaged around while Zachary sat at the table. Rhys pulled leftovers out of the refrigerator and stacked them on the counter. He pointed to Zachary and raised his brows. *You?*

Zachary shook his head. "Kenzie and I had Thai tonight. I'm stuffed."

Rhys nodded and prepared his evening snack. In a few minutes, he sat down at the table with a heaping bowl of food. He shoveled a couple of forkfuls into his mouth before his eyes finally met Zachary's. He moved his hands wide, eyebrows raised. *So…?*

"I want to know about Aster. How you met her. How Luke met her. Anything I should know about her."

Rhys frowned. He pointed to Zachary and then made a zero shape with his hand, looking questioning. *You don't know anything?*

"Nothing."

Rhys thought about it some more, munching away. He started thumbing through pictures or videos on his phone. Eventually, he showed Zachary another picture. Luke was front and center, but someone was standing in the background behind him.

"Was this the first time you saw Aster?" Zachary guessed.

Rhys pointed at him with a pistol-shaped hand. *You got it.*

"But Luke already knew her."

Rhys nodded his agreement.

"Had they met at a club? Or somewhere else?"

Rhys shrugged. He indicated the picture again off-handedly. *First time I knew anything.*

"And Luke didn't tell you where they had met?"

Rhys shook his head.

"Do you have any idea? A guess?"

Rhys flipped past the photo of Luke and Aster and the next couple of pictures and then showed it to Zachary. Clearly a dance floor. Kurt had said that Luke had been going out to meet people and not be so isolated. He needed to be with people, not just at home alone with Joss.

"Dancing? Or drinking?"

Rhys nodded at the first, then shook his head emphatically at the second guess.

"Not drinking? You're sure?"

Rhys shook it again. Kurt had also said that Luke wasn't drinking. Just out to have a good time. To socialize and make new friends. Zachary remembered how difficult it was moving from one place to another as a child. Landing in a place where he didn't know anyone and had to start all over again. It got to be too hard after a while. So that he didn't even want to try. He just kept his head down and tried not to do anything to irritate his guardians, and otherwise to be invisible everywhere he went.

"And Aster? She was just looking for some company too?"

Rhys nodded.

"What do you know about her?"

Rhys scratched his chin, considering. Eventually, he took a deeper dive into the photos on his phone, searching for something he remembered. Zachary had hoped to see snippets of conversations between Rhys and Luke or Aster, but apparently Rhys wasn't going to share that. Maybe he had deleted his conversations with Luke to ensure that his grandmother wouldn't find them and realize Rhys and Luke hadn't ended their friendship after all.

Eventually, Rhys handed the phone over to Zachary.

Zachary studied it, frowning. It was a picture he knew, of Luke—at the time, going by Noah—and Madison. Madison had gone missing and Rhys had been concerned about her. He'd had some inkling of the fact that she was involved in trafficking and that Luke wasn't really just the attentive boyfriend everyone thought him to be. It was before Rhys had been attracted to Luke. Or at least, before he'd let anyone know it.

Zachary tried to bridge the communication gap. He'd asked Rhys to tell him about Aster, and Rhys had shown him a picture of Madison. Aster, then, was like Madison. Zachary's gut tightened at the thought.

"Do you mean that Aster was being trafficked too?"

Rhys nodded and took another bite of his meal.

"By Luke?"

Rhys shook his head adamantly. He crossed his hands in an X and pushed them away from him.

Zachary was relieved at that answer. At least, temporarily. Rhys could be wrong. Luke and Aster might have kept those details from him. Luke was a good liar. And when Zachary had first found Madison, she had not understood what she had gotten herself into. She was doing her boyfriend a favor, and Luke was carefully leading her down the path, with each step getting her more and more comfortable with doing things she had never dreamed she would be doing before she had met him.

"Do you know who she is under? Who her boss is?"

Rhys mimed stabbing himself in the heart and slumping over dead. Zachary found his meaning pretty clear.

"Eyler?"

Rhys nodded and pointed at Zachary.

Zachary swore. "Eyler was Aster's boss? She worked for him?"

Rhys made a motion behind his back. Zachary tried to fathom his meaning.

Rhys held one fist upright, then grabbed his wrist with his other hand and pulled it up as if lifting himself up.

"Helping hand?" Zachary asked. "Rescue! Aster was rescued from Eyler?" Rhys was nodding his agreement. "Aster was working for Eyler, but she was rescued?"

Rhys pointed at him, nodding.

Zachary took out his own phone and looked at the picture that Rhys had sent to him of Luke and Aster together. He studied her face and tried to remember the descriptions of the hotel clerks of the young people who had been in and out of Eyler's suite. Blond girls. One of them with a rounder face, like a fresh-faced farm girl. Had they been describing Aster?

He looked at her, looked at Luke, looked at the background. They had been laughing and enjoying themselves, dancing. What had happened between that moment and Luke entering Eyler's hotel room to kill him? Why hadn't he just stayed with Aster?

After gazing at the picture for a moment, he went to his browser and searched for the Duck and Dog. Rhys leaned in, trying to see what he was doing. Zachary found the website for the bar. A series of video thumbnails ran down the side of the screen, and Zachary looked for the fight between Luke and the other man. It wasn't there, but he could see reasons for the bar not to put that particular one on the website. He clicked on another and, as he had hoped, it took him to the videographer's social media channel. Looking down the list of videos, he was able to find the one of the fight. He turned his phone slightly as he watched it so that Rhys could see it as well.

Rhys watched the action and made several gestures of surprise. Zachary played the video again. He watched it two more times. The flash of movement was difficult to see, but Zachary managed to pause the video and step through a few frames at a time to get a reasonably clear still from the first few seconds of the video. He showed it to Rhys and pointed.

Rhys nodded his agreement. At the very beginning of the recording, Luke was pushing a young lady back and stretching his arms to block the other man, protecting her.

Aster.

*She* was the reason for that fight.

"Where is Aster now?" Zachary demanded.

Rhys spread his hands out, palms up. *I don't know.*

"She could be in danger. You need to tell me. If we're going to get this all straightened out, I need to talk to her."

Rhys shook his head, eyes wide and innocent, shrugging dramatically.

"You've been messaging with her."

Rhys pushed his phone toward Zachary, pointing to it and motioning for him to look at his phone and find any messages. So he had deleted them, or they were in an app that was hidden or protected. Zachary didn't bother to pick it up.

"She's the one who told you that Luke had been arrested."

Rhys hesitated, then gave a slight nod.

"And then what? Have you talked to her since then?"

Rhys shook his head and made the familiar hand gesture. *No.*

"It's pretty hard for me to do anything if everyone keeps lying to me and withholding information from me. I thought you really cared about Luke."

Rhys opened his mouth. "I do!" he blurted.

"But you're not doing anything to help him. Aster may know a lot of the details that we're looking for. She was around, hanging out with Luke, and knew Eyler. *She's* the connection, not Connor."

Rhys mouthed the name "Connor" and shook his head.

"Connor was... someone in the organization that Luke was close to, who was killed by Eyler."

Rhys's brows went up in surprise. So, there was still plenty that Luke had not told Rhys. It made sense for him to withhold anything too personal or too ugly to tell the younger boy about. Luke had, so far, kept Rhys well out of the way of the trafficking business.

Rhys picked his phone back up and thumbed a brief message.

*DON'T KNOW WHERE*

Zachary took a deep breath and let it out slowly. If Rhys didn't know where Aster was, it didn't matter how firm and persuasive Zachary was. Rhys still wouldn't know.

# 45

Heather had gone back home after supper, so it was just Kenzie when Zachary returned from his visit with Rhys.

"Did you find anything out?" Kenzie asked. She had put on her pajamas and was rubbing cream into her heels.

"Not a lot, but a little more progress. There was a girl."

"Aster?" Kenzie asked.

Zachary nodded. "Aster. A girl that Luke was trying to protect who had been trafficked by Eyler."

"Do you think *that's* why he went after Eyler?"

"I guess so, yes. I thought that it was because of Connor, but I couldn't figure out what would have triggered him to kill Eyler now, when Connor was killed years ago and Luke did nothing about it then."

"Maybe he feels more empowered now. Or is afraid to see the same thing happen again. So… he jumps into action and confronts Eyler."

"And that does not end well."

"Or it *does* end well," Kenzie said, tilting her head to the side slightly. "Eyler is eliminated."

"Well… yes," Zachary admitted. "He can't prey on any more girls —or boys. But Aster is still out there somewhere, and there are plenty more people prepared to step in and take over where Eyler left off. And Luke is headed for prison, maybe for the rest of his life. Is anything really any better?"

"No. I know. I just thought… Luke got what he wanted. And it sounds like this Eyler was worse than most. Why would he provide Connor to a john that he knew was dangerous?"

"Because he wanted to get back at Connor."

"What did the poor guy do?"

"He used to be owned by Eyler. But he caused such problems that Eyler beat him and left him for dead. Only Connor had the gall not to die, and one of the other bosses took him in. And then—"

"There's an 'and then'? How many lives did this guy have?"

Zachary nodded. "And then he turned out to be a really valuable asset for Peggy Ann. When she didn't have to pay anything to Eyler for him."

"Then…" Kenzie paused as she tried to sort the narrative out. "How did Eyler arrange for Connor to see this dangerous john?"

"Promised him enough money that he'd be able to break free and start a new life somewhere else, with a new identity. It was a side gig. A secret from Peggy Ann."

Kenzie shook her head. "Then Eyler really did want to get back at her and Connor."

"Yeah."

And that was the kind of man who'd had Aster in his stable. Zachary remembered Luke's description of how harshly Eyler treated his assets and shuddered to think about what Aster would have gone through at his hands. Possibly snatched off the street, drugged, beaten, and turned out.

It wasn't a particularly nice thought to dwell on before going to bed.

---

Despite Zachary's concerns, He didn't sleep too badly. At least, not compared to his worst nights. After waking up, he worked on the deep background checks that Heather had mentioned he needed to do. And was finished two of them by the time Kenzie woke up and rolled out of bed.

She got her first cup of coffee from the kitchen and stood there looking adorable with her sleep-mussed hair and pajamas, rubbing her eyes.

"Are you going back south again? Looking for this Aster?"

Zachary nodded. "Yeah. I don't know if I'll be able to find her, but... I need to try. Knowing what Madison and Luke and Connor went through... I can't just leave it alone, thinking someone else will help her. I have no idea if she's back in their hands or hiding. She could still be in town, or she could be long gone. If she's skipped town... that's probably the best thing for her. As long as she didn't leave a trail for anyone to follow."

"But where would she get the money to leave town?"

Zachary nodded at the question. "Yeah. They're pretty careful about how much spending money they give to these kids. Keep them close to home. And if they think they're going to run, or if they do run and get caught..."

"I hope you can do something to help her. But don't be too hard on yourself if you can't. You can't take care of everyone."

Zachary flashed a look at her and nodded. He knew she was probably thinking about his fixation with Bridget and her babies. It was a battle every day not to think about them and to go by the house to check on them. His need was so deep and primal, he knew it bordered on being pathological.

Forget bordering; he knew it was well into obsessive territory.

It was true that Zachary couldn't help everyone. But if he had let that stop him in the past, there were a lot of cases that would have gone unsolved. It was being obsessive about a case that led to him being able to find the things other investigators had missed and to chase them down to a successful conclusion, even when at times it had put his life in peril.

"Don't do anything dangerous," Kenzie said, her mind apparently running in the same track as his. "Slow down and think before you put yourself into a bad situation."

"I won't do anything dangerous," Zachary agreed.

And he would try not to.

---

When Luke saw Zachary waiting in the visitor room, he stopped and pulled back, turning his head away to indicate to the CO that he didn't want to stay there.

"I got nothing more to say to you, Zachary."

The CO looked from one to the other, brows raised.

"You need to talk to me if I'm going to help Aster," Zachary told him.

Luke stiffened. He looked at Zachary in disbelief. "How did you…? You gotta stop, man! Stop digging and just stay out of it."

"Staying or going?" the CO asked Luke sharply.

Luke hesitated. He wanted, of course, to say no and show Zachary that he was still in charge, even if he was in jail. He wanted to assert that Zachary couldn't know anything or do anything unless Luke decided to speak to him. But if everything he had done had been for Aster, then he couldn't very well abandon her to her fate now.

He let out his breath in an angry huff. "Stay," he announced.

"Get in there, then." The CO shoved him forward. Luke lurched forward and managed to avoid falling despite his leg shackles. He sat down. The CO anchored him into place and left them alone together.

"How are you going to help Aster?" Luke demanded. "What's wrong?"

"I know that you rescued her and were trying to help her. That's why you killed Eyler, wasn't it? To protect her from him? So that what happened to Connor wouldn't happen to her too?"

Luke stared at him, face impassive, and didn't answer one way or the other.

"Aster is missing. If she's been taken by the cartel again, I need to know that. And where they're likely to stash her."

"Missing? She's not at the—" Luke cut himself off. Zachary actually saw him wince in pain from biting his lip. He scowled at Zachary. "How am I supposed to know whether you're telling me the truth or not? She's supposed to be safe. What do you mean, she's missing? Who told you she's missing?"

Zachary could see that not having all of the details made it impossible for Luke to refuse him. Luke had to assume that Zachary knew more than he did about the current situation. Zachary was on the outside, where he had freedom of movement and could talk to who he liked. If Luke could get any information on the inside, the pipeline was probably pretty slow and unreliable.

"How am I supposed to tell whether *you* are telling the truth?" Zachary countered. "I know one thing, and that is that you haven't told me everything I need to know. Especially everything about Aster."

"I haven't told you *anything* about Aster," Luke said grumpily, slouching down in his chair.

"Yeah. Exactly. Why not? If I'm going to help you—" Zachary could see the expression on Luke's face that he was going to protest that he didn't want or need any help, "—or help Aster, then you need to tell me everything. You can't just sit there and say nothing."

"No one asked you to get involved in this case."

"Yes. Joss did."

Luke sat there fuming. "She should have left you out of it. I told her to just let it be. I told her and told her to keep it in the family."

"I *am* family."

"Not that kind of family. The kind of family that chooses each other. Joss never chose you."

Zachary was stung by the comment. On the one hand, he knew that Luke meant they were only thrown together by an accident of genetics. But on the other hand, he felt as though he had been rejected by everyone in his family after the fire. Even though the social worker had never said the other children didn't want to be with him anymore, Zachary couldn't help but wonder if that was were case. She had told him in the beginning that he'd be able to see them after everyone was settled, but then that never happened. Of course the children hadn't had any say in what families they went to. But the fact that they had never been reunited as children gutted him.

No one had wanted him. His entire family had disappeared from his life.

Refusing to be distracted from his goal, Zachary sat there as if Luke's words hadn't hurt him and repeated. "Where would Aster go? Or if the cartel got her again, where would they take her?"

"She didn't have anywhere else safe to go. That's why she was with —" Luke again stopped himself. This time Zachary actually saw a fleck of blood on his lip.

And Zachary knew where she was supposed to be. They had just been talking about it. *Joss.* Zachary's biological family, but Luke's and Aster's chosen family. Luke had told Joss not to get Zachary involved, because Zachary would find out about Aster.

And that could change everything.

# 46

Luke's face was as white as a sheet. He could see that he had given Zachary too much information. He, who had told Joss not to give anything away, was the one who had put his foot in it. He scowled furiously when Zachary waved for the guard to take Luke back to the cellblock, but there was nothing he could do to stop Zachary.

Back in the car, Zachary forced himself to sit and consider the possible outcomes. The pros and cons of going to Joss's house now that he had the rest of the information he needed. Kenzie would have been proud of him for stopping to think before he dove right in.

But in the end, he dove in anyway.

Joss answered the door and scowled at Zachary. "What are you doing here?"

"We need to talk."

She stood there for a moment, more to let him know that she had the upper hand than because she actually didn't want him to enter, Zachary suspected. She sighed deeply, took a quick look behind her, then opened the door wider to let him in. Maybe it hadn't been a power move; maybe it was to ensure that anyone who had been in the living room had time to clear out and hide in one of the bedrooms until he was gone.

Zachary followed her in. He stooped to put the box he held onto the coffee table. "I brought donuts for the girls," he said in a voice raised loudly enough that others in the house would be able to hear it.

Joss's eyes blazed. "I don't know what you're—"

"Did someone say donuts?" A tiny slip of a girl, a blond teen, stood in the doorway to the hall, peering around the wall to scope out the treats.

Joss opened her mouth to rebuke the girl but, before she said anything, the girl flitted into the living room and opened the box. "He brought the good stuff," she called out to the rest of the house. "And look at that, I'm the only one home. I guess I get all of them."

There was movement from the other rooms. The other girls came into the living room, some of them slowly and cautiously, and others boldly, a tall one pushing the others out of her way so that she could reach the donuts first and have her pick. Zachary looked carefully at each of them, looking for Aster's round farm girl face and seeing if any of them might match the description of one of the girls at the hotel.

But Aster was not there.

"Is this everyone?" Zachary asked.

Joss was glowering at him. "Anyone ever tell you you're a pain?"

Zachary chuckled. "I might have heard that a few times."

"You guys shouldn't have come out," Joss told the girls severely. "You're supposed to be keeping a low profile. We don't want people to know that you're here."

"There's keeping a low profile," the small blond said, licking chocolate glaze off her fingers, "and there's missing out on donuts."

The others giggled and nodded in agreement. Most of them were painfully thin—the result of drugs, neglect, and a society that idolized thin as beautiful. The traffickers wanted girls that the johns thought attractive, and fat wasn't on the list of desirable qualities. It gave Zachary hope that Aster had not been with the traffickers for very long, or she would have lost the comfortable roundness of her cheeks. If she hadn't already become conditioned to the rules of the trafficking ring and bonded to her boss, maybe it would be easier to get her out and give her a chance at a normal life.

Zachary turned his attention back to Joss, who was looking down at the box of donuts and eventually bent over to pick one out before sitting down to talk to Zachary.

"So… Aster…" Zachary ventured.

The other girls quieted, the jokes and giggles dying on their lips.

Joss shook her head, frowning. "Who told you about Aster?"

"I keep my sources confidential. I was hoping that I would find her here. She's not with you?"

"She should be. She was supposed to be."

"And Luke thought she was safe here?"

"Did you tell him she wasn't?" Joss's voice rose sharply.

"I asked him where she was. Then I figured out that she was here. Or that Luke thought she was here."

"I can't believe he told you."

"He didn't. At least, he tried not to, but he gave it away."

"My brother, the private investigator."

"I do have some experience in worming information out of people. I'm pretty… persistent."

"That's one word for it," Joss said sourly.

"You're the one who asked me to help."

"To help find a way to get Luke off or get his sentence reduced. Not to interfere in other things."

"I'm doing my best, but how can I do that when I don't have the full story?"

"You do. I told you everything you need to know."

"No, you didn't."

She avoided his eyes, looking at the girls seated and standing around the room.

"Did she go somewhere else?" Zachary asked. "Or did something happen?"

"She wasn't careful enough." Joss looked significantly at the young girls. "They need to follow the rules to stay safe."

"Do you know where she is?"

"I know who she's with," Joss corrected. "Location—no."

Zachary's stomach twisted.

At least Eyler was out of the picture.

But there were still plenty of predators out there who would be happy to add another girl to their offerings. Eyler's territory was open. Who would try next? Who would take it over?

## 47

Zachary wasn't familiar enough with all of the players in the trafficking business. He only knew one of Eyler's close competitors. One who had outstripped him while he had been on probation with the cartel, climbing the ladder and growing her business while Eyler was held back.

"Tell me it's not Peggy Ann."

Joss rolled her eyes and let out a sigh. Another expression of her disgust at Zachary figuring out things he wasn't supposed to know about.

"We have to get her back," Zachary said, his heart giving an extra thump or two as it sped up. He remembered the burn marks on Luke's shoulder, the looks that both he and Madison had shared when they talked about her. Peggy Ann might be more civilized than Eyler, but that wasn't saying much. She would still use drugs and pain to force Aster to do what Peggy Ann expected her to. Maybe Aster would be lucky, and there was a more experienced prostitute like Luke helping her out, showing her the ropes and ensuring that she didn't get into too much trouble. Someone who could make sure she knew what to do to avoid getting hurt.

"We?" Joss repeated. "How are *you* going to get her back? You don't know where she is. If you try to go in there guns blazing, you're going to get killed."

"Maybe there's a way we can negotiate for Aster."

"Do you think that I'm not already doing that?"

Zachary was a bit taken aback by her vehemence. But if she had been fighting to get Aster back the whole time Zachary had been investigating Luke's case, she was undoubtedly tired and frustrated. Of course she would be irritated by Zachary's ignorant suggestion.

"How can I help?"

"There isn't anything you can do to help. You don't know anything about this business or about Peggy Ann."

"I know a little," Zachary protested. "It might not be much, but I've been figuring it out. I know about Eyler and Peggy Ann. And Connor, Luke, and Aster. I know about Luke running into one of Eyler's men at the club and defending Aster."

Jocelyn stared at him. She frowned. "Who is Connor?"

"Connor was one of Eyler's assets, but then he ended up with Peggy Ann, and Eyler wasn't happy with that. Got his revenge by setting Connor up with a john known to be dangerous." Zachary raised his brows at Joss. "You haven't heard the story before? About how Eyler got sanctioned by the cartel? He wasn't allowed to advance...?"

Joss frowned and shook her head. "I heard that, of course. But... Peggy Ann didn't have anything to do with that."

"No," Zachary agreed. "She didn't know about it. Connor took a job on the quiet. She didn't know what was happening until it was too late."

"You're sure? Connor was Peggy Ann's asset?"

Zachary nodded. "According to Luke. I don't have independent confirmation, but that's what he says happened, and he was around at that time and very close to Connor."

"I heard about it... I was still in the business, then. But I was pretty messed up, and I don't remember much other than that a boy was killed and Eyler was punished for it because the john was supposed to be embargoed."

"Well, that's the story that Luke tells. Eyler tried to kill Connor once before. Left him for dead. But Peggy Ann nursed him back to health and he was working for her. That pissed Eyler off because Peggy Ann was using his asset without having had to pay him anything, and I guess Connor turned out to be pretty good at recruiting other kids, like Luke."

"He was Luke's Romeo?"

Zachary nodded.

"Then he would know." Joss sat there, frowning, a deep crease between her eyebrows.

"I think I smell something burning," one of the girls teased. "Smoke's coming out her ears, those gears are turning so fast."

Another girl slapped her arm. "Leave her alone!"

"I'm just teasing!"

Joss turned her head to glare at the two girls, and they were immediately silenced. She looked back at Zachary again. "Was Connor's murder ever solved?"

"No. But the organization knew who it was. They knew the john and they knew it was Eyler who had set it up."

Joss nodded. "But the police? They didn't know? Eyler didn't go to prison for it."

"No, he tidied things up so the police didn't know where Connor had come from."

"If someone were to tell the cops that Connor belonged to Peggy Ann…"

"Oh." Zachary understood in a flash. "Then they would go after her for the identity of the john—"

"And after her as an accessory. Because if she owned him, then she must have set up the meet."

"But she didn't know anything about it. It was Eyler."

She shrugged. "So? He's not around to confirm Peggy Ann's story. Not that he would anyway. Nobody has any proof. It was years ago. As far as the cops are concerned, whoever set up that date is partially to blame for the outcome. Prosecuting the pimp who set it up would be a warning to anyone else in a similar situation. 'You put together a match and something happens, and we'll come after you.'"

Zachary nodded slowly. "You think you can get to Aster if you get the police to arrest Peggy Ann? It's kind of a long shot."

"Yeah, it would be," Joss agreed dryly. "Especially since it would probably be months before they were ready to make an arrest. They're not going to do anything on my say-so. They have to get evidence to back it up first. By that time, getting Aster away would be a lot harder. No. I'm just thinking… maybe Peggy Ann doesn't want to hang on to the girl if there's that much risk." Recognizing that Zachary hadn't yet caught up, she filled in. "If there's a risk that *someone* could tell the cops that she was involved in Connor's death."

"You're going to blackmail her?"

The girls were whispering back and forth, not loud enough for Zachary to make out what they were saying. But they were obviously surprised or concerned that she would consider it.

"I think I could make it part of the negotiation process. Up until now, I haven't had much leverage. But with something as explosive as this, I might be able to push a little harder."

"You need to be careful," Zachary warned, worried at this suggestion.

"Look who's talking!"

Zachary laughed weakly. "Well, I didn't say you should do what I would. I would try to be careful. It's just that sometimes…"

"You go off like a bull in a China shop?"

"I try," he protested. "I stopped to think about it before I came to see you today."

"And you figured I wouldn't answer the door with a Glock in my hand? Shoot first and ask questions later?"

"Well, I was right, wasn't I?"

Joss pushed her long shirt aside to show the butt of a gun protruding from a holster on her hip. "Were you? You're lucky I'm not as impulsive as you are, or you could be in a world of pain."

Zachary cleared his throat. Sweat broke out on his forehead. "Do you really think you should be carrying that around?"

"With these girls to protect," Joss indicated the teens, "do you really think I shouldn't?"

It was difficult to argue the point. Zachary wiped his forehead and smiled weakly at the girls. "You haven't had to use that, have you?"

"Do you think I would tell you if I had?"

Another good point.

Joss waited for him to voice any further stupid questions or objections, but Zachary was finished and stayed quiet.

# 48

Joss excused herself to make a call or reach out using some other method to contact Peggy Ann. Zachary was left sitting with the girls, who giggled and stared at him and whispered to each other. Zachary could feel his face getting red. He hadn't been in such an awkward situation with a bunch of girls since he had been a teenager himself.

"Are you really Madam's brother?" one of them asked him. She laughed and looked away again, blushing herself.

"Madam?" Zachary repeated. Remembering how Luke had been arguing with Eyler's man about territory, his gut twisted. The cop he had talked to at the police station the first day had said that Joss was rescuing girls and kicking the traffickers out of her neighborhood, but what if she were setting up shop herself? What if her "rescuing" was just taking girls away from their bosses and using them for herself?

"It's a joke," the girl said, shaking her head. "It's funny because she's *not*. She's just helping us out. She doesn't want us to be in the game. She's not in it herself."

"Not anymore," another agreed.

"But you know that she used to be like you," Zachary said.

"A loooong time ago," the first girl giggled.

Zachary opened his mouth to point out that Joss had still been in the game until quite recently, then closed it again. Joss didn't need him telling stories on her. And maybe they just meant she hadn't been young and beautiful for a long time.

"Well... I am Joss's brother, yes. But until recently, we hadn't seen each other for a long time. We didn't actually grow up together. Not after I was ten, anyway."

"She acts like she doesn't like you," one of them told him. "But when you're not here, that's not how she talks about you."

Zachary raised his brows. *Was that so?*

He knew Joss wasn't quite as tough and cold as she pretended to be. But it was hard to catch the flashes of affection, and they were gone so fast that he was left wondering whether he had imagined them.

It was a while before Joss returned to the living room. The girls had gone their different directions, but a couple were still in the living room, chatting and reading books.

Joss's cheeks were flushed and her eyes bright. She looked surprised to find Zachary still there.

"You're going to have to go. I can't leave you here with the girls."

"Where are you going?"

"To see if I can get Aster back."

"I'll come with you."

Joss shook her head. "No, you won't. Why don't you go home? I'll let you know if I need anything."

"You need me. I'll help you with Aster, and then we'll get this thing with Luke straightened out."

"What makes you think Aster has anything to do with Luke?" Joss shook her head. "It's nice of you to care, but stick to one thing at a time."

Zachary laughed. "You don't tell someone with ADHD to stick to one thing at a time. It's impossible."

"Well, maybe, but I don't need you to do anything else. Just trying to help Luke. And if that's not possible..." She trailed off and shrugged. Not the shrug of someone who didn't care, but of someone who was carrying a heavy burden.

"If I'm going to help Luke, then I need to talk to Aster."

Joss stopped in her preparations to leave and looked at him. "Why?"

"Because I think she knows about it. She was there when Luke got into a fight with one of Eyler's men. I want to hear what she has to say about it."

Joss gave her head a quick shake. "Then you can talk to her when she gets back. If I can get her."

"I'll help," Zachary repeated.

"I don't need you."

"No, but it looks better if it's both of us together."

Joss appeared to consider that for a moment. "I don't think so," she decided.

"You're going to go see Peggy Ann all by yourself? And you get after me for doing stupid things? It's not smart to go there by yourself. *She* won't be by herself. When I saw her when we were rescuing Luke, she wasn't by herself. She had a guy with her. Some... troubleshooter, Luke said."

"You're going to come along to be my troubleshooter?" She gave a short laugh. "Can you even shoot?"

"I won't be shooting. You're the one with the gun. But I think... it just looks better if you have *people*. One person by yourself, she might decide to do something on impulse. If there are at least two of us, she has to think it through. She doesn't know me. She won't know if I'm carrying or what my skills are. Who I know or whose protection I might be under. There's a lot to think about if you don't know a person."

"You're hoping she doesn't just blow both of us away and ask questions later."

Zachary took a deep breath and blew it out. "Yes. And I'm trusting that you've already laid the groundwork to make her think twice about that."

Joss nodded, conceding the point. Zachary figured that if Eyler and the previous trafficker hadn't eliminated Joss, she had enough dirt to worry them.

"Fine," Joss said finally. "But you do what I say and no arguing. This is not exactly... the safest mission."

Joss gave the girls various instructions on what they needed to do and on avoiding detection and other security issues. Zachary guessed from the rolling eyes that it was all ground Joss had covered more than once before. But he had to hand it to her—the girls were safe and comfortable. Joss had told Zachary before that there was nothing he could do to get kids away from the trafficking rings permanently. But there she was, with five of them. And up until recently, Aster and Luke too.

He followed Joss out to her car, a black SUV with dark windows that would make it easier to transport people without their being seen. Zachary climbed into the passenger's seat without comment and let Joss get on her way. Too much talking right away, and she'd pull over and make him walk back to his car. He was sure of it. He waited until they were well on their way on the highway before speaking.

"So, where are we meeting her?"

"You'll see."

"You think she'll deal? Let you have Aster?"

"Maybe. She wasn't happy talking to me on the phone, but she's agreed to meet. That's more than I expected."

"You think it's a trap?"

"If she could guarantee that nothing I know will get out after I'm dead, yes. But she doesn't know what arrangements I've made to disseminate information about her and the rest of the organization if something happens to me."

"And you *have* made arrangements, right?"

She looked at him for an instant, then turned her attention back to the road. "Of course."

Zachary couldn't tell from the flat tone of her voice whether she really did have all of those safety measures in place or whether it was just a bluff.

If Zachary couldn't tell, then how could Peggy Ann? She had to assume that there was a chance Jocelyn was telling the truth. She had to protect herself and her organization.

Zachary watched the road. It helped him to relax, despite the fact that they were going to face a dangerous woman who was part of an organized crime syndicate that would just as soon see him and

Jocelyn both dead. He had faced criminals before. But not usually this way. Not intentionally confronting them with the truth and trying to coerce something out of them. He really did *try* to stay out of trouble, even if it did seem to always find him.

"Can *you* shoot?" he asked Joss.

"Would I carry a gun if I couldn't?"

"A lot of people carry guns who can't."

"Well, I'm not one of them. If you're going to carry, you should know how to use it. And not just a couple of test fires at a tree stump or on a gun range. You should practice regularly and not be afraid to use it."

He wasn't sure whether he was reassured or not. It was good, of course, that she knew what she was doing and was comfortable using a weapon. But he really didn't like the part about not being afraid to use it. He was hoping that she wouldn't use it today.

# 49

T he area that they drove to was not a neighborhood that Zachary had hung out in or done any jobs in before. The houses were huge, some of them with full-sized tennis courts or swimming pools, which were not at all common for Vermont. Zachary stared at the towering mansions.

"You're meeting her at her house?"

"One of them."

"I can't believe… she lives somewhere like this."

Zachary had only caught one glimpse of Peggy Ann before. She hadn't exactly been a society lady. She'd been dressed fashionably in a red leather jacket, but not made up to look glamorous. A sour-faced, hardened woman who had a job to do.

"Where did you think she would live?" Jocelyn demanded. "You think she's going to be in some run-down rat hole? She may put her girls up in places like that, dirty little places that could be condemned at any minute. But the kind of money that she makes on the backs of these kids is not just a few extra dollars. This is… an empire."

Zachary swallowed and nodded. He'd read the stats about human trafficking, so he shouldn't have been surprised. He knew that it was a billion-dollar business. Of course mid-to-high-level bosses would make enough for a fancy house. Or several fancy houses. They wouldn't choose to live in the drug and rat-infested dens they kept their employees in.

Joss checked the numbers on the gates with the one on her phone and eventually pulled to a stop in front of one of them. She checked the number one more time, then inched close to the speaker with a red call button. She pushed the button firmly and kept it held in for a few seconds longer than Zachary would have dared. She was not trying to be polite and inconspicuous. She was there for a reason and believed that she held the upper hand.

"Who is it?" a male voice inquired.

"Joss."

They had undoubtedly been told to expect her, so the pause while the security guard pretended to check a long list of authorized guests was just for show.

"One moment, please."

He clicked off. Several minutes passed without any further response.

Joss rolled her eyes and put the car into "park." She picked up her phone and started to thumb through content and read.

"Yes, you may enter," the speaker finally announced.

Joss didn't move or acknowledge the guard.

"Hello? Are you still there?" There was a murmur as the guard talked to someone else in the room. "Hello? Miss… Goldman?"

Joss continued to play with her phone.

There were a few more squawks from the speaker. Looking around, Zachary spotted several surveillance cameras. They could see Joss and the fact that she was ignoring them. Eventually, Joss put her phone away and pressed the button on the speaker again. Probably making the guards jump if they were close to the speaker on their end and expecting her to speak rather than to ring the bell.

"Yeah, it's Joss. Is she ready yet?"

"Come in," the voice responded. The gate clanged and started to move.

Zachary smiled to himself. Power play met with power play. Joss knew how to give as good as she got. They drove along the winding drive. The leaves were just coming out on the trees. It was still cold at night, but the trees knew it was spring. They reached the house, and Joss drove part way around the parking area so that the van was not neatly pulled into one of the stalls, but in the middle of the lane, pointing outward. Good for a quick exit. Though Zachary suspected that if there was trouble, they wouldn't make it all the way to the van.

Joss got out of the van. Zachary stepped down and walked along beside her.

"You keep your mouth shut," Jocelyn warned. "Let me handle this. You're just here for appearances."

"Yes, ma'am."

She glared at him.

The door was opened for them before they had to knock or ring, by a man who was not dressed like a butler on TV, but more like a hood, in jeans and a jacket. He looked the two of them over.

"Miss Goldman," he said curtly, with a nod. "And who is this? He shouldn't be here. You shouldn't have brought anyone."

Joss shrugged, looking bored. "Look. I have an appointment. Is Peggy Ann ready or not? I'm not going to deal with a bunch of delays and nonsense. Ready or not?"

He nodded, his head at a bit of an angle as if he were considering something else or didn't really want to say that Peggy was ready. "We'll need to search you."

"You will not," Joss snapped. "Where is she? Upstairs?" She motioned to the grand staircase on their right.

"We can't let you walk in there with a concealed weapon. We need to protect the boss—"

"I'm sure she has a gun of her own. She certainly doesn't need you stepping in to protect her from a washed-up hooker. She's not helpless."

"Well, no!" the guard agreed, his neck turning red. "Of course not."

Joss pulled back her shirt, tucking it behind the gun on her hip. "There's mine. She'll have hers. But she knows that if she kills me, she loses. All of the information I've collected over the last few decades gets spread all over the state. Even farther than that. And if I shoot her, how am I supposed to get what *I* want?"

"It's our standard protocol. It's routine. We *have* to do it."

"That's bull. Peggy Ann knows I'm not going to meet her unarmed. So quit the nonsense. No more stalling."

The man looked at her for a moment, then shrugged. He apparently knew that Joss might not cooperate and had a standard protocol for *that* too.

"In her office. At the top of the stairs and to the right."

Joss headed for the large staircase without any expression of thanks. Zachary moved briskly to keep up with her. It wouldn't do to have him trailing behind her like a lost puppy. He needed to look like he was supposed to be there and was strong and prepared to deal with whatever nonsense they might like to throw at him. The staircase was curved so that the stairs were wedge-shaped rather than rectangular. The stairs were deeper than standard household stairs. While they were probably easier to walk up and down in a ballgown, they were the wrong distance apart for Zachary's stride, and he had difficulty figuring out how to take them comfortably. He was fine with walking and going up and down regular stairs, but the physiotherapy he had done after injuring his spine had not covered stairs that were the wrong distance apart. He lagged behind Joss by a stair or two all the way up, and she was waiting for him and glaring when they got to the top. Zachary didn't bother trying to explain the reason for his awkwardness.

They entered the hall together. Jocelyn put her hand on the doorknob of the first door to her right and looked back at Zachary to make sure he was ready.

His heart was pounding hard, but he was ready. They were just there to talk, after all. And whether they succeeded in getting what they wanted or not, they would walk away in a few minutes, safe and sound.

# 50

Joss pushed the door open without any apparent hesitation. Zachary admired her. She was tough as nails, that was for sure. She was not cowed by anything. She stepped into the room ahead of him, but he was close behind, and then moved up beside her so as not to be relegated to a subordinate position.

Peggy Ann's desk was large and ornate. Very dark, maybe black walnut, with fancy carved edges. The kind of thing Zachary might expect to see in the White House or a museum. It looked heavy and very old, but was polished to a high sheen.

Peggy Ann sat behind it. She was a petite woman with dark hair and a hard, angry face. She pretended to be engrossed in her work and unaware of their arrival. Or at least, unconcerned by it. There was a man standing a few feet away from her. A goon with a thick neck, his arms folded across his chest, looking like the bouncer at a biker bar. There were only the two of them. So their numbers were matched, even though it was clear that there was no way Zachary would ever be able to fight someone that big and well-muscled. At least Joss wasn't outnumbered. It looked better.

Joss marched up to the desk, not waiting to be acknowledged. Zachary stayed with her. He could have stood back like the goon and tried to fade into the background, but he wanted to be right there with Joss, presenting a united front. So that to Peggy Ann, it would *feel* like two-to-one, even if it wasn't.

"I'm here to talk," Joss declared. "Don't try to put me off with the fake work you're trying to finish."

Peggy Ann looked up, her pen still hovering over the paperwork. "Who is this?" she demanded. "You were supposed to come alone."

"We didn't discuss that. I brought my acquaintance with me. I'm sure you don't mind. You're surrounded by your men." Joss looked around, sneering at their surroundings. "Like you're afraid of getting assassinated or something."

"I'm not afraid," Peggy Ann corrected coldly. "I merely take precautions. Like you, wearing that gun like a talisman."

"Your guy downstairs wanted to see it. It's not like you thought I was going to come here unarmed."

"This is tiresome," Peggy Ann said, pushing her papers to the side. "Are we done with the posturing?"

"I'm not here to show off. I'm here to get Aster."

"Aster," Peggy sneered. "What kind of a name is that?"

"It's a flower," Zachary offered.

Joss turned and gave him a poisonous look. She had told him to keep his mouth shut, and here he was already jumping into the middle of her negotiations without being asked.

Peggy Ann gave a harsh laugh. "Can't keep this one under control, Joss? I thought I remembered you being better at getting men to do what you wanted."

Joss stared at Peggy Ann, not taking the bait. Zachary didn't know whether Peggy Ann actually knew anything about Joss's past. He was pretty sure that Joss hadn't been in Peggy Ann's stable or in any way associated with her. But it was a small world. She imagined that the different players heard about what workers were good and which were troublemakers, about who belonged to whom and what their special talents might be. And Joss had been in the business for a long time. Long after the blush of youth had faded.

"Aster," Joss repeated icily.

"I don't know what makes you think that I have her or would give her back to you. If you can't keep track of your own girls..."

"You know she is mine."

"I know she was Eyler's," Peggy Ann countered. "I'm not sure how that would make her yours."

"Eyler is dead. She left him before he died and came to me. I told Eyler and everyone else to stay out of Kent."

"It's not yours, dear. Living somewhere doesn't make it your territory. You have to *earn* territory."

"I have. I took it from Maxwell and I won't let anyone else operate there. It's the desert; you're not going to get anything out of it. Ever."

"Because the almighty Joss says it is so?"

"Yeah. I know you. And I know the organization. If people infringe on my territory, I will use what I know to get rid of them."

"Snitch to the cops, you mean."

"Whatever it takes. A few well-placed words here and there can ruin a business. You get a reputation for mismanagement and unhappy clients, raids on your cathouses, girls who won't stay or who refuse clients… it's not long before your name is mud in a small, close-knit community."

"I'm not worried about you," the small woman said, straightening her papers and putting down her pen. "You and your rescued girls and little house in the suburbs. You think you could take down someone like me?"

"Aster."

"You ridiculous woman! Aster is mine now, and I will use her to control you. If you cause problems, she is going to suffer for it."

Zachary's stomach twisted at the thought. That pretty young girl, being used as a pawn by Peggy Ann. Being tortured if Joss didn't do what she was told. And of course, Joss wouldn't do what she was told any more than Zachary would.

Joss didn't blanch or turn a hair at Peggy Ann's threat. She looked utterly unaffected. "I know about Connor."

Peggy Ann raised an eyebrow and looked at Joss as if she didn't know what she was talking about. "Connor?" She feigned ignorance. "Who is Connor?"

"You know who Connor is. A boy in your stable who died at the hands of a john."

"Oh…" she tilted her head to the side, brows drawn down, "that sounds vaguely familiar. But that was years ago."

"The case is still open. The police would love to have some new leads on it."

Peggy Ann shrugged. "Nothing to do with me. I can't help it if someone makes a date outside of my purview. I do my best to protect my assets, you know, but sometimes things are out of my hands." She looked down at her shapely hands with their red, manicured nails as if distracted by them.

"There is no way that Connor could have been introduced to that john without you. And you knew, like everyone else, that he was embargoed. But you let it go ahead. You contributed to his death."

"Even if that were true—and of course, it is not—the police would never come after me for it. I didn't make the arrangements."

"You had to know about it."

"I did not. But if I had, I would still not be guilty of anything."

"You have withheld information about the commission of a crime. If you had given the police what you knew, that scumbag would be rotting in a prison cell. But instead, you let him go free. All of you who knew about his previous crimes and about him torturing Connor to death just turned a blind eye and pretended it didn't happen."

"The appropriate action was taken at the time," Peggy Ann said smoothly. "I was not in the position that I am in now. I did not have the power to change anything. Eyler was responsible, and he was the one who was disciplined. Regardless of any of that…" Peggy Ann made an airy motion with one hand. "The police cannot arrest people for what they know. Knowing who committed a crime is not a crime."

"You contributed," Joss insisted. "He was your boy. If I tell the cops you set it up, they will come after you."

"I had nothing to do with it," Peggy Ann said sharply, her voice rising. "I had no knowledge until it was too late. You think I would have let one of my top assets be slaughtered like that?"

"You think you can convince the police of that? Once they know that you owned him, they'll know that *you* arranged for the date between him and the john, and they'll come after you."

Peggy Ann shook her head. "That is not going to happen. I am not afraid of the police."

Zachary could feel Joss's frustration that she was not making any headway with Peggy Ann. And Peggy Ann was probably right. Even if Joss told the police that Peggy Ann had been the one to set up the encounter between the john and Connor, the chances that Peggy Ann would go to prison over it were very slim. They would have to prove Peggy Ann knew the john was dangerous.

# 51

T here are rules in this organization, right?" Zachary asked.
Peggy Ann and Joss both looked at him in irritation. Joss's mouth was a thin, straight line. She would take the stuffing out of him once they were out of the house. It was the second time he had spoken up, and this time was a bigger infraction.

"We have rules," Peggy Ann agreed. "And we have our own system for dealing with infractions. Eyler was disciplined, whether or not anyone thinks he deserved a harsher punishment. And that's the end of it. We don't deal with the justice system."

"There must be rules against stealing other people's assets. Like when you took Connor from Eyler."

Peggy Ann looked at Joss. "Who is this guy? I didn't take Connor from Eyler! Eyler disposed of him and I took care of him on my own. This was all adjudicated years ago. It's ancient history."

"But *Aster* isn't ancient history. And her case hasn't been adjudicated."

There was silence in the room, like everyone had taken a breath in and held it. Zachary looked deliberately from Joss to Peggy Ann.

"Didn't you take Aster when you knew she belonged to someone else?"

"You're an idiot!" Peggy Ann snapped. "You don't know what you're talking about. Aster was Eyler's, and he's dead."

"And who gave you his assets?"

Peggy stared at him through narrowed eyes, not answering. Zachary's heart was thumping hard. Joss and Luke had both indicated that Peggy and Eyler were competitors. Luke had told him before that when one trafficker died, his boss absorbed his business. So Eyler's girls would not go to Peggy, but to Eyler's boss. More than likely, Peggy Ann had snatched Aster and she was only bluffing about it being a legitimate acquisition.

"Besides," Zachary went on, going all-in on his own bluff, "Aster wasn't Eyler's anymore. She was Joss's. Eyler gave her to Joss before he was killed."

"He did not," Peggy Ann said tightly.

"She kept running away. Joss was… trying to convince Eyler to leave town, and he didn't want anything else to do with her. So he said that Joss could have Aster. He didn't want to have to deal with her anymore."

Peggy Ann's eyes cut to Joss, considering this. Joss's chin went up a little, challenging her. Neither one said anything as they measured each other up and Peggy Ann weighed this new story.

"There had already been trouble between you and Eyler," Zachary pointed out. "Are you really going to try to convince Gordo that Eyler gave *you* Aster?"

There was a gasp from Joss when he said Gordo's name. Zachary belatedly remembered her warning not to even mention it out loud.

His use of Gordo's name seemed to have the same effect on Peggy Ann, whose face drained of color. Zachary decided to push it further.

"First, you take Connor from Eyler. He's furious, but the organization rules in your favor and says that you can keep him. Without having paid or traded Eyler anything. Then you supply Connor to an embargoed john, and he's killed, getting lots of attention from the cops. And now, someone knifes Eyler in his own hotel room and you somehow acquire one of his girls. You think that Gordo is going to give Aster to you? Why? Because he gave you Connor? You screwed that up royally, didn't you?"

Peggy Ann's face was a white stone mask. Zachary didn't even see her signal her bodyguard but, out of the corner or his eye, he saw the big man peel himself away from the wall and take a run at Zachary.

Zachary was much too slow to react. Never athletic even as a teenager and having had to relearn how to walk and move after his spinal cord injury, his reaction to seeing the guard come at him was delayed by what seemed like hours. Before he could turn and attempt an escape, the guard had a tight hold on Zachary with his beefy arm wrapped around Zachary's throat. Zachary first gagged and then tried to inhale and found his air supply had been cut off.

"You want *another* body to explain?" Joss asked coolly.

Peggy Ann didn't say anything, but must have made a sign to the bodyguard. He released the pressure on Zachary's throat, allowing Zachary to take a deep breath.

"I don't know what game you're playing at," Peggy Ann growled, "but those accusations will not stick. I'm well-respected. I follow the rules and everyone, including my bosses, knows it."

"You think you're safe," Zachary's voice was higher than usual and raspy. "And then someone stabs you in the back." He tried to remember exactly what it was Luke had said. "You put your trust in someone, and they pull the rug out from under you. How many people in the organization do you really trust not to turn on you the first minute they smell blood in the water?"

"Get them out of here," Peggy Ann said. "I need to think. Lock them up while I figure this out."

The guard released Zachary's throat, but held on to his arm. He jerked his head at Joss, indicating that she should go with him. Zachary didn't know whether to hope that she cooperated and came with him and kept him company or made a break for it, realizing that the guard would be occupied with Zachary already and would not be able to go after her. She probably couldn't make it out of the house, but she could try.

Joss took a quick look around the room and did not try to run. She went along with the guard, with Zachary, out of the room, down the hall, down the stairs, and down another set of stairs in the back of the building that led to a cool, windowless basement.

## 52

"hat the hell was that?" Joss demanded when the guard left them, shutting the door behind him. "Didn't I tell you not to say anything? You were supposed to be here just for numbers. Just for moral support. Not to insert yourself into the middle of the discussion and stir things up! You haven't got a clue how things work in an organization like this!"

"You weren't getting anywhere with your threat to take it to the police," Zachary pointed out, trying to stay calm in the face of her anger. As the oldest child, tasked with the responsibility for all of the others, Joss had been a disciplinarian. If he stepped out of line, she was fully within her appointed family role to smack him around or impose whatever consequence she thought appropriate. And while she had only been a child, some of those punishments had served as very painful lessons he would remember for a long time. It wasn't easy to face her fury without flinching.

"Maybe not," Joss snapped. "But at least with my approach, we would be leaving here alive."

"Without Aster."

"There was only ever a slight chance that we were going to be able to get her. I wasn't counting on it."

"Well…" Zachary tried to think of a bright side to the situation or an excuse for doing what he had done. But he couldn't think of either. He sat down on the floor, his back against the wall. The cold floor was really going to be a pain. "We're not dead yet."

"Always little Miss Sunshine, aren't you?"

Zachary closed his eyes, thinking that it would only be a few minutes before Peggy Ann figured out the best way to dispose of them. But after sitting there like that for what he estimated was half an hour, he was getting too restless to stay still. He opened his eyes and looked around, cataloging everything he could about the room. There wasn't much to see. It was probably intended to be used as a storage room. Hard tile floor over concrete. No windows. No furniture. A suspended ceiling, above which they could probably see the pipes leading to the upper floors if they were to pop one of the tiles. There was a plugin on each wall, but no cords plugged into them. The walls appeared to be poured concrete rather than wallboard. Not something anyone could break through.

A good room to hold someone prisoner in.

Maybe when Peggy Ann had built extra storage rooms into her basement, she had planned to use them as temporary detainment areas. As a human trafficker, she would frequently have people on her hands who needed temporary housing while she and the other traffickers dealt with business arrangements. Zachary didn't think she would use her house for them regularly, but she might occasionally need to house a person or two.

The bodyguard hadn't needed any prompting as to where to put them when Peggy Ann had said to lock them up.

"What are we going to do?" he asked Joss.

"*Now* you want my direction? What we are going to do is wait here like sitting ducks until she decides what she wants done with us. Then we're not going to have much choice but to go along with whatever she decides."

They sat in silence.

"Do you really have a system set up that will leak information about them if something happens to you?" Zachary asked.

Joss looked at him and didn't answer.

Zachary felt his pockets. "They didn't take our phones. We can call for help."

Joss paid him no attention as he turned his phone on and tapped the phone app.

*No service*

"There's no signal down here," he told her.

"Brilliant."

Of course there wasn't any signal. Joss hadn't even needed to check. But then, she had been in the business for a long time. As she had been trafficked, she had probably sat in a number of rooms like that one. Completely cut off from the world. So much that she might start to wonder if the rest of the world even existed anymore. Whether everyone other than her bosses and johns she dealt with had ceased to exist.

*We are going to sit and wait.*

---

Something changed even before Zachary could hear footsteps in the hallway outside. A drop in the air pressure when a door was opened, maybe. Something stirred and alerted his animal brain that someone was coming.

Joss looked up too, and they both strained their ears, then eventually heard the footsteps. Just one set, Zachary thought. Not the two people that would be required to handle them both securely. But then, maybe all he needed was a gun or a couple of pairs of handcuffs. Zachary wasn't exactly a ninja.

It didn't occur to him until then that they hadn't even bothered to take Joss's gun from her. Joss had gone with the bodyguard as directed and had not tried to shoot her way out. She had been put in that room with him without protest, and she hadn't discussed any escape plan with Zachary while they had been in there. But what was she going to do? Shoot whoever opened the door to get them? And then what? They wouldn't be able to get out of the building without running into other members of Peggy Ann's crew. Zachary didn't know how many bullets a gun like Joss's had, but it wasn't a TV show. They weren't going to be able to shoot their way out.

The door opened. Zachary followed Joss's lead and stayed sitting on the floor, waiting. It was a different man, not the bodyguard. He looked at the two of them and scowled.

"Get up. Time to go."

"Where are we going?" Zachary questioned as he got up. He couldn't help himself. Even though he might not want to know the answer, he couldn't just follow without asking.

"Shut up."

Zachary glanced at Joss, hoping for some sign from her as to what he should do. She got to her feet, saying nothing. She didn't reach for her gun. She didn't complain about their treatment or ask what was happening. She looked as if this were all routine. Boring, even. He didn't know how she could not show any anxiety over what was going to happen to them. His guts were writhing so bad he didn't think he could stand up straight to go with the man.

Joss touched him lightly on the back to usher him ahead of her. He was soothed by her touch, even though it was fleeting and she barely touched him. Just feeling her there, knowing she was behind him, was comforting. She didn't have to say anything. He knew that she was telling him to stay cool and not say or do anything stupid. In his head, he promised her that he wouldn't.

They went with the man, back upstairs to the main floor, then up the grand staircase to the second floor, and into Peggy Ann's office. She wasn't there. The room was empty.

"Sit down." The man pointed to the upholstered chairs in front of Peggy Ann's desk. Zachary looked around. There was another door in the corner of the room. It did not look like a closet.

"Is that a bathroom? I could really use one... you know... while we're waiting..."

The man rolled his eyes and gave a nod. Zachary got up, made a beeline to the door, and let himself into a small, sparkling clean bathroom. He let out a sigh and was as quick as he could be, not wanting to be caught with his pants down—literally—when Peggy Ann returned to deal with them.

He returned to his seat in the office, feeling much more relaxed and human. He was still anxious and had no idea how everything would play out, but felt more in control of himself and his body. Joss gave him a look of exasperation when he sat down beside her. Zachary shrugged. Despite his varied childhood and private investigator experiences, this was not the way he was accustomed to being treated.

The door opened and Peggy Ann walked in and sat down at her desk. Zachary assumed the big, black desk made her feel stronger and more secure. It was physically imposing when she was not. She looked directly at Joss.

"Take my advice and don't ever bring him here again."

Joss raised an eyebrow but didn't say anything. Zachary's heart started to thump, finally hopeful. If he and Joss were going to come back, they would have to be alive. There wouldn't have been any point in saying it if Joss and Zachary, or even just Zachary, was going to be dead.

"You are going to stay away from anyone in the organization." Peggy Ann leaned forward on her desk, her jaw set, speaking through gritted teeth. "You are not going to keep stirring things up and getting in my way. You are not going to communicate anything to... anyone over my head."

As Joss had suggested, Peggy Ann would not even say Gordo's name.

"Is all of that understood?" Peggy Ann barked.

Zachary was nodding, but Joss sat there impassively. "You seem to think that you're the one with the negotiating power here."

Peggy Ann's face flushed a deep red.

"I have no desire to have anything to do with anyone in your organization," Joss said. "When I left, I planned on never having contact with any of them again. I don't want any of you operating in Kent. If you do... then expect me to get irritated by it. And that means I will have the cops in your business any time I can. And that any girls who come to me for help are going to find asylum and are not going to be forced back into service."

The tendons in Peggy Ann's throat stood out. She tried to stare Joss down, but Joss looked unconcerned.

"I know all kinds of things about you and the organization. All I'm asking for is peace and quiet. For your kind to stay out of my town and leave me alone."

Peggy Ann seemed to be speechless. Eventually, she signaled the guard. Zachary braced himself for attack. Fists, gunshot, or another arm around his throat. He didn't know what to expect. But the guard stepped out of the room. There were voices in the hall, and then the man returned. Leading a blond, round-faced girl by the arm.

Aster.

Zachary didn't know whether to believe it.

Maybe all three of them were going to be executed. That would show everyone not to threaten a cartel boss in her own house. Maybe Peggy Ann had decided she didn't care what would leak out once Joss was killed.

"Go." Peggy Ann made a flicking motion with her fingers. "Take her and go."

Zachary was the first one to his feet. Joss was slower to get up. She nodded vaguely in Peggy Ann's direction.

"Thank you. I trust we won't have to see each other again."

She looked at the guard as they approached him. "Let her go."

The man looked surprised. He looked at Aster, then released her arm. Joss touched her gently on the shoulder.

"Come on. Let's go."

Aster walked beside Joss. Zachary brought up the rear. They walked out to the car without a word. The sky was beginning to get dark. Zachary opened one of the back doors and slid in, letting Aster ride shotgun. Aster's arms were crossed and her hands pulled into her long sleeves. She walked like a zombie, uncertain as to what was going on, without a will of her own. Zachary didn't say anything as Joss shifted the car into drive and hit the gas. When they got past the big, barred gates, he sighed in relief but still didn't speak until they got to the highway.

"That was… something."

Joss glanced over her shoulder at him. "You did okay," she said grudgingly.

"I did good?"

"You did good."

## 53

Z achary sat back. Joss didn't give out praise lightly. He couldn't remember the last time she had praised him for anything. He wasn't sure she ever had. It was a new experience.

He watched the scenery pass by the window, feeling drowsy. The aftereffects of the adrenaline. Now that he was safe, it was time to replenish his stores. He watched the soft glow of the sunset changing from oranges to deep blue, with the stars creeping out.

"Wake up, baby brother. I'm not carrying you into the house."

Zachary rubbed his eyes and looked around. He hadn't intended to let himself fall asleep.

"Though I probably could," Joss went on. "What do you weigh? A buck? Buck twenty-five?"

"I don't know," Zachary groaned. He stretched and stumbled out of the car. Though, of course, he did know. The doctor tracked his weight closely, making sure he didn't stall in his weight gain.

Joss opened Aster's door and encouraged her to get out and go into the house. She must have fallen asleep too. Zachary could certainly understand why. He was exhausted after just a few hours languishing in Peggy Ann's basement room. Aster had been there for days, or maybe somewhere worse. Jocelyn had said that Peggy Ann would not have her girls living in the house, but somewhere else. Some dirty little apartment like Madison had been living in when Zachary tracked her down. Probably several of them in one apartment.

Zachary let Joss and Aster go ahead of him again, Joss nudging Aster along until they reached the house. The outside light was on, and the door, when Joss tried it, was unlocked.

The other girls were watching for them and crowded around Aster when she walked in the door, hugging her and greeting her with high-pitched, excited voices. Aster stood there, seeming not to even be taking it in. Eventually, the excitement died down, and Joss led Aster to the couch and let her sit down. The other girls were quiet, whispering to each other.

"Why don't you girls go clean up the kitchen and let me talk to Aster?" Joss directed.

Eventually, the other girls left them alone. Just Joss, Aster, and Zachary. Zachary studied Aster with concern. He wasn't sure whether she was drugged, hurt, or traumatized. Maybe all three. She seemed very distant and unsure, curled up into herself.

"Can you tell me what happened?" Joss asked gently. Zachary appreciated this soft, gentle version of Joss. He didn't jump in, but let Joss take charge. She was the one who knew Aster. Zachary only knew her from her pictures.

Aster shook her head.

"Come on," Joss coaxed. "I need you to tell me what happened. You left the house? You were supposed to stay here and keep safe." Joss shook her head. "I blame Luke for always going out, making you feel like you were missing out on something."

Aster sniffled. "Not Luke's fault."

"Not this time, no. You made that decision for yourself. What was it? You wanted to go out to meet with friends? Dance? Where did you go?"

"No. I just... I wasn't feeling good. I needed to get some fresh air. That's all." She blinked; eyelashes wet with tears.

Zachary's heart went out to her. Who knew what she had been through at Peggy Ann's hands and, before that, with Eyler. Was she one of Eyler's "grabs"? Someone he had just snatched off the street and forced into working for him? Where had she been before that? With her own family? Homeless on the street?

Joss frowned at Aster, the crease between her eyebrows deepening. "You weren't feeling good and needed some fresh air," she repeated flatly.

Aster nodded. She rubbed both eyes with the heels of her hands.

"Sounds to me like you were jonesing."

"I never said that!" Aster's voice rose in pitch.

"Tell me you weren't."

Several seconds passed in silence. Aster shrugged, her lips forming a pout. "Maybe. I needed some air. I couldn't just stay cooped up here."

"So you went for a walk."

"Yeah."

"To get some fresh air."

"Yeah. That's what I said."

Joss shook her head. "You can't BS an old addict. An addict doesn't go out for fresh air. She goes out for drugs."

Aster's mouth twisted into a snarl. "No."

"Yeah? If I tested you right now, what would I find?"

"Peggy Ann gave me something. That's not *my* fault."

Luke had said that the traffickers would get new recruits addicted to get them to do what they wanted. Someone hurting for a fix would do almost anything for the next dose. But Joss's expression was hard. She wasn't buying Aster's excuse.

"You didn't go out for a walk. You went out to buy."

"No." Aster shook her head again, tears falling down her cheeks. "I didn't!"

"Why do you think there are rules about staying in the house? When you go out there, especially to buy, people can see you. They're watching for you, and they'll act the moment they see you."

"I don't have any money."

Joss was being too hard on Aster, assuming she knew what had happened based on her own experiences. But Aster wasn't Jocelyn. Zachary opened his mouth to interrupt and point this out. Joss was victim-blaming, acting like it was Aster's own fault she'd been kidnapped by Peggy Ann's goons. It wasn't Aster's fault that she'd been targeted. All she had done was go out for a walk to clear her head.

---

## 54

J oss shot Zachary a look before he could voice his opinion. "You don't need money to get drugs if you know the right places to go," she told Aster, but Zachary knew she was talking to him. "The people to go to."

"You think I wanted to go back there?" Aster's voice was teary. "You think I deserved what I got?"

"I think you needed a fix and would do anything to get it, including turning yourself back in to the organization, because you knew they would give you what you needed if you went back to work for them."

"You think I wanted to hook?"

"I think you needed drugs."

"It might be easy for you," Aster snapped, "but it isn't for everyone. Just because you managed to get out, you think it means anyone else can. As long as they're strong enough." She wiped her nose on her arm. "But not everyone is as strong as you!"

"I don't expect you to just go cold turkey all by yourself. There are other people here to help you. I told you about the detox I could get you into. You didn't have to just tough it out without any help."

"You're all high and mighty. Think that you're better than any of us."

Joss shook her head. "Where do you want to go? Whatever program you want, I'll get you into it. Or back to your family. You just say what you're willing to do, and I'll help you."

"I don't know." Aster pulled at a lock of hair and wrapped it around her finger. "I'm not like you."

Joss sighed. "Until you're ready to commit... I can't help you."

"You're kicking me out? Well, why not? You already kicked Luke to the curb."

Zachary looked at Joss, shocked by Aster's accusation. Joss shook her head. "I didn't kick Luke to the curb. I didn't kick anyone out. I haven't kicked you out. Luke isn't here because he got himself into trouble. That had nothing to do with me."

"Is he okay?" Aster continued to sniffle. "If anything happened to Luke..."

"Okay? I guess he's okay. He's alive. They'll make sure he stays that way so they can take him to trial and put him in prison for twenty to life. Sure, he's fine."

A fresh burst of tears from Aster. "He's the only one here who understood me. He cared. He would go out with me, and we would just have a good time, and he would listen. He—he was a really good listener."

"I wish he hadn't taken you out. Taking you where you could be seen, where Eyler's men could find you and take you back or report to him on your movements... he didn't do you any favors. He put you in danger."

"It wasn't Luke's idea. It was mine. He just came along to keep me company."

"He should have told you to stay home."

"It's all my fault. If it wasn't for me, he wouldn't have..."

Aster was the reason Luke had gone to see Eyler. To tell him to back off and leave her alone. He knew about Eyler through Connor, and knew what had happened to Connor. He didn't want to see it happen to another kid, especially fresh-faced Aster, who was happy to hang out with him and dance. She had met Rhys virtually and exchanged messages with him. They had sent photos back and forth. Involved Rhys in the happy times, even though he couldn't join them, and it all had to remain a secret from Zachary, Vera, and Joss. Luke took on the role of her protector.

"Luke made his own choices," Joss said. "And some of them were not good choices."

Zachary rubbed the bridge of his nose, thinking over his notes and the various interviews he had done since first finding out that Luke was in trouble.

"Where were you the night Eyler was killed?" he asked Aster.

"I was here!" Aster looked at Joss for her to confirm the fact to Zachary.

Joss nodded. "She was here."

"All night?"

Joss's eyes slid over to Aster. "Why?"

"Are you sure she didn't go out for a few hours to get drugs or do something with Luke?"

Joss leaned her head back and sucked in her cheeks, studying Aster. "I can't sit up all night making sure that no one leaves her bed. I check at night. I know who is here in the morning. But if they sneak out and put themselves in danger, there isn't anything I can do about that."

"I didn't," Aster insisted. Fingers poking out of her sleeve, she pulled on a lock of hair, twisting it around and around.

But Zachary was starting to put it together. For years, Luke had stayed away from Eyler. He didn't go after the man when Connor was killed. He'd probably only been fourteen at the time, small and vulnerable. Not able to face off against a big man like Eyler. When he had gone out with Aster and been approached by someone wanting to take her back to Eyler, Luke had been quick to defend her, but he didn't kill the messenger or go to Eyler's hotel room to confront him at that point, at the peak of his anger. He had made threats, but he hadn't been violent.

But a few days later, he had gone to Eyler's room. Possibly unarmed. And had killed him.

Why?

"You went back to Eyler," Zachary suggested to Aster. "You were looking for drugs, and you knew he had the good stuff. Eyler was more generous with drugs than most of the bosses. Gave you more, higher-quality stuff. You didn't have any money, but you knew he would give it to you if you went back to work for him."

"He was a pig," Aster spat. "First client of the night was always him."

Joss nodded her understanding. "And once you'd satisfied him, you would get your drugs. The next dose, anyway."

"He was..." Aster covered her mouth to hide her expression. Her eyes squeezed shut and more tears ran down her face. Joss looked unmoved by her emotion. Joss had been in the business for a long time and had probably seen it all. She was of the opinion that the best thing to do was to compartmentalize. Lock it away in a box and, if possible, don't revisit it. Aster covered her face with both hands. "He likes to hurt," she said, voice muffled by her hands. "He said not to tell anyone, but the things he does..."

She sobbed, unable to tell them any more. Zachary looked at Joss, wondering if maybe he should leave. Maybe Aster would be able to tell Joss more, woman-to-woman. Zachary being there was probably hampering her. Joss gave a slight shake of her head, surprising him. He raised his brows in question, but stayed where he was.

He was the one who Aster has started talking to, so maybe something about him made her trust him. Like she had trusted Luke. She hadn't stayed at home with the other girls, relying on their help and association, but had gone out with Luke to have a good time.

"He hurt you," Zachary repeated. "Luke said he was like that. He enjoyed hurting his girls. Or making them suffer by withholding drugs."

Aster nodded.

"What did he do to you?"

Joss widened her eyes at Zachary, asking him if he really wanted to know.

Of course he didn't. Zachary felt sick asking the question. He didn't want to know what sorts of torture Eyler enjoyed. Zachary didn't want to think about the things that had been done to him by Archuro. He didn't want to know any of it. But Aster had been waiting for him to ask.

"He had…" Aster was gasping with sobs, her sentence broken up into bunches of words, "… a knife. Kept threatening… me and he'd start to cut me… and I screamed. He'd cover my… mouth or kiss me to muffle it… laughing. No one… would hear… me over the music…" She took a deep, shuddering breath, trying to collect herself. "I wouldn't do it… tried to get… away. Said I didn't want to… but he put his hands… around my throat…"

She broke off, sobbing more. Zachary had been trying to keep himself aloof, to be alert to the fact that she could be lying and dramatizing to make herself look good. Some people were great at turning on the waterworks and garnering sympathy. But he didn't believe that Aster's distress was faked. He touched her hand tentatively and, when she didn't pull back, he covered her hand with his own as if he were trying to warm it up.

Joss moved as well, first putting her hand on Aster's shoulder, and then moving it to unbutton the top couple of buttons on Aster's blouse. There were dusky bruises around Aster's throat. She was not lying about the fact that he'd choked her.

Aster turned her hand to hold Zachary's, her grip painfully tight. "He was gonna kill me." She breathed shallowly, no longer sobbing, but forming her words carefully. "I knew he decided I wasn't worth his time and was gonna kill me."

Zachary could have tried to argue, to say that she couldn't know what Eyler had intended, that Eyler surely wouldn't dispose of a valuable asset so soon. But Luke had told him Connor's story. Maybe he'd told it to Aster too.

# 55

The knife was right there," Aster squeezed harder, making Zachary wince. He was worried that she was going to end up breaking bones. But he was too engrossed in her story to make her let go. He didn't want to do anything to interrupt her. She had started to unburden herself and, as she got it out, she was calming down. She was no longer sobbing, maybe past the point where she could feel the fear and anxiety anymore. "I guess he thought it was out of my reach, or that I would pass out right away. Maybe he just thought... I wouldn't dare."

Zachary nodded, encouraging her to go on.

"I could reach. And I... I just drove it in as hard as I could. He kind of... collapsed on top of me, and I rolled him over. And I stabbed him again. I don't know how many times, until he stopped moving or making noises."

Zachary pulled his gaze away from Aster to look at Joss. He wondered, at first, if Joss had known this all the time and been part of the cover-up. But Joss's pale, pinched expression told him she had not. She had believed that it was Luke, had not guessed that Luke was covering up for someone else.

Aster had been there at bed check, and she had been there in the morning when Joss got up. Joss hadn't guessed that Aster had been gone for several hours in the middle.

"When did Luke get there?"

"Not until it was over. I was trying to clean up. Get all the blood off so I could..." she sniffled, "go home." She let go of Zachary's hand and looked down at her own palm. It was crossed with several deep cuts. Zachary realized that both he and the police had failed to recognize the significance of Luke's unmarked palms. He had not been the one to drive the knife into Eyler again and again, his hand slipping from the handle to the blade.

"What did he do?"

"He said Eyler had been shouting." Aster shook her head at this thought. "I don't even remember that. I just... I was so scared. I just wanted him to stop, to let me go. I went because I needed drugs, but he was going to kill me."

"Luke told you that Eyler had been shouting. When? Was he shouting at you before you killed him? While he was choking you? Or when you stabbed him?"

"I don't know!" Aster's voice cracked. She waved his question away in irritation. "Who cares? He said people would be calling the police. He told me I had to get out of there before the cops got there. They couldn't find me with Eyler's body. All covered with blood. *Luke* was shouting at me, telling me how I should have kept Eyler quiet so no one would call the cops." She was outraged at this. "How was I supposed to keep him quiet?"

"He was worried about you. Trying to keep you safe."

Aster nodded. "I know. I just... I was so messed up. I couldn't think straight. Being attacked like that, and him dying... I just wanted to go home and hide."

"And he got you out of there before the police showed up."

Aster nodded. "Told me to be quiet. To take the stairs down. Pretend..." Aster tried to suppress a smile. "Pretend like I was sneaking out on Joss." She wiped both cheeks.

"Maybe if there'd been less sneaking out, this wouldn't have happened," Joss pointed out.

THEY CAME FOR HIM

"I know. But… Eyler shouldn't have done that. He shouldn't have tried to kill me!"

"No," Zachary reassured her. "He shouldn't have done that."

Joss rolled her eyes at Zachary. He sighed. "What are we going to do?"

Joss rubbed Aster's back. "I'll call a lawyer. He'll tell us how to get this sorted out."

"I'm not going to jail," Aster said, sniffling and wiping her eyes, which were getting very red and puffy. Looking at the bruises on her throat, Zachary wondered how many other marks were on her body from the encounter with Eyler, who liked to hurt people.

"Honey, it was self-defense," Joss told her. "You're not going to go to prison."

"But *Luke* is," Aster protested.

"Luke isn't going to prison either, because he wasn't the one who did it. We've been trying to figure out how to get his sentence reduced all week. You should have told me what happened."

"Luke said not to say anything. Just to go home and pretend that I'd been home all night. So that's what I did. I did what he said. He said he would get me off."

Zachary shook his head. "He shouldn't have interfered. This mess could have been avoided if the police had known what happened from the start."

## 56

*Z*achary made a large carafe of coffee in the kitchen and helped himself to a mug. He looked at his phone and frowned when he realized how late it was. It had been dark when they had reached Joss's. He should have been home long before. He was already too late to have supper with Kenzie. He was surprised that she hadn't called him. He tapped on his phone and text apps, which were not showing any alerts or recent calls. That never happened. Especially if he was so late getting home. He tapped Kenzie's name to call her, and the phone just gave three beeps and told him that the call had failed. He looked at the service icon in the top corner to make sure that he had coverage.

*No service.*

Zachary swore. Joss, pouring herself a cup of coffee, turned and looked at him. "What?"

"There's something wrong with the phone. No service."

"Try shutting it off and restarting it. Sometimes if you've been out of service for long enough, it stops looking to preserve battery life."

Zachary swore again, but this time just in his head. He shut the phone down, watching for everything to disappear from the screen, waited for a slow count to ten, and then held down the power button. By the time it finished going through its warm-up cycle, he could see that he had service bars. The counts of his missed calls and new texts rocketed up. Which meant he was in big trouble.

"You're looking a little green there, little brother."

"Yeah, I missed all kinds of calls and messages. Kenzie is going to think I drove off a cliff or something."

"You'd better call her."

"Good idea."

She smirked at his sarcastic tone. Zachary stared up at the ceiling rather than looking at Joss or any of the girls going in and out of the kitchen, helping themselves to coffee or trying to talk to Aster or Joss. No one wanted to talk to him, which was good. He had enough problems to deal with.

"Zachary?" Kenzie's voice was high-pitched with worry.

"I'm here. I'm sorry, everything is okay."

He braced himself for a stream of invectives. And Kenzie would be right with all of them. He'd been stupid. He should have noticed the time hours ago and checked his phone to see what was wrong with it. He should have called her before supper to tell her where he was and what was going on. He should have acted like an adult and let people know what was going on, instead of just dropping off the face of the earth.

"You're okay?" Kenzie repeated, sounding thick and choked up. "What happened?"

"There was no service. For a while. And I didn't realize that my phone hadn't reconnected when I got out of there. So I thought... I don't know what time I thought it was. I should have noticed how late it was getting. I'm so sorry."

"Did you check your messages?"

"No. I saw there were a bunch, but I just called you first. I can listen to them later."

"Yeah, and laugh at how freaked out your partner was getting. You missed therapy. Dr. Boyle called."

He hadn't even thought to call her and cancel. He'd lost track of what day it was or where he was supposed to be. He had been so caught up in the developments of the case that he'd been oblivious to the rest of the world.

"Oh, no. I lost track."

"Your calendar reminders should still go off, even if you're out of service."

"Yeah, they probably did. I've just been so focused on everything else, I never heard or felt them."

"Well, call Dr. B and let her know you're still alive. We were really worried."

"You know I'm okay right now," he pointed out. "I'm not depressed."

"You could have had an accident. Or something to do with that trafficking ring... Or something might have upset you. You were really having a hard time after hearing about what had happened to Connor. I didn't know if things had gotten worse. I don't know. I was imagining all kinds of things."

"I'm so sorry."

How was he going to tell Kenzie what had actually happened? That he'd been sitting in a basement wondering whether they were going to execute him or if there was any chance of escape. He had never really thought that they would just let him and Joss walk out of there with Aster. It had been every bit as bad as she had worried. Because he thought that they could just walk into Peggy Ann's house and negotiate for Aster's release because of some secret information that Joss held. Which he was beginning to think was just a bluff. Sure, she had worked with the cartel for a long time, but did she really know enough to have them all convicted? And if she did, did she really have the information secreted away somewhere with a release protocol if she disappeared? He was beginning to doubt all of it. She was just really good at head games.

"Where are you, then? Are you coming home?"

"Yes." Zachary pulled the phone away from his face for a moment to look at the time. It was already late and, in the morning, he was going to come straight back to talk to Luke again. "I'm at Joss's now. I'll get on my way."

"Maybe you should stay over there. Are you alert enough to drive?"

"I just had a big cup of coffee." He hadn't yet finished what was in his cup, but he would before he hit the road. "I won't fall asleep."

He expected her to tell him again to just sleep over on Joss's couch. But she didn't. She must have really been worried about him and wanted to see him, even knowing that neither of them would get very much sleep before going back to work in the morning.

"I'll be back as soon as I can," he promised.

"Don't speed. I'll see you when you get here. I'll be okay now that I know you're fine."

"Good." The guilt was a tight knot in his stomach. He knew, despite her calming words, that she'd been really upset. He didn't know whether she had gone as far as to call the police, maybe a personal call to Campbell to find out whether he knew anything. She wouldn't have been able to file a missing person report yet, but she could have called around to hospitals and morgues.

"You're going?" Joss questioned after Zachary ended the call.

"Yeah. I didn't realize that there was a problem with my phone and it had gotten so late. She was really worried. I want to get back there and reassure her that everything is fine."

Joss nodded.

"What about you?" Zachary looked toward the living room where Aster and the other girls were talking. "Are you going to get any sleep tonight?"

"No. I don't expect so. Need to get things straightened out with Aster. She's coming down hard. It isn't going to be a soft landing, and I'm going to have to talk her into talking to a lawyer."

"Do you know what's going to happen?"

"She'll probably have to turn herself in, but should be able to get out on bond because it was self-defense and nobody's going to be crying for justice for that scumbag."

"I'll be back in the morning to talk to Luke."

"Maybe we'll see you over at the jail, then."

"Good luck."

Joss nodded. "You too. I don't know that I'd want to be facing Kenzie after that stunt."

"It wasn't a stunt!" But with the way she had stood up to Peggy Ann, unflinching, he knew that Joss would never have had any problem facing Kenzie's anger, no matter how bad. He had to keep reminding himself that Kenzie wasn't Bridget and wasn't going to react like she would. Bridget would have torn a strip off of him when he called. She would not have been polite and requested that he come home. He probably would have had to sleep on the couch for a month.

# 57

Zachary parked the car and, by the time he had opened the door and climbed out, Kenzie was standing in the open front door waiting for him. He walked as quickly as he could without getting overly awkward and tripping. When he reached her, he put his arms around her and pulled her in close.

"I'm sorry, I'm so sorry."

"Shut up. Quit apologizing and just hold me."

"I am."

She gripped him tightly, pressing herself against him. Zachary remembered how worried he had been when Tyrrell had disappeared. Not that he had known the first day, or anywhere near the beginning. By the time he knew Tyrrell had disappeared, it had been weeks, and Zachary was frantic to find him or to find out what had happened to him. He tried to imagine what it would be like to suddenly not be able to get ahold of Kenzie. If phone calls and texts and every other imaginable method failed and he had no idea what had happened to her. It was inconceivable. He had no idea how he would have handled it. A nervous breakdown, probably.

Eventually, Kenzie's grip on him relaxed and she pulled back a little. "Better come in. The neighbors are going to be wondering what's going on."

Zachary stepped into the house. Kenzie touched his face, looking into his eyes. She took a deep breath and let it out. "Do you need anything? A bite to eat before bed? I don't suppose you remembered to eat, if you didn't even think to look at the time."

"No. But it can wait. I'm not hungry."

"You're late on your night meds."

"Uh, yes." Zachary nodded his agreement. And she was right to point it out, because he needed to take some of them with food. "I guess I'd better have something small, then."

She kept a hand on his arm all the way into the kitchen as if to reassure herself that he was okay, that he was there, not just a figment of her imagination.

"What can I do?"

"Sit." She pointed to his chair. "I don't want you in the way today. I don't have the emotional resources."

If he were helping her get things ready, it should be less for her to deal with, not more. But Zachary kept his mouth shut and didn't argue the point. He had asked her what she wanted, and she had answered clearly. Arguing opinions was not going to do anyone good, particularly when they were both so drained.

Zachary sat down as he was told. He looked through the doorway to the living room to check his car through the window and make sure that it was safe. He didn't even remember shutting and locking the doors, but he could see that they were all shut. He pulled out his key fob and hit the lock button a couple of times to lock and arm it. Then he noticed the dark form lying on the couch in the dim living room.

Tyrrell.

It made sense, of course, that he had come over when Kenzie had called around looking for anyone who might have heard from Zachary. He had been there to support her and do what he could to try to track down Zachary, just as Zachary had once helped to track down him.

"How long has Tyrrell been here?"

"Early evening. Dr. B called to say that you had missed your appointment, and I wasn't really worried for a couple of hours. I know that sometimes you just get distracted and might have forgotten about it. But when you didn't come home and didn't answer any calls or texts, we started to get concerned. I couldn't find you on that app. Location unknown. I guess that's just because you didn't have service, but I was thinking all kinds of things."

Kenzie warmed up some leftovers, put them on the table in front of Zachary, and filled a glass of water before sitting down to join him. She didn't have anything to eat, but she sat and stared at him. He ate a few bites of the food and tried to think of what to say other than to apologize again, which she was tired of. He downed his night meds and looked down at his plate, considering whether he was going to eat anything more. Maybe a couple more bites, just to make sure that the pills didn't give him heartburn or nausea.

"So... find anything out today?" Kenzie asked casually.

"Um... yeah. Big day." Zachary took a deep breath in and let it out. "It wasn't Luke who killed Eyler."

"What? Are you kidding me? But he admitted it."

"He was covering to protect someone else. I'll get his story tomorrow. I just... believed everyone who said that he had done it."

"Well... there was plenty of evidence pointing in that direction. Found holding the murder weapon, dripping with blood."

Zachary nodded. "But that didn't mean that he'd just killed Eyler, like they said. There was a few minutes between the disturbance and when the police got there... enough time that he should have been out of there. He could have ditched the weapon in a sewer grate and gone somewhere to arrange an alibi. But he didn't do that. He intentionally stayed there to get caught so that the police wouldn't be looking for anyone else."

## 58

L uke." Kenzie shook her head. "Somebody needs to give that boy a talking to."

"You and Joss can flip for it. Or maybe you should both give him a talking to and hope that it will actually stick."

Kenzie nodded her agreement. "So, how did you figure that out, Mr. PI? You were still convinced this morning that he was the culprit and were looking for ways to get his sentence reduced."

"Well... I went looking for Aster, the girl in the background of the video. And I guess... that triggered the rest. Started all of the dominoes falling."

"Well, good job for noticing her in the video. I guess no one else did."

"Oh, I'll have to message Rhys tomorrow. He was the one who gave me Aster's picture so I *could* recognize her. He'll be glad to hear that Luke will be getting out."

"I'm sure he will," Kenzie agreed. "What happened when you went to talk to Luke about her?"

"He gave away that Aster was supposed to be at home with Joss. So, I went to Joss's to find out."

"And was she there?"

"No. Turns out that she had gone out... looking for drugs."

"She's an addict?"

"Most of these kids are. It's one of the ways the bosses keep them on the hook. Keep them supplied with drugs. If they ever try to leave, they have to leave that supply pipeline behind. If they ever refuse to do a job, their boss withholds the drugs. An easy way to keep them under their control."

Kenzie nodded. "These poor kids. When I think about the stuff that they have to go through."

"They're not all kids. Joss was in the business for a long time."

"I know, but they generally start as kids. That's the best time to get them. When they are the most vulnerable. And what happens after that... well, it's not exactly their fault. Once they're trapped in this cycle of addiction and abuse, and with how powerful these cartels are. It's scary."

"Yeah. So, she went back looking for drugs. Back to Eyler. One thing led to another..." Kenzie didn't need to know all of the sordid details of what had happened to Aster. "And she ended up killing him in self-defense. Luke shows up, gets her out of there, and covers up for her. Taking all of the heat himself."

"But if it was self-defense, then it was justified. She can get off free, or with a minimal sentence."

"Yeah. I have to talk to Luke about it tomorrow. I don't know what he was thinking. He should never have been there in the first place, but when he saw what had happened, he shouldn't have stepped in like that. It would have been better if Aster had stayed and faced the cops, told them that she had been attacked."

"Wow. That's quite a revelation. You managed to track down Aster...?"

"Uh, yes. She had been picked up by another trafficker. Peggy Ann." Zachary frowned, thinking about it. "I don't know whether she just wanted to run Aster, to pick up another asset for free, or whether she did it to try to control Joss..."

Kenzie's eyebrows went up. "To try to control Joss? How? In what way?"

"Well, Joss has been rescuing girls from the organization. She had rescued Aster already and she was living at the house with Joss. She's got a whole house full of them. Joss has been a thorn in the side of these traffickers, calling the police to report them, trying to drive them out of town. I guess maybe Peggy Ann figured that if she got her hands on one of these girls, she could hold her hostage. Force Joss to back off."

"Jocelyn doesn't strike me as the type to be intimidated too easily," Kenzie said dryly.

"Uh… no. You should have seen her today. I couldn't believe the way she stood up to Peggy Ann and her goons."

"Oh…?"

Zachary licked his lips. He should have kept his mouth shut. He should not have told Kenzie that he had seen Joss stand up to the traffickers. If he explained the details to her, she would not be happy about it. She would realize that all of her worries about him when he had been unreachable had been justified. And then the next time she couldn't reach him, it would be that much harder for her to believe that everything was okay and he just happened to be out of service or not have noticed her phone call.

He took a sip of the water, looking around the kitchen, trying to think of something else to tell her about. If he could just distract her so that she wouldn't realize he had not answered her inquiry…

"But how was your day at the morgue? I've been telling you all about my day, but you haven't told me anything about yours. I shouldn't be monopolizing our time together." He looked at his phone to see what time it was. "We should be in bed."

"Tell me about Joss facing Peggy Ann." Kenzie's voice was even and firm. Zachary swallowed.

"That's kind of a long story. We should probably leave it to tomorrow, so we can get a few hours in tonight. If you want to be in good shape for work…"

"Whose idea was it to confront Peggy Ann? And why were *you* there?"

"It wasn't my idea," Zachary protested immediately, and was glad that he could tell the truth about this point. "Joss decided that the only way she was going to be able to negotiate successfully for Aster's release was to go in person."

"Really."

Zachary nodded eagerly. "Yes. It was her idea, not mine. I didn't just dive into it."

"And… she asked you to go with her?"

"Well…" Zachary looked down, studying his fingernails. He needed to take better care of them. A couple were ragged and needed to be smoothed down with an emery board. He thought that he had probably messed them up on the concrete in the basement room. While he had done his best to copy Jocelyn's lead and remain calm, it had been hard to keep his body still and under his control, and he had scratched and scraped at the concrete floor while trying to think his way out.

"You volunteered?"

"I couldn't let her go by herself. That would have been too dangerous. Just Joss, and all of Peggy Ann's crew? I had to go with her, at least make it look like she had other people behind her."

"Because it isn't as easy to shoot two people as it is to shoot one?"

"Well…" Zachary struggled to explain his thought processes to her. "You see… Joss has been threatening these guys. Peggy Ann and the other traffickers. Telling them that if they don't get out of her territory, she is going to leak information about them to the police." Kenzie opened her mouth to respond, but Zachary held up his hand to stop her, not yet finished with his explanation. "And she has said that if they kill her, the information will leak out after she dies. That she's made contingency plans so that killing her won't solve their problems, it will make them worse."

Kenzie looked bemused. "Okay…?"

"So… I needed them to see that she wasn't alone. That she had friends and other people behind her. That she wasn't just bluffing, but might have set up this plan to have other people spread the information if she died."

"But you couldn't very well spread it if you were dead."

"Well, we never said it explicitly that way. It was just… to give an impression. And I knew that Peggy Ann wouldn't see Joss alone, that she would have at least one other person in the room to keep her safe. It would look unbalanced if Joss met her by herself."

Kenzie stared at him, processing this. "And you managed to convince Joss of this?"

"Yes."

She shook her head slowly. "You and Joss thought that the best way to get Aster back, rather than going to the police about this girl being held hostage by human traffickers, was to go and confront this boss face-to-face."

## 59

Zachary chewed on the inside of his cheek. The way that Kenzie said it made it sound so ridiculous. "The police are already trying to get enough evidence to prosecute these people. They've already got all different agencies trying to shut them down. Going to them about this one hooker that we think is being held by this one pimp against her will won't get anything done. When Madison was with Luke, and I got the police to go to bust him, there was nothing they could do. She told them that she wanted to stay with him, denied that anything was going on, and they didn't have any evidence, any way to take her back away from him. It would have been the same with Aster. If they could find her—and Joss and I didn't know where she was being held—then she would just say that she was there by choice."

"Why? If she was being held against her will, why wouldn't she say so? If she knew that the police could get her out, and she could go back to Joss, that's what she would do."

"No. She wouldn't. They are conditioned to only do what their bosses tell them to. If they don't, the drugs will dry up, they will be hunted and beaten, their loved ones will be killed. They don't have control over their own lives. They have to do what they are told."

"If Aster turned on Peggy Ann and told the police that she had been held against her own will, then they would arrest Peggy Ann. She wouldn't be able to do anything to hurt Aster."

"She'd bail out in a day. Or her goons would go ahead and track down all of Aster's friends and family and hurt them. She wouldn't be able to get drugs anymore and would have to find a new source. Even if she tried to stay away from the organization, they could still have hurt her. And if they did track her down in person..."

Kenzie could fill in that part herself. She looked like she still wanted to argue that Joss and Zachary should have gone to the local police, but didn't have enough ammunition to do so. "So, you and Joss formulated this brilliant plan to go negotiate for her release."

"It worked," Zachary pointed out, a little stung by her remark. "We did it. We managed to get Aster out of there. She's back with Joss. And Peggy Ann knows that Joss has dirt on her that would make her look bad in front of her bosses, not just give the police a reason to arrest her."

"What dirt?"

Zachary waved his hand, tired and not wanting to get into it all. If he could just gloss over what had happened at Peggy Ann's house, they could get to bed. He really wanted to just lie down with her and cuddle and let the stress and anxieties of the day roll away.

"Another time. I'm beat."

Kenzie grunted, dissatisfied. "When exactly did you lose your phone service? You forgot to mention that part."

"Uh—when we were at Peggy Ann's. And I didn't realize that my phone hadn't reconnected when we got away from there."

"Does she have a signal jammer or something? How can she make calls if she has no service? I don't see how you could run a cartel like that without any phone service."

"Well, even with a jammer, there could still be places where she *could* get a signal. Or she could shut it off when she wanted to make a call..."

Kenzie stared at him, clearly seeing that he was just throwing out whatever he could to distract her from the fact that he wasn't answering. "I think there's more to it than that," she said quietly. "Don't lie to me. You know the ground rules we laid down in couple's therapy. If you don't want to answer, tell me you don't want to answer. Don't lie to me."

"I didn't lie…"

"Are you going to tell me the truth? Or tell me that you don't want to answer?"

Zachary considered, weighing one against the other. He could just tell her that he didn't want to answer, and they would be done with that part of the conversation. Kenzie would be forced to talk to him about other things rather than continuing in the same vein after he had told her no. But then she would know that he was keeping something from her, and she would probably guess that it was because he had been in danger and didn't want to tell her about it.

He sighed. "It wasn't because of a signal jammer. As far as I know. There could have been one, but… there was a lot of concrete in the building. It was probably blocking the signal."

"Were you in some kind of bunker? Or is this some kind of industrial building?"

"Uh… bunker would be a closer guess. We were in the basement. For a while."

"I see."

She probably did see far more than he wanted her to know.

"We were fine. No one hurt either of us. We were just… detained for a while so that Peggy Ann could figure out what to do and get Aster back from wherever she was being held. It was good, really, because it meant that she was considering what Joss had and deciding how to respond."

"Or whether to take the chance of just getting it over with and killing both of you. Take the risk that Joss was bluffing or that the information wouldn't be enough to get her in trouble."

"I don't think that was ever a serious consideration," Zachary told her uncomfortably.

"No? You felt safe and secure the whole time you were there?"

Of course he hadn't, and Kenzie knew it. She saw right through him, even when he tried to shade the truth. It was a wonder she had gone into medicine instead of into private investigation like he had.

She would have been brilliant at it. Or maybe a psychologist or one of those behavioral analysts. She was better at reading him than anyone else was.

Zachary shook his head. "I'm sorry. I know we put ourselves in danger, but we were trying to rescue Aster. But it was… a calculated risk."

"I don't like it. I got a taste today of what it would be like to have you drop off the face of the earth and never come home and, in case you're wondering, I didn't like it. That really freaked me out. Please…" Kenzie's voice was breaking, "don't put yourself into dangerous situations. And check your phone more often."

Zachary got a lump in his throat at Kenzie's emotion. He nodded, feeling like an even worse heel than he already had. He knew he needed to be more careful to check in with her. Too often, he lost track of time when he was working on a project and didn't think to call Kenzie and let her know where he was or what he was doing. But then, she didn't often call him during her workday either. Sometimes at lunchtime, and then again toward the end of the day to let him know how late she was running so he knew when to expect her home. The rest of the time, she did her work and he just assumed everything was fine.

But Kenzie wasn't a private investigator, poking into people's lives, putting in hours on surveillance, or trying to negotiate with human traffickers. There was a bit of a difference. Unless she told him otherwise, he assumed that she was at the morgue, working on the computer or assisting with an autopsy. Not out somewhere she might be putting herself in danger.

"I'm really sorry about the phone," he said miserably. "I wish I had realized earlier that you weren't able to reach me."

She nodded. Looking at the clock on the wall, she let out a sigh. "Well, you're right. We'd better be getting to bed. I already know I'm going to be tired in the morning. Might as well at least get a little bit of sleep under our belts." She stood up, scraped the remains of Zachary's dinner into the garbage, and put his plate in the dishwasher.

"I'm not planning on wearing my belt to bed," Zachary

attempted humor, hoping she wasn't too tired to appreciate it. "Are you?"

Kenzie gave him a light slap on the arm as she walked by him. "You're going to be sharing the couch with Tyrrell if you're not careful!"

# 60

Zachary was up before Kenzie in the morning, as usual. He had managed to get a couple of hours of sleep, but his brain was too active, running through everything that had happened, trying to sort out all of the little unanswered questions about the case, and then wondering what was in his email inbox and whether he was falling behind on his other work. He still had surveillance to do. And deep background checks. There might have been other stuff that had come in since he had looked at his inbox last.

He had forgotten, while in bed, that Tyrrell was on the couch, which was where Zachary usually sat to do his work. He looked at the lump under the blanket for a moment, considering. He did not want to wake Tyrrell up. Even if he suggested that Tyrrell retire to the guest room, which would be more comfortable than the couch, Tyrrell might not get back to sleep. Zachary didn't want to do anything else that might affect Tyrrell's fragile mental health. Too little sleep could lead to depression, and depression could lead Tyrrell back to the bottle.

He picked up his laptop from his work table. He could sit at the kitchen table, but the light might wake Tyrrell up, and the table was not at a good height for him to use his computer. Instead, Zachary retreated down the hall to Kenzie's home office and set up there. They hadn't ever discussed this being Kenzie's territory, somewhere she wanted for herself. She had never told him not to use it, but he still felt a little guilty for assuming that he could use it for his own purposes without getting her permission first. He would have to seek her forgiveness later.

Pushing the discomfort and distraction of a new environment out of his mind as much as he could, Zachary opened up his laptop and started to work.

When he saw that his inbox was nearly empty, he just about had a heart attack, thinking he had been hacked. But he saw an email from Heather about their new workflow and opened it up. She had set up the project management account that she'd said she would, and listed the URL, login, and password, as well as the fact that he could download it onto his phone. Each actionable email that had come into his inbox had been sent to the new program, where it was sorted by client and type of task, linked back to the original email. Junk had been routed to the spam folder, and anything that was personal or she thought he might want to read had been filed into a new "personal" folder.

Following Heather's instructions, he processed the new emails that had arrived in his inbox since she had last looked at it, sending them to the project manager app or the appropriate folder. Then he stared for a minute at his empty inbox, analyzing the anxiety he was feeling. This time, it wasn't worry that he was forgetting something important or was buried under an avalanche of email. Instead, it was because he'd never had an empty inbox before and felt like he'd become unimportant or invisible. The many emails in his inbox had always been a testament that people wanted him, needed him, or considered him important. It felt like he had been erased. He clicked on his personal folder and looked at the emails there. He still had people who felt like he was an important part of their lives. They were just in a different folder now.

He tried to shake off the unsettled feelings and clicked over to the project manager to see what he needed to do.

"Ah, here you are."

Zachary was startled at Kenzie's voice. He swiveled the chair to turn and look at her in the doorway. "I hope you don't mind; T was still on the couch and I didn't want to wake him. I can move somewhere else if you want. The guest room or kitchen table."

"No, this is fine. Why shouldn't you use the office? I always thought you preferred the couch, but you can use the office whenever you want. As long as I'm not using it, I mean, and honestly, that's not very often. You need it more than I do."

"It's your space, though. I don't want to just take it over."

"No, it's fine," she waved a hand at him. "Please do. Use it whenever you like."

Zachary stretched and arched his back. "It is a better setup than hunched over my computer on the couch."

"Yes. I hate to think of what kind of problems your bad posture will cause in the future. You should be using an ergonomically correct setup. I have a chair and desk fitted to me at work so that I don't end up with carpal tunnel or back problems. Even the autopsy table raises and lowers so that I'm not operating at the wrong height." She looked Zachary and her desk over with a critical eye. "If something doesn't fit right, or you're getting a sore back after using it for a few hours, let me know. We can get a better chair. You could even use a standing desk, if you wanted to. There are lots of options."

"I don't think I would like a standing desk. I like being able to sit down and relax."

She nodded. "Whatever works for you. Some people find that a standing desk helps them to focus better, or to move around more. With your ADHD, you might even find it helpful. It doesn't mean you can never sit. Just that you have options."

Zachary nodded. "I'll just finish this search, and then I'll join you for breakfast." He looked at the system time on his computer. It was later than they usually ate breakfast. "Do you still have time?"

"Yes. I'm not giving up my coffee or my breakfast."

"I'll leave this." Zachary looked at the screen one more time, then closed the lid to force himself to break away from the screen and focus on Kenzie and real life going on around him.

He followed her out to the kitchen, and they worked together as usual to set the table and get out what was needed for their preferred breakfasts. Toast and marmalade for Kenzie, and a granola bar and whatever else Zachary could get down after taking his morning meds.

There were a few noises from Tyrrell, and then he sat up, rubbing his eyes, to look around.

"Oh! You're back!" Tyrrell bounced up from the couch and made a beeline for Zachary. He clasped him tightly. "Where were you yesterday? You had us worried."

"Sorry," Zachary gave his brother a squeeze. "I had phone trouble." He glanced at Kenzie and didn't fill in any other details. Tyrrell didn't need any extra stress.

"Is that all? Man, you should have called!"

Zachary and Kenzie both gave him a look.

"On someone else's phone," Tyrrell clarified, laughing.

Zachary nodded. "Yeah. I should have. I lost track of time and didn't realize how late it had gotten. As soon as I did, I called Kenzie."

Tyrrell shook his head. He punched Zachary lightly on the arm as a reprimand or to reassure himself that Zachary was really there, then considered his own state. "Sheesh. You'd think I slept in my clothes. I'll at least go wash up."

He went down the hall to the bathroom.

"You're going back to talk to Luke this morning?" Kenzie asked.

"Yeah. Need to get his full story. If he'll tell the rest to me now that we know half of it. I can't believe he fooled everyone with his phony confession."

"I don't think anyone can be blamed for assuming that the guy holding the knife dripping with blood was the killer."

## 61

Zachary was so eager to confront Luke with the truth that he forgot all of the protocols for getting into the jail and kept having to repeat everything. He hadn't left his personal items in the car. He went through the security gate too fast and didn't hold still properly when the CO tried to wand him to confirm that the extra metal in his arm was what was setting the metal detector off, rather than that he was trying to bring a weapon or some other contraband into the jail.

"You're so jittery," the CO complained. "Are you high on something today?"

"No. Sorry. Just... I know that Luke didn't do it. I'm going to talk to him about it to get all the details of what happened. Before long, he'll be out of here."

"But then we won't be seeing you every day anymore," she teased, her face still serious. "Aren't you going to miss us?"

"Definitely," Zachary agreed.

He tried once more to hold still while she checked him with the wand, and eventually she nodded.

"Okay, you're clear."

"You already know I have metal in my arm. I don't see why it's such a big deal to wand me each time."

She rolled her eyes. "Because it could be something else. You get our guard down with the first few visits, then bring something in. You certainly look like you could be up to mischief today."

Zachary laughed. "I'm not, I promise. I'm just excited that we're going to get him off. You'll see."

She escorted him to the visitor room, and one of the male CO's came in with Luke. Luke looked at Zachary for a moment, considering whether to stay and talk to him or not.

"Come on, Luke," Zachary invited. "This is probably the last chance you're going to get to talk to me here."

Luke frowned. The CO hooked him into the anchor and left the room. "What's that supposed to mean?" Luke demanded.

"I mean that you're not going to be here anymore."

Luke's eyes went back and forth across Zachary's face as if trying to read him. He didn't like this new development, didn't know what to think of Zachary's announcement.

"We found Aster. She's back home with Joss."

"Uh… good. Glad to hear it. I wouldn't want anything to happen to her."

"You like her, don't you? Quite a bit."

Luke shrugged. "Yeah, sure. She's a nice girl. Lots of fun."

"Is she the only one who would go out with you? Dancing or to the bars or clubs? The rest of them listened to Joss and followed her rules?"

"No one followed them all the time," Luke said with a hint of a laugh. "She makes *lots* of rules."

Zachary allowed himself one short foray into the past, smiling as he remembered Joss bossing them around, telling them all of the rules, either of what they were supposed to do when they got home, or the newest game that she and Heather had cooked up. Yes, Joss had liked making rules back then. Trying to fence them in so they couldn't get into any trouble. But Zachary always managed to get into trouble. As much as she wanted the order and control that rules would provide, it didn't happen.

"Yes, I'm not surprised. But Aster was just a little bit more special to you?"

Luke considered the question, looking at it from various angles, frowning at Zachary and trying to see what he was getting at, what he was trying to pull over on Luke. "I like her," he said finally. "Like I said. She was fun. Funny, intelligent, rebellious."

"And you were protective of her. When one of Eyler's men saw her and tried to take her back to him, you defended her. Wouldn't let him take her away."

"I would do that for anyone," Luke said firmly. "No one should be owned or made into a slave."

If anyone knew what he was talking about, it was Luke. He knew what Aster had faced if she went back to Eyler. He had known all of the dangers and tried to keep her from making that mistake. He remembered Connor and, Zachary was sure, wanted to prevent the same thing from happening to anyone else. But especially not to his new friend, Aster.

"Tell me about the night Eyler was killed."

Luke shook his head.

"Did you hear Aster leaving? Or did you wake up and realize she was gone? Maybe she messaged you to let you know where she was going, so you wouldn't be worried."

Luke shook his head slowly. "I don't know what you're talking about."

"You knew you had to keep her from going back to him. He couldn't be trusted to keep her safe. He was sadistic, hurting the kids in his stable if he felt like it. And you probably knew that Aster had already had some trouble with him. Worried that she might be going down the same path as Connor had. What if Eyler decided that he didn't want her around anymore? What would he do?"

Luke's face was white. "Why would I think that?"

"Because he was. He decided to kill her. To strangle her to death while she was at the hotel. Then, no more trouble from Aster."

Luke rolled his eyes. "He wasn't trying to kill her."

"She has bruises around her throat."

"It was a fetish. He would have let go."

"Aster said he was trying to kill her."

Luke took a deep breath in and released it. "She's not very experienced. She would have learned. Like we all did."

"That's why she stabbed him. Because he was strangling her. It was self-defense."

"You don't have any proof of that. There's no evidence to back that up."

"There's Aster's own story."

"The cops need evidence. Not just a confession. Confessions are a dime a dozen."

"She and Joss are going to the police today. They may be here in the building already. Aster is going to confess what really happened. And once they re-examine the evidence and confirm her story, they'll release you. You can go back home."

"While she goes to prison? No."

"She won't go to prison. It's self-defense. It's the law."

"And you think the cops are going to believe some teenager? A hooker? They won't. They think we're all liars. Making up stories. They only believe what they see with their eyes. And you know what they saw with their eyes?"

"You, holding a bloody knife."

Luke nodded and sat back in his chair, looking smug.

And of course he was right. The police had immediately believed what they had seen. They didn't look any further than that. But they would have to know that there was a competing story. They would have to look at everything again to see which story held up under scrutiny. And Zachary believed that they would accept Aster's story. It made more sense than Luke going over there after years of avoiding Eyler, unarmed, killing him with a kitchen knife found at the scene.

Besides, Aster had cuts on her hands and Luke did not.

## 62

"Tell me what happened when you followed her," Zachary coaxed. "I know everything else. Just fill in the details."

Luke stared at him for a long time. "This is confidential," he said eventually. "Like lawyer-client privilege. You can't talk to anyone about it. If you repeat anything, I'll deny it. Say that you made it up because you wanted a relationship and I turned you down."

Zachary gulped. He hadn't been expecting that. He would never repeat Luke's words to anyone in authority without his permission, so he really didn't have to worry about it, but just the thought of some of the people in his life or of his clients thinking that he'd been pursuing an illicit relationship with a teenage prostitute was enough to make his heart pound like it had been announced all over the media. It would destroy his business. His friendship with Rhys. Who knew how many other people in his life would believe it? Hopefully, most of those he was close to would recognize it for what it was, lies to discredit him, but who knew how many friends he would lose because of it?

"I'm not going to tell the police. That's up to you," Zachary told Luke, trying to keep his voice as calm and soothing as he could despite the tightness of his throat.

Luke nodded slowly, still watching Zachary as if he might suddenly change his mind or give some indication that he was lying.

"You followed her to Eyler's hotel?" Zachary asked. "Or did you know that's where she was going?"

"I had a pretty good idea she needed to score, and that was the easiest source. She didn't know a lot of other people in town. She could have found something on the street, but then you never know what kind of quality you're getting. Eyler, she knew he had the good stuff."

"Didn't it bother you that she was going to him?"

"Of course it did. You think I wanted her having anything to do with that piece of—" he broke off, shaking his head adamantly. "She had gotten away from him. She was safe with Joss. We could have helped her. We could have kept her safe from him if she would just stay away. I get that there were too many rules, that you have to get out sometimes before you go buggy… but going back to Eyler? But she was desperate. I understood it even if I didn't like it."

"And you didn't confront her or follow her to the room?"

"I knew where she was going. I didn't need to be right behind her. I figured I'd hang around there while she did whatever she had to do to score some dope from him, and when he was done with her… I'd try to get her back home to Joss's."

Zachary didn't ask for further details, letting the silence do its work and get under Luke's skin.

"She went up and I hung around downstairs for a while. Didn't figure she'd be down right away. Eyler would want his turn with her. Watched the doors to see if he lined up some clients for her. Didn't spot any. I went upstairs just to take a look around, see what the setup was. Whether they had the whole floor. If there were any of his goons around."

Zachary hadn't thought to check whether Eyler had booked more than one room. He probably had, if he wanted to have several of his stable working at the same time under his close supervision. He would need more than just the room he was sleeping in.

"Did you see any others?"

"Didn't see anyone patrolling the hallways. Couldn't tell whether the other rooms were all occupied or not. Everyone was out of sight." Luke's eyes went up to the ceiling as he told his story. "Eyler was yelling. The guy was supposed to be a professional, but he was bellowing over the music that was supposed to cover up the noise of what was going on in those rooms. Berating her for leaving him, for thinking she could go back to him for drugs without any punishment. Calling her every filthy name he could think of." Luke licked his lips. "Gem of a man."

Zachary gave a short laugh. "Oh, yeah."

"With him being so loud, I figured people would be calling the police or the front desk complaining about him. I mean… there was no doubt he was out to hurt her. You could tell, listening to him, that he was going to do something to her."

"But you didn't go in."

"We've all dealt with guys like that. Best to let it blow over. The ones that blow up like a bomb are usually over it quick. He'd figure Aster had learned her lesson. And with the noise he was making, I figured the cops or at least hotel security would be along before long to put an end to it. It was best I wasn't in there when they got there. No point in trying to tangle with Eyler or get myself arrested."

Zachary nodded his understanding.

"And then…" Luke pursed his lips and seemed to be searching for the words. "I never heard anyone make that kind of noise before. I've had some pretty vocal clients, but not anyone who sounded like that."

"When she stabbed him?"

Luke nodded. "He… screamed and screamed. I wasn't sure what to do. Kept waiting for someone else to come and take care of it. Thought security would be there any minute, but they weren't. Just the music playing then… couldn't tell what was going on in any of the other rooms, or whether the hotel staff were going to take care of it. He could have paid them to look the other way no matter what noises came out of his rooms. Probably did. Money will get you a lot of privacy in a place like this. People are happy to look the other way if they're getting something out of it. They'll chance losing their jobs because it's worth it…"

"And then…"

"No one was coming. I broke in. Those doors are easy to bypass. Went into the suite, through the living room area into the bedroom…"

"And found Eyler dead and Aster shell-shocked," Zachary suggested. Aster had said that she hadn't even been aware of Eyler yelling at her, had no idea how much noise he had made when she had stabbed him. That showed that she was traumatized. Had perhaps dissociated to escape the abuse.

Luke rubbed his chin. "Eyler was dead all right. And Aster… naked, covered with blood, shooting up."

Zachary shuddered at the mental picture. So desperate for her next fix that she hadn't bothered to tend to any other necessities first.

"I got her into the bathroom. Yelling at her to get cleaned up and dressed so that she could get out of there before the cops showed up. She was moving so slowly. Like she didn't have any idea what she had done or that there was going to be trouble. Got the worst of the blood washed away and helped her dress. She was so high she would have walked right out of there starkers. And trying to get her into her clothes… it was like dressing a toddler. Arms and legs going every direction. Distracted, flirty and playing around…"

Zachary could hear the anxiety in Luke's voice over how long it had taken to get Aster presentable. He could feel the time pressure, knowing that the police could be there any minute.

"I told her to go home. To go straight back to Joss's and wait for me there. Not to tell anybody what had happened. I didn't know whether she'd be able to follow my instructions or whether she would just wander around the hotel or out into the street. But I couldn't take her myself. I needed to… clean things up a little."

Zachary remembered the handprints in the bathroom. Smudges of blood all over the place. The police hadn't lifted Aster's prints there. "You intentionally put your prints over hers."

"Yeah. Anywhere I could see. It was a mess. But I knew if they caught her, she was going away for a long time. Eyler might be scum, but they would still want to make an example of her. Hookers can't just go around killing their bosses or anyone else they think is being abusive. Society says that if you put yourself into that position, choose that lifestyle, then you better be able to take what they dish out. There are consequences to your choices."

"That's victim blaming."

Luke raised a brow. "And…?"

"Well… I thought we were supposed to be past that. That we're more civilized now and understand about abuse and PTSD and the way that these predators control the people they traffic."

"Welcome to my world," Luke snorted.

"And then the police got there before you could finish obscuring all of the evidence and leave."

"I'd done enough to make it work." Luke's chin lifted slightly. He *had* done a good job. He had done what he had set out to do, ensuring that the police saw only the evidence that he had planted.

"Yes, you did. But now… it's time to admit what really happened. Aster is going to confess. When they investigate her story and realize that it is true, you're going to get out of here. You need to confirm her story instead of saying that you killed Eyler. She'll get off. She still has bruises on her neck. There will be proof that he was trying to kill her, and she can get off with self-defense."

Luke stared at Zachary, chewing on his lip. "You really think that they'll believe her? The guy deserved to be killed. I'm happy to take the heat for it, if it keeps Aster out of prison."

"You killing him because of your past and what happened to Connor will send you to prison for decades. Even saying that you were defending Aster or trying to keep Eyler away from your neighborhood is going to get you time. But she was being assaulted. She's allowed to defend herself under the law. No prison time for her."

"If they believe her."

"She has the injuries. You need to give them the same story as she does. They'll believe her."

"You think so?"

Zachary nodded. He could understand why Luke was so distrustful. For a lot of years, the police had pulled out all the stops to prosecute the victims of human trafficking rather than the traffickers or the johns. Prostitutes were seen as the lowest sort of criminals, despite how they were victimized by the traffickers. The tide had turned, with a number of states adopting the policy of prosecuting pimps and johns and providing counseling and services for the victims. Hopefully, there was enough awareness of the issue that no court would consider putting Aster in prison for what she had done.

But there were always wild cards.

"I'm *sure*," he told Luke. "She's going to be okay."

# 63

After he finished his visit with Luke, Zachary texted Joss as he walked around the building to the police station to see if she had taken Aster to the police station.

*Dealing with it now,* Joss replied.

He walked in through the front doors of the police station and looked around. He couldn't see either one of them; they must have already been taken to another room and were giving a statement, or waiting to give a statement to a policeman.

A cop walked out of the secured area to bend down and talk to the officer of the day, and Zachary realized it was Detective Richards, the homicide cop on Luke's case.

"Detective Richards."

Richards looked at him and didn't recognize him immediately. Then he clued in. "Goldman, right? What are you doing here?"

"I was just checking in with Joss. I knew that she was planning to be here with Aster this morning."

He nodded. "Yeah, the girl is making her statement." He rolled his eyes. "That's quite some story."

"It's not just a story."

"Yeah, well, if we find out that she's lying and that you're the one that fed the story to her in order to get the kid exonerated...."

"It isn't anything like that. I just followed the evidence to her. I didn't know she existed before I started. And once she told what really happened, we made arrangements for her to talk to you."

"You really think she did it, not the boy."

"Yes. And she's got the bruises to prove it."

"She can't prove where she got the bruises. They could be from anywhere."

"Well, maybe her DNA was found on Eyler's body. Or maybe his is under her fingernails."

Richards shrugged. "We'll see where the evidence leads. It can take months to get DNA back."

"How long do you think they're going to be in there?" Zachary nodded toward the offices and meeting rooms.

"Couple of hours, at least. To do it right."

Zachary looked at his watch. "I'll pop back in later, then."

"Why? They don't need you here. You don't have any direct testimony to add to her case."

"No. I just want to see that what I started… ends well."

"It won't be over for some time. But you do what you like. No skin off my nose."

---

Zachary could have sat in his car for a couple of hours doing what work he could on his phone and laptop. But he decided to reward himself for bringing the case to a successful conclusion by taking some time off for his own photography, which he hadn't been spending much time on lately.

He worked his way through several parks and open spaces, exploring the spring growth, stalking and snapping pictures of birds and squirrels, and watching people who were out enjoying the pleasant weather. Not people who were just hurrying from one place to another, with work or family trouble on their minds. No cheating spouses. People who actually looked happy and relaxed.

He returned to the police station when Joss said they would be getting out soon and met them when they returned to the public welcoming area.

"How did it go?" Zachary asked immediately, checking both of their faces. Aster was pale, probably not feeling very good after whatever drugs she'd been on the previous evening had worn off. She looked tired, but not upset, not what he would have expected if they had told her that she was going to have to serve time for Eyler's death or hadn't believed the story she had told them.

Joss nodded, giving a grim smile. "Aster did what needed to be done. I'm sure it will all work out. One less scumbag for us to deal with here. Maybe now they'll leave my girls and me alone."

"You need to be careful," Zachary warned her. "Don't antagonize them. You're lucky that so far, everyone has backed off when you said that you have information that could be detrimental to their business. One day…"

"Someone might decide to shoot first and ask questions later?" Joss finished. "Take me out and take their chances with the rest?"

Zachary nodded.

"I know." Joss sighed, folding her arms across her chest. "Believe it or not… I sometimes have trouble backing down once I've drawn a line in the sand."

Zachary chuckled. "Oh, I think I can believe it."

She pretended to punch him in the shoulder. "Don't get so cocky. Why are you looking so cheerful and pink-cheeked, anyway?"

"Just been out doing some photography. I forget sometimes how much I enjoy just getting outside with a camera."

"What do you take pictures of? It wasn't a job?"

"No. Just some wildlife. The local flora and fauna. And a few of people. It's nice out."

Joss nodded as she exited the building with Zachary and Aster. "It is nice." She put her hands on her hips for a minute, taking in a lungful of air. "The trouble is… it doesn't stay like this. Sooner or later, a cold front rolls in, the sky gets dark, and everything changes."

"So, I should enjoy it while it lasts?"

"So you should always be prepared for what's coming next."

Did you enjoy this book? Reviews and recommendations are vital to making a book successful.

Please leave a review at your favorite book store or review site and share it with your friends.

Don't miss the following bonus material:
Sign up for mailing list to get a free ebook
Read a sneak preview chapter
Other books by P.D. Workman
Learn more about the author

# UNLOCK ACCESS TO ZACHARY GOLDMAN'S CASE FILES!

Get a peek inside Zachary's case files and see what other intriguing tales are in store!

## SCAN TO UNLOCK OFFER

books.pdworkman.com/sign-up-zg

# PREVIEW OF
# UNLAWFUL HARVEST

More books will be coming in the Zachary Goldman Mysteries series, but they are not ready for preview yet!

The next book in the timeline after They Came for Him is Posed for Death, book #6 in the Kenzie Kirsch Medical Thriller series.

If you have not started the Kenzie Kirsch Medical Thriller series yet, read Kenzie's origin story in Unlawful Harvest. Here is a free preview!

# 1

MacKenzie reached for the ringing phone, trying to drag herself from sleep, but her hand encountered only the empty base of the phone, the wireless handset missing.

She pried her eyes open while feeling for it on the bedside table, knocking off keys and a glass and an empty bottle and other detritus. She swore and blinked and tried to focus. Where had she left the handset and who was calling her so early in the morning? The phone rang five times and went to her voicemail. Too late to answer it. She sank back down onto her pillow and closed her eyes. Whoever it was would have to wait.

But no sooner had it gone to voicemail than it started ringing again. MacKenzie groaned. "Are you serious? Come on!"

She turned her head and squinted at the clock next to her. It was hard to see the red LED display in the bright sunlight. It was almost eleven o'clock. Certainly not too early for a caller, even one who knew that she would sleep in after a party the night before. She rubbed her temples and scanned the room for the wireless handset.

There was a man in the bed next to her, but she ignored him for the time being. He wasn't moving at the sound of the phone, so he'd probably had more to drink than she had. She slid her legs out of the bed and grabbed a silk kimono housecoat to wrap around herself. The caller was sent to voicemail a second time. MacKenzie took another look around the bedroom without spotting the phone, then went out to her living room, also bright with sunlight streaming in the big windows. Outside, the pretty Vermont scenery was covered with a fresh layer of snow, which reflected back the sunlight even more brilliantly. MacKenzie groaned and looked around. The newspaper was on the floor in a messy, well-read heap. The remains of some late-night snack were spread over the coffee table. Some of their clothing had been left there, scattered across the floor, but no phone.

It started ringing again. Now that she was out of the bedroom and away from the base, she could hear the ringing of the handset, and she kicked at the newspaper to uncover it. She bent down and scooped up the handset. She glanced at the caller ID before pressing the answer button and pressing it to her ear, but she knew very well who it was going to be.

No one else would be so annoying and call over and over again first thing in the morning. She couldn't just leave a message and wait for MacKenzie to get back to her, she had to keep calling, forcing MacKenzie to get up and answer it. Her mother didn't care how late MacKenzie might have been up the night before or how she might be feeling upon rising. It was a natural consequence of MacKenzie's own choices. MacKenzie dropped into the white couch.

"Mother."

"MacKenzie. Thank goodness I got you. Where have you been?"

Her mother had been calling for all of two minutes. Where had MacKenzie been? She could have been in the bathroom, having a shower, talking to someone else on the phone, or at some event. Granted, she didn't go to a lot of events at eleven o'clock in the morning, but it *could* happen. Mrs. Lisa Cole Kirsch had a pretty good idea where MacKenzie had been. In bed, like most any other morning.

"What is it, Mother?"

"It's Amanda. She's sick."

MacKenzie nodded to herself and scratched the back of her head. One of the things that would definitely set Lisa into a tizzy was Amanda being sick. She worried over every little cough or twinge that

Amanda suffered. She had good reason, but it still made MacKenzie roll her eyes.

"What's wrong with Amanda?"

"I don't know. Maybe it's just the flu, but I'm really worried, MacKenzie. The doctors said to just wait and see, but they don't understand how frail Amanda is. They think that I'm just overreacting and being a hypochondriac. You know that I'm not just a hypochondriac."

"I know. So, how is she?"

MacKenzie had to admit that even though her mother worried about Amanda, her worry was well-justified. Amanda's health could get worse very quickly, and with the anti-rejection drugs suppressing her immune system, she was prone to picking up anything that went around.

"She's not good. She was up all night, throwing up, high fever, she's just not herself. I called an ambulance at eight o'clock. She just can't keep anything down and I don't like the way she's acting. So... weak and listless."

MacKenzie felt the first twinge of worry herself. Amanda had spent much of her life sick, but she was a fighter. She usually did her best to look like nothing was wrong, not letting on unless she was feeling really badly. She would laugh and brush it off as just a bug and smile and encourage MacKenzie to tell her about what was going on in her far-more-interesting life. MacKenzie closed her eyes, focusing on Lisa's words.

"But the doctors don't think that there's anything to worry about?"

"No, but you know... they never do. She has to be at death's door before they'll admit that there might be a problem."

"Have they given her anything or did they just send her back home again?"

"They've got her on an IV and have said that they'll keep an eye on her. But you know they don't really think there's anything wrong. They're just humoring me."

"Yeah. Do you want me to come?"

"Would you? I'm really worried."

"Okay. I'll need a few minutes to get myself together. I'll be there as soon as I can."

"Thank you, MacKenzie. I don't know what I would do without you."

The sad thing was, Lisa would do just fine without MacKenzie. Even though she said that she needed MacKenzie, MacKenzie wouldn't really be able to do anything that Lisa couldn't do herself. She'd been dealing with doctors for a lot of years, and though she didn't pick up on the medical jargon as quickly as MacKenzie did, she could hold her own very well and was stubborn as a mule when it came to Amanda's care. She would protect her baby at all costs, and Amanda would get the best of care whether MacKenzie were there or not.

But if Lisa wanted the extra comfort of having MacKenzie around, who was she to argue? She didn't have anything else going on that prevented her attendance, and even if she did, it was easy enough to beg off of any event with an excuse, especially if the excuse were that Amanda was sick. MacKenzie had used it as an excuse even when it wasn't true. Although technically, even when Amanda was feeling well, she was still sick, so it wasn't really a lie.

MacKenzie hung up the phone and put it down on the brass and glass side table. She scrubbed her eyes with her fists, and when she opened them again, Liam was standing in the front of her.

"What's up?" he asked. "Everything okay?"

He hadn't yet recovered anything more than his boxers and, for a minute, MacKenzie just let her eyes rove over the piece of eye candy, remembering the night before through a slight haze of alcohol. They had gone to the Cancer Society fundraiser, had made the rounds there and let themselves be seen, and then had returned to MacKenzie's apartment for more drinks, some real food, and private entertainment.

"MacKenzie? What's up?"

"Amanda. She's in the hospital and Mother wants me to go over there and reassure her." MacKenzie yawned.

Liam bent over to pick up the various items of clothing he had dropped the night before. "Is she okay?"

"I'm sure both Amanda and Mother will be just fine. But she sounded pretty worried, and she said that Amanda was listless, which isn't like her. A really bad flu, maybe. I hope that's all it is."

"I was going to have a shower before heading out. Do you want it?"

MacKenzie weighed the options. Amanda was in the hospital, so she would be getting the best of care. Did it really matter whether MacKenzie had to wait an extra ten minutes for Liam to shower before she got herself ready?

"Or," Liam suggested, a dimple appearing in his cheek, "we could shower together and be done twice as fast."

"I have a feeling I wouldn't be out of here very quickly if we did that," MacKenzie laughed. They could easily be another hour, and Lisa would be on the phone again, ringing insistently, demanding to know where MacKenzie was and why she wasn't at her sister's side yet.

"Okay," Liam agreed. "So, do you want it?"

"Yes. I guess so. I need to pull myself together even if I am just going to the hospital." Lisa would not want her to show up looking bedraggled. She'd expect MacKenzie to be well turned-out even if it were the middle of the night, which it wasn't.

Liam nodded agreeably. He pulled on his white shirt from the night before, but didn't put on the pants or the rest of his outfit. "Shall I make you some breakfast while you're in there so that you can get out more quickly?"

"Would you? Just a couple of pieces of toast and some juice," MacKenzie requested, heading toward the bathroom. She looked back over her shoulder at him. "And coffee."

He smiled. "I think I know by now that you don't start any morning without coffee."

"Well, I need to fortify myself with *something* this morning before facing my mother."

---

She had a quick breakfast while Liam got into the shower, but he wasn't out by the time she was finished. She poked her head into the bathroom.

"Will you be much longer?"

She could see his shadow through the shower curtain as he turned his head toward her. "Oh… I can just lock up when I leave. You can go ahead."

MacKenzie shook her head. "I don't like to leave people here when I'm not around. Sorry. Can you be quick?"

"Yeah, sure." His tone was agreeable, but clipped. He obviously didn't appreciate that she didn't trust him enough to leave him alone in her apartment. But MacKenzie had been burned in the past by people who didn't respect her privacy, and she wasn't about to leave him there without supervision. She didn't know him well enough. Just because she could go with him to an event, and maybe bring him home afterward, that didn't mean she knew enough about his essential character to leave him there alone. She valued her privacy and there were a few things around the apartment that were quite valuable. Not that she thought Liam Jackson was going to steal them. She knew where to find him if he did. But it just wasn't good policy. If she didn't notice that something was missing right away, she might never be able to track it down again.

"I'll just be two more minutes," Liam promised.

"Thanks."

She went back to the bedroom and, since she had the time and couldn't leave until he was finished, she actually went ahead and pulled her bed into some semblance of order. It didn't look as good as when the maid did it, but it was better than leaving it all rumpled. She would appreciate it when she got home later.

If Lisa could only see her now. Twenty-seven years old and actually making her own bed. On a roll, she went into the living room and picked up the newspaper, which she threw in the garbage, and her clothes, which she threw in the laundry. Liam was out of the shower but not yet out of the bathroom. She threw a random assortment of dishes into the dishwasher and had the place looking pretty tidy when Liam made an appearance, dressed, hair wet but neatly combed, and his face still stubbly, not having taken the time to shave.

She stood on her tip-toes to give him a kiss. "Thanks. Sorry about having to rush you out of here. It's my sister. Mother wants me there, so I have to make sure she's okay."

Liam nodded, looking down at her and letting his fingers linger on her jaw for a moment. "That, or you got one of your girlfriends to call to break up the party so that you could get rid of me."

"Ugh. I wouldn't do that when I was still in bed."

He smiled. "Give me a call later, then. Let me know how it goes. And we'll see each other again… soon."

They didn't have anything lined up, no dates, no fundraisers, nothing on the horizon. Liam was a nice guy, good looking, and MacKenzie might add him to her regular coterie of admirers, but she hadn't made up her mind yet. She wasn't one hundred percent sure that he was her type. Whatever that was.

After seeing him out the door, she put on her coat and winter gear and headed for the hospital.

---

When she managed to find her way to Amanda's hospital room, not in the renal unit where she usually was, Amanda was asleep. Lisa sat next to the bed, watching her sleep. Not reading a book. Not looking at her schedule for the week. Just watching her sleep. MacKenzie would have gone crazy. She couldn't stand to have people staring at her.

"Hi, Mom," she said softly.

Lisa looked over at her, automatically making a motion for her to be quiet before she evaluated MacKenzie's voice and the deepness of Amanda's sleep and decided that she probably wasn't being too loud after all.

"How is she doing?" MacKenzie looked over her kid sister. Amanda was twenty years old, but when she was asleep, she looked about ten. She was shorter than MacKenzie, and MacKenzie wasn't exactly an Amazon herself. Amanda was small and elfin, and people often mistook her for a kid if they weren't paying attention. She had a beautiful face, when she was feeling well. She wasn't looking too bad.

Her weight was good, her cheeks round rather than sunken like they had been when she'd been through her worst times. She had long, dark hair that got tangled if she didn't take care of it, which was hard to do when she was in a hospital bed all day, but she didn't like to cut it short so that it would be easier to take care of. She said she needed her strength, like Samson.

Amanda was pale, and that bothered MacKenzie. But if she had the flu and had been throwing up for hours, then of course she was going to be pale. It was just a virus. She would be feeling better soon.

"She's sleeping," Lisa stated the obvious. "She's been so sick all night... I'm glad she was finally able to drift off. Maybe she's on her way to feeling better."

"Probably just a bug."

"Yes. Hopefully."

There was an IV hanging, but Lisa had said that Amanda needed it to stay hydrated. It didn't necessarily mean that she was back on some treatment again.

MacKenzie pulled the other chair in the room closer to her mother's and sat down. Amanda had been given a private room, of course. There was no way she was going to be left in some hallway or emergency room curtain. Lisa would see to that.

"Do you want to go get something to eat?" MacKenzie suggested.

"Well..." Lisa's eyes flicked over to Amanda. "I don't know. I don't want to leave her alone."

"I'm here. And you haven't had anything to eat, have you? You've been with her since last night?"

"Yes, you're right."

"Well, you're not going to be any good to her if you're fainting from hunger or all angry and irritable from low blood sugar. So go. I'll be with her if she wakes up. She's not going to be alone."

"Are you sure?"

"Why don't you take advantage of the fact that I'm here, because I'm not going to be here all day. Go have something to eat."

"Okay," Lisa agreed, but she still made no movement to get up, watching Amanda with worried eyes.

"She'll be fine for now. I'll have them page you if something happens."

"Would you?" Lisa brightened at that suggestion. She could go have something to eat and still be sure that Amanda hadn't taken a turn for the worse. She clutched her purse on her lap, then nodded and got up. "Thank you so much, MacKenzie, I appreciate you coming and being here for your sister."

"And for you," MacKenzie reminded her. "Don't you try saying that I never do anything for you."

"I would never say that."

MacKenzie raised her eyebrows as her mother left. She might say it and she might not. But she would certainly imply it the next time she wanted MacKenzie to do something for her and MacKenzie had something else going on or didn't want to be there.

Lisa's heels clicked sharply as she walked away. MacKenzie watched her go. She leaned back in her chair and looked over Amanda once more. The hospital chair was far from comfortable. She was going to have to get used to it if she were going to be there for a few hours.

"I should have brought a book," she murmured to Amanda. She hadn't thought to bring anything with her. She'd just gotten herself together and headed over. And she couldn't go down to the gift shop to pick something up. Not after dismissing her mother and saying she'd stay with Amanda while Lisa was eating. MacKenzie sighed and resigned herself to just sitting there and napping while she waited either for Amanda to wake up, or for Lisa to return from lunch.

## 2

---

She had nodded off, and when she opened her eyes and rubbed the stickiness away, she realized that Amanda was awake, her head turned to look at MacKenzie.

"Oh, hey sleepyhead," MacKenzie greeted.

"Hi," Amanda said in a soft little voice. MacKenzie waited for the rejoinder about how MacKenzie had been falling asleep in her chair. But Amanda didn't tease her. MacKenzie bit her lip. That was what Lisa was so worried about. Amanda might look like she was just a little tired, but that shouldn't change her personality. Her lassitude suggested that there was something more wrong, not just a twenty-four-hour flu bug. She shouldn't have been experiencing that level of fatigue with just a virus.

"How are you feeling?"

"I think I'm better now," Amanda said faintly.

MacKenzie waited for her to go on, but she didn't. "I guess you had a pretty rough night of it,"

Amanda nodded. She turned away from MacKenzie again and her eyes closed. MacKenzie frowned watching her. It was just the flu. Just a fever and throwing up. It could be any number of viruses. They had her on IV. She was going to be just fine.

Lisa returned, and looked worriedly over to Amanda lying in the bed, as if she had expected her to be sitting up talking by the time she got back.

"She was awake for a minute," MacKenzie said. "She didn't throw up, so that's good news."

"I think they put something in the IV to stop her."

"Oh. Well, that's good. At least they're taking it seriously."

"She really does need to sleep," Lisa said, but MacKenzie knew she was trying to reassure herself. They were all used to Amanda's high energy level. Even when she was sick, she still joked and teased and tried to keep everyone around her in a good mood. She didn't like long faces around her hospital bed.

"If she was up all night throwing up? She sure does. I was up half the night and I could still use a few more hours of sleep. And I wasn't throwing up."

"You were up late?"

"I was at the fundraiser."

"Oh, the one at the Phelps's house?"

"Yeah. That one."

"Who did you take?"

"Liam Jackson."

"He's a nice boy."

"He seems that way," MacKenzie agreed. She focused on looking out the window on the opposite side of the room. She didn't want to blush and have Lisa detect it. MacKenzie smiled and raised her eyebrows as if she weren't thinking immoral thoughts about Liam Jackson.

"How is Daddy?"

"You know your father. Always occupied with very important meetings with very important people."

MacKenzie nodded, smiling. Lisa hadn't said it in a way that was sarcastic or critical, but with a little bit of humor, as other women might talk about their husbands' interest in cars or collectibles. *Boys and their toys.* Was that how her mother saw Walter's lobbying? As a hobby that occupied her husband and kept him out from underfoot?

"Does he have anything interesting going on right now?"

"I'm not sure what he's working on. I don't really pay much attention, unless it is something that could have an impact on one of my causes."

Lisa always had plenty of causes on her agenda. There were an infinite number of foundations, societies, and fundraisers that needed her attention and support. Lobbying kept her father busy and fundraising kept her mother happy. MacKenzie just didn't know what it was that kept *her* happy. When was she going to find her way in life? She didn't want to be a lawyer, lobbyist, or politician. But she didn't want to be a socialite or drum-beater either. She had done well enough in school and had taken enough classes in college to get herself a degree, but that hadn't helped her to find her place in the world. She wasn't passionate about anything.

Lisa's eyes were quick and perhaps took in more than MacKenzie had expected. She reached over and patted MacKenzie's hand. "You'll find something," she said. "You're just a late bloomer. You need to be patient and give yourself some time."

"When you were a kid, what did you think you would be when you grew up? Did you have any dreams?"

Lisa shrugged and looked away from MacKenzie. "I don't know. I wanted to be a wife and mother. I was never really interested in a job. I felt like children were my avocation." She shrugged. "I know that's not a very popular answer these days. We're supposed to think big and take the bull by the horns, to make our mark on the world. But I can't help but think... that the marks being made on the world wouldn't amount to very much if it weren't for the mothers."

MacKenzie gave her a smile. "The hand that rocks the cradle, and all that?"

"Yes. Exactly. Mothers shape the thinkers and the soldiers. The scientists and the astronauts and the Nobel laureates. They all had mothers. They all had people to help them along the way and give them support at various parts of their lives, like a mother would, even if they didn't have a mother. I happen to think that's a very important position."

"Of course," MacKenzie agreed. "I never thought that you should be required to give up your family and have a high-power job."

"I could have, you know," Lisa said. She obviously didn't want MacKenzie thinking that she had only stayed home to be a mother because she couldn't do anything else. She had chosen to be there and not to hire a nanny to raise them. That had been her choice, not a fallback position.

"I know, Mother. You have a brain. You're very organized and I'm always amazed at what you can accomplish. I know you could have chosen to do other things."

Lisa nodded, satisfied.

MacKenzie looked back at Amanda. They had been lucky to have a mother who stayed home to look after them. Amanda probably wouldn't have survived without a strong, proactive mother watching over her. How many times had Lisa been the one to take her to the hospital and insist to the doctors that something was wrong, and she wasn't taking Amanda home until they had figured out what it was? She had insisted that Amanda wasn't just a whiner or a hypochondriac, but that she was really ill. She could have died if they hadn't been forced to dig deeper for the answers.

---

MacKenzie and Amanda hadn't really been playmates. MacKenzie had been too much older than Amanda to consider her a real friend and peer. Instead, Amanda had been MacKenzie's baby as much as she had been Lisa's. MacKenzie had been fascinated with her care and had happily fed and changed her. It was like having a living doll. MacKenzie had never even liked dolls. But she liked having stewardship over the tiny new person in their home. Lisa had encouraged her interest rather than shooing her off to go play or insisting that she diaper her dolls instead of her sister.

At first, no one had known that anything was wrong. Amanda got sick a lot, but children picked up viruses everywhere, it wasn't really that unusual. As she got older, she didn't outgrow it, and MacKenzie realized that she was sick a lot more often than MacKenzie or her friends, or little Amanda's other friends. She remembered the day when she had been out at the playground with Amanda, about nine years old by then, and MacKenzie a teen. Amanda had been playing tag or grounders or some other schoolyard game on the climbing equipment with her friends, but she had to sit down at the edge of one of the platforms, her face white, trying to catch her breath and get up the energy to go back to the game. The other girls teased her for calling timeout too often and told her that she couldn't be safe, but there wasn't any point in tagging her while she sat out, because she wouldn't run after the rest of them and the game would grind to a halt.

MacKenzie walked over to Amanda.

"Mandy-Candy," she singsonged, "what's wrong? Don't you want to play anymore?"

Amanda was breathing shallowly, too fast. "I want to play," she protested, her arms folded across her stomach, "I'm just too tired. I need a break."

"Do you want to go home?"

Amanda looked at the other girls still playing and having a fun time on the playground equipment around her. She looked sad. Not just sad, but desolate, as if they had all run away and left her behind where she could not follow.

"I guess so," she said finally. "I can read, I guess."

"Do you really want to?" MacKenzie pressed. "I'm not saying you have to. If you want to stay and play…"

Amanda shook her head. "I can't," she said hopelessly. "I don't know how they can run around all day."

MacKenzie sat looking at her as the seconds ticked by, a knot growing in her stomach. She walked home slowly with Amanda, back to the big house on the hill. It was a long way for a child who didn't have any energy left. Partway there, MacKenzie boosted Amanda up onto her back and carried her piggy-back to the house. Amanda lay against her, body limp, arms around MacKenzie's neck.

When they got home and MacKenzie settled Amanda in bed with

a book, she went looking for Lisa. Lisa was, luckily, home for the evening and not on her way out to some fundraiser.

"Mother... I think something's wrong with Amanda. I mean... really wrong."

Lisa looked at her for a long time, then finally nodded. "I do too. And I think it's time we found out what."

So many doctors had said that Amanda was just a girly girl, that she didn't want to participate in activities and was overly sensitive to every little ache and pain that came along with growing up and roughhousing with friends. There wasn't really anything wrong.

But when they had insisted that it was time to figure out what was really wrong with Amanda and that they weren't going away until they got some answers, everything changed.

And it would never be the same again.

---

*Unlawful Harvest*, Book #1 in the *Kenzie Kirsch Medical Thriller* series by P.D. Workman can be purchased at pdworkman.com

# ABOUT THE AUTHOR

P.D. Workman is a USA Today Bestselling author and multi-award winner, renowned for her prolific output of over 100 published works that span various genres. With a knack for crafting page-turners, Workman captivates readers with everything from cozy mysteries like the Auntie Clem's Bakery series to gripping young adult and suspense novels.

A prolific reader and writer since childhood, P.D. Workman crafts emotionally powerful stories that don't shy away from hard topics. Her books tackle mental illness, addiction, abuse, and trauma with raw honesty and compassion, giving voice to the often unheard. If you crave authentic, character-driven page-turners that hit deep and stay with you long after the final page, you're in the right place.

With each new release, fans eagerly anticipate another thrilling blend of thought-provoking storytelling and relatable characters that define P.D. Workman's brand as an author of unforgettable page-turners— gripping tales that leave a lasting impact long after the last page is turned.

> P. D. Workman, does not shy from probing the deep psychological scars of childhood trauma, mental illness, and addiction. Also characteristic of this author, these extremely sensitive issues are explored with extensive empathy, described with incredible clarity, and portrayed with profound insight.
>
> ——KIM, GOODREADS REVIEWER

Some of Workman's titles have been translated into Spanish, French, Portuguese, German, and Italian.

Workman began writing at an early age and is a prolific reader as well as writer. She is also passionate about teaching and learning, expresses her creativity through art and cooking, and loves exploring the Calgary parks and green spaces where the Parks Pat Mysteries are set. She was a legal assistant for many years and has done extensive charitable work.

Workman was born and raised in Alberta, Canada, and is married with one adult son.

---

Please visit P.D. Workman at pdworkman.com to see what else she is working on, to join her mailing list, and to link to her social networks.

---

If you enjoyed this book, please take the time to recommend it to other purchasers with a review or star rating and share it with your friends!

tiktok.com/@pdworkmanauthor

facebook.com/pdworkmanauthor

x.com/pdworkmanauthor

instagram.com/pdworkmanauthor

amazon.com/author/pdworkman

bookbub.com/authors/p-d-workman

goodreads.com/pdworkman

linkedin.com/in/pdworkman

pinterest.com/pdworkmanauthor

youtube.com/pdworkman

Find P.D. Workman's books at

**PDWORKMAN.COM**

Scan the QR code below